THROUGH A FRACTURED DOOR

The search for love and acceptance never ends

Colin Mellor

Matador
9 Priory Business Park,
Wistow Road, Kibworth Beauchamp,
Leicestershire. LE8 0RX
Tel: 0116 279 2299
Email: books@troubador.co.uk
Web: www.troubador.co.uk/matador
Twitter: @matadorbooks

ISBN 978 1800461 703

British Library Cataloguing in Publication Data.
A catalogue record for this book is available from the British Library.

Printed and bound in Great Britain by 4edge Limited
Typeset in 12pt Gill Sans Nova by Troubador Publishing Ltd, Leicester, UK

Matador is an imprint of Troubador Publishing Ltd

This book is for my wife, she is my world, my Oxygen.

Also to all readers everywhere:
You know who you are, I thank you.

Lastly to the teacher who almost blinded me in one eye.
Keep looking over your shoulder...

About the Author

Colin Mellor is a Hampshire-based author who, after spending many years in the paper industry working in graphic design and photography, is now retired. Diagnosed with dyslexia in his late 50's Colin has written an engaging novel, *Through a Fractured Door* which illustrates how undiagnosed Dyslexia can affect lives.

Preface

Here is a story of human life, maybe yours, maybe mine. Not much in life is as straightforward, or as easy, as we think. Life is full of surprises.

People we think we know well, including friends and family, sometimes cause the biggest upsets in our lives, with unexpected results.

If this happens, we need time for reflection. Some of us have an innate confidence in ourselves and our abilities. But we are not all the same... are we? What do you see when you look beyond your mirror? Be prepared for the unexpected, life can be difficult. With a small amount of forethought, we might be able to make our time on Planet Earth a little more peaceful.

If you think you see yourself in this story, go and have another look in the mirror.

All characters in this book are fictitious, as is the name Tillshott, the road names, maps, etc. Any similarity to anyone either living or dead is coincidental.

Author's Note

With this story I hope to illustrate to everyone, including those living with, or suffering from, dyslexia, as I do, some of its idiosyncracies. Dyslexia can affect far more than reading and writing and still appears to be widely misunderstood today. Many normal everyday tasks we perform (without a second thought) can be affected. Some of the more common indications can include: mental confusion, becoming easily stressed, annoyance with noises in our surroundings, low self-esteem and tolerance levels, spatial awareness issues, and bad balance. The typeface and the lack of full-text justification have been chosen with this in mind.
The British Dyslexia Association recommends the use of sans serif fonts, as do other dyslexia organisations. Several excellent organisations have been created to help deal with this condition. If you think you are affected by dyslexia, please seek advice from your medical practitioner or, for more information, visit
https://www.bdadyslexia.org.uk/

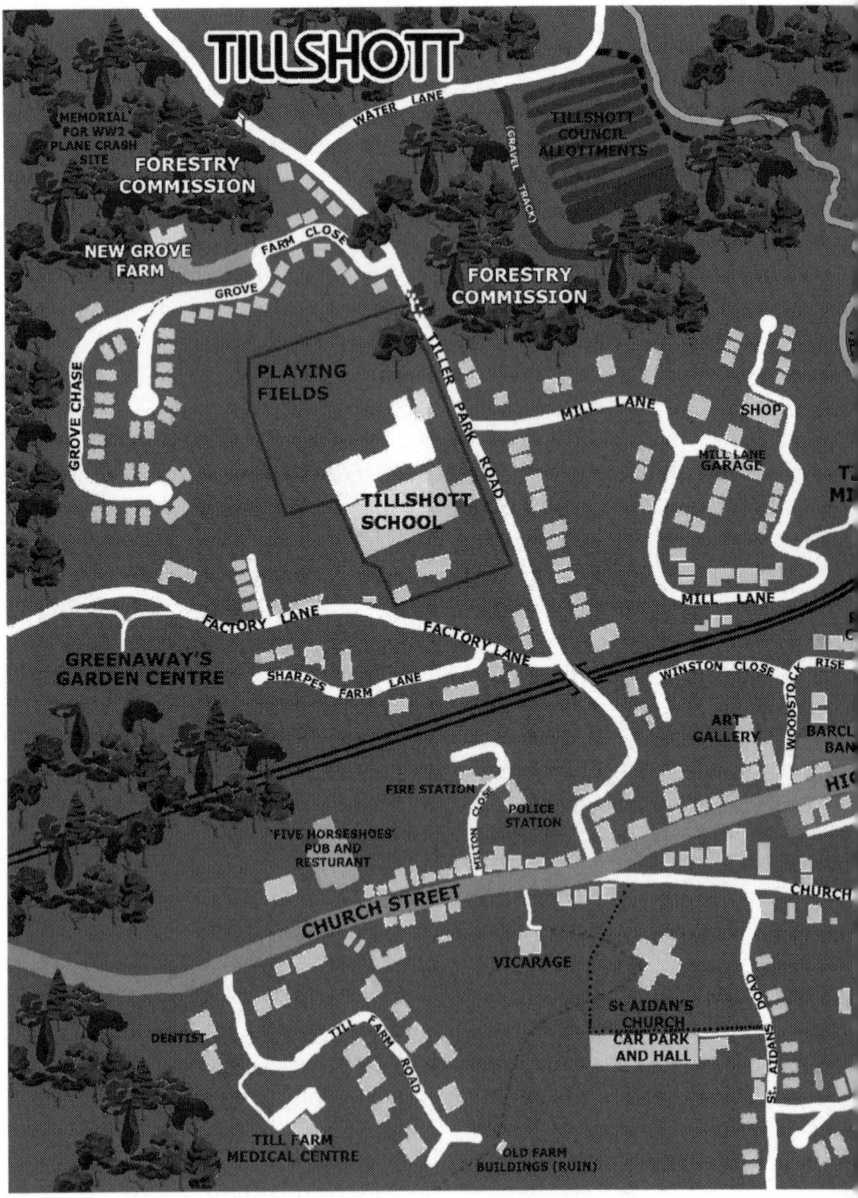

TILLSHOTT
'MEMORIAL' FOR WW2 PLANE CRASH SITE
FORESTRY COMMISSION
WATER LANE
TILLSHOTT COUNCIL ALLOTMENTS
(GRAVEL TRACK)
NEW GROVE FARM
FARM CLOSE
GROVE
FORESTRY COMMISSION
GROVE CHASE
PLAYING FIELDS
TILLER PARK ROAD
MILL LANE
SHOP
MILL LANE GARAGE
TILLSHOTT SCHOOL
MILL LANE
FACTORY LANE
FACTORY LANE
GREENAWAY'S GARDEN CENTRE
SHARPES FARM LANE
WINSTON CLOSE
WOODSTOCK RISE
ART GALLERY
FIRE STATION
MILTON CLOSE
POLICE STATION
'FIVE HORSESHOES' PUB AND RESTURANT
CHURCH STREET
CHURCH
VICARAGE
ST AIDAN'S CHURCH
CAR PARK AND HALL
ST. AIDANS ROAD
DENTIST
TILL FARM ROAD
TILL FARM MEDICAL CENTRE
OLD FARM BUILDINGS (RUIN)

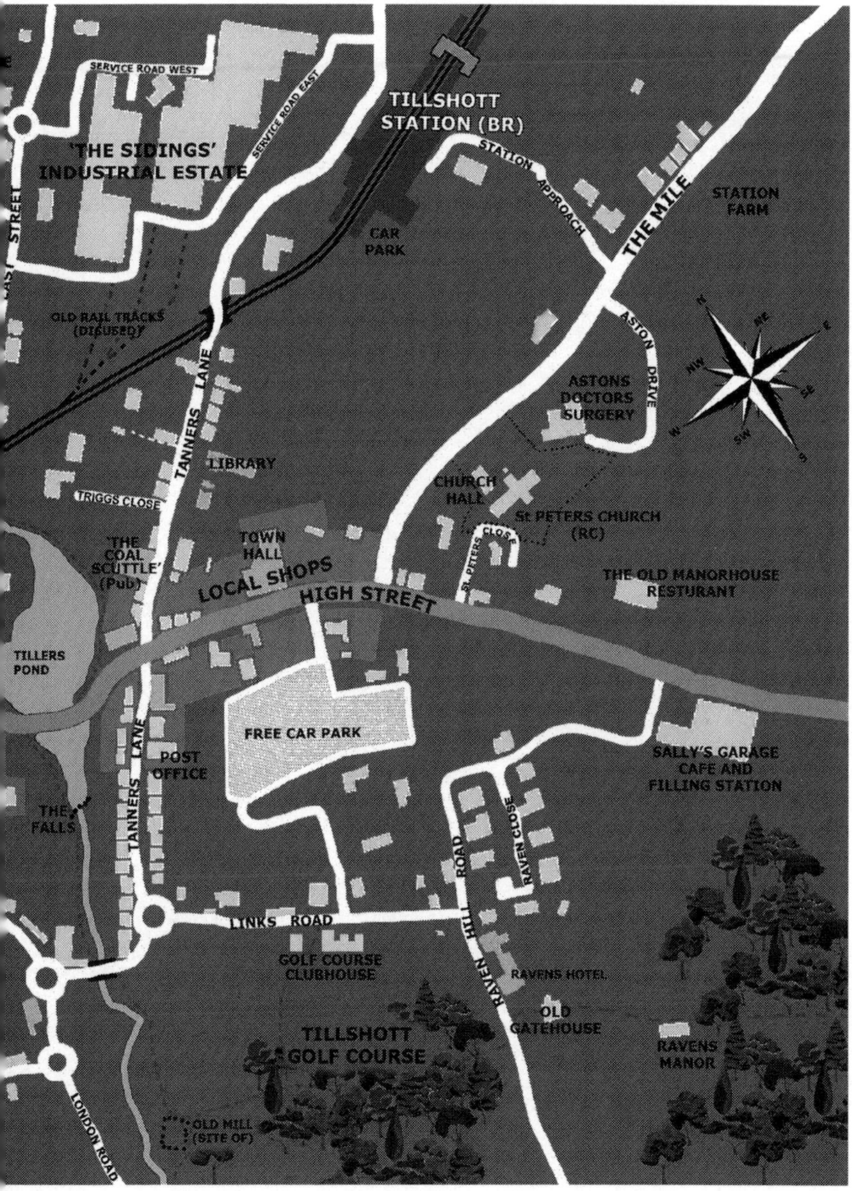
SERVICE ROAD WEST
SERVICE ROAD EAST
TILLSHOTT
STATION (BR)
'THE SIDINGS'
INDUSTRIAL ESTATE
STATION
APPROACH
THE MILE
STATION
FARM
EAST STREET
CAR
PARK
OLD RAIL TRACKS
(DISUSED)
ASTON DRIVE
ASTONS
DOCTORS
SURGERY
TANNERS LANE
LIBRARY
CHURCH
HALL
TRIGGS CLOSE
St PETERS CHURCH
(RC)
ST PETERS CLOSE
'THE
COAL
SCUTTLE'
(Pub)
TOWN
HALL
LOCAL SHOPS
HIGH STREET
THE OLD MANORHOUSE
RESTURANT
TILLERS
POND
FREE CAR PARK
POST
OFFICE
SALLY'S GARAGE
CAFE AND
FILLING STATION
THE
FALLS
RAVEN HILL ROAD
RAVEN CLOSE
LINKS ROAD
GOLF COURSE
CLUBHOUSE
RAVENS HOTEL
OLD
GATEHOUSE
TILLSHOTT
GOLF COURSE
RAVENS
MANOR
LONDON ROAD
OLD MILL
(SITE OF)
N
NE
E
SE
S
SW
W
NW

PROLOGUE

July 2001

Giovanni Stefano Agazzi wanted to tick off every item on his list.

He had prepared his paperwork in such a way that no one could misunderstand his wishes. His Will was up to date. His share certificates for various Australian mineral and mining companies, which he'd bought for a song back in the early 1980s, were placed, together with current valuations, in a new plastic folder. His solicitor had told him he was a lucky man because his investments had grown into a considerable fortune. He'd even joked with his client about it, saying he would add his name to the "rich list". Giovanni smiled at this, making no comment. He had only paid a few pounds for his initial investment. He wasn't a gambler.

His latest bank statements were placed in large brown envelopes; other files were put in plain manila folders. He had also updated his inventory of the house contents. It didn't take him long as he always kept it current, completing a check every year for the insurance company. Most of it was of little value, but Giovanni was obsessive about having everything "tickety-boo".

The last thing he dealt with was the letter to his son. He wouldn't make this too long, but he wanted it to be correct and as detailed as he could make it. He tore up his first two efforts and burnt them in the grate. After reading the third, he signed, dated and folded the pages to ensure an exact fit as he licked the envelope's seal, and wrote "Private and Confidential: for Stanleigh Agazzi" on the front. Then he tucked it out of sight below the other items.

He wanted his well-organised paperwork neatly laid out on the dining-room table, with each item clearly marked in black ink.

Oh, yes, this was exactly how he'd meant to present his affairs.

Wearing his best suit, a clean blue shirt and matching tie, he checked his chin for smoothness. Then he rubbed his hands over the rest of his face. Good. No roughness, no bristles and no stubble.

He thought that, maybe for the first time in his life, he would be doing the right thing. It wasn't going to benefit him but would hopefully begin to make up for all the hurt he had caused. From a financial viewpoint the action he planned would help his son Stanleigh and lovely wife Anna, and certainly benefit dear little Denise, Giovanni's only grandchild, whom he'd got to know and love so much in recent months.

But although his plan was well intentioned, this was still about him, about Giovanni. The distress to others, and probable repercussions from the actions he was about to carry out, never entered his mind.

After his wife died, he'd become a lost soul, depressed and devoid of hope. The sudden loss had made him realise how badly he had messed up their lives and that of their son Stanleigh. But he couldn't rewind the clock. Now, his decision made, Giovanni felt stronger and more positive than he had for years.

The letter he'd received from his doctor a few days ago had made everything so much clearer to him. The biopsies showed some evidence of abnormalities and the consultant was concerned enough to want him back for further tests, to ascertain the exact cause of his ongoing discomfort. Giovanni couldn't cope with illness at all. The last thing he wanted was to be "cut up and poked about", and he didn't want to end up being cared for in a nursing home, or as a burden on his son and family.

He'd considered, for a few brief moments, returning to Italy, but dismissed the idea as pointless, even dangerous.

In the kitchen, he prepared an excellent hearty feast: what Giovanni called "an Italian full English breakfast".

This consisted of a large cup of the best Italian coffee alongside a plate laden with two fried eggs, some rashers of bacon, his favourite Italian sausages, fried bread, tomatoes and a handful of olives, all covered with shavings of Parmesan cheese. The wonderful aroma made his mouth water as he stood over the cooker. To the empty room, he mumbled, "Yes, this will be the finest breakfast I have eaten in ages."

As soon as he'd finished the last drop of coffee, the plates, knives, forks, spoons and pans were washed, dried and put into the correct cabinets.

He folded his napkin and placed this neatly in the kitchen drawer.

His mind was made up. He was ready. It would be now or never. His hands shook because of the vast number of antidepressant tablets he'd consumed before starting to eat his breakfast.

With some difficulty, he climbed the stairs to his bedroom, went in and closed the door. From the back of the drawer in his bedside table, he removed a few 9mm cartridges and an automatic pistol, a Browning Hi-Power. He had secretly brought this weapon with him from Italy in 1945 and had managed to keep it well hidden ever since. It was the gun he'd used when ordered to take out the local police chief by the Partito Nazionale Fascista, the PNF, in 1941. But that was a long time ago during WWII. No one had ever suspected him of committing such a dreadful deed. Even so, he'd been glad to leave Italy, pretty damn' quick, when hostilities came to an end.

Sitting on the comfortable double bed, Giovanni hesitated for a moment before he picked up the gun and some cartridges.

Out of the bedroom window, he stared at the trees opposite as they moved a little in the light breeze. He forced himself to concentrate, unable to focus clearly. The drugs were now working and causing his vision to blur.

He played with the slide mechanism for a brief moment, to ensure everything was in working order. Two rounds were loaded into the magazine. A third slipped out of his hand and fell on the floor, rolling under the bed. Two rounds would be more than enough, he thought. With a shaky hand, he pushed the loaded magazine firmly into the butt where it locked with a solid click. The slide was pulled back and released, snapping into place with a sharp jolt. This forced a cartridge into the firing chamber.

Giovanni, now with tears in his eyes, was talking aloud to himself as he disengaged the safety catch. Holding the pistol against his right temple, he closed his eyes and started breathing heavily as his finger tightened on the trigger.

"Oh, Stanleigh, I so wish that…"

Chapter 1:

A Lesson in History

1976

Lee Agazzi woke with a jolt at about 8:30 in the morning, quite a bit later than usual. He leapt out of bed in a tizzy, and almost lost his balance in the gloom. He fumbled his way around the bedroom seeking the light switch, in the process stubbing his toe against the doorframe. He swore aloud from the sudden sharp pain and hobbled about as he tried to locate his slippers. He couldn't find them. Throwing his arms up in the air, he decided to forget them and put on an extra pair of socks instead. After a moment, he found and flicked the switch up and down a few times.

Sod it. No bloody power... again. He opened the striped curtains to allow some light into the room so he could see a little better.

The unusually cold and dark October morning, and the fact his toe throbbed with pain, did nothing to improve his mood.

He shivered, rubbing his hands rapidly up and down his arms, which were covered in goosebumps.

All night long his and Anna's sleep had been interrupted, on and off, by bursts of heavy rain. Lee had finally dozed off at around 4 a.m. Within an hour he was disturbed by his wife trying, as quietly as possible, to dress and get ready for work at the hospital, where she was on earlies all this week.

The severe weather during the night and his lack of sleep caused Lee to feel tired, pissed off, and playing catch-up for his meeting with the Vicar of St Aidan's Church. While walking from room to room, he talked to himself as he often did when on his own.

"Shit! I'll have to skip breakfast. I wish this bloody rain would stop."

The tantalising aroma of toast lingered in the air from Anna grabbing a bite to eat a few hours ago before the power cut.

She would often prepare breakfast for them both when her nursing rota allowed. This morning it hadn't.

The smell of toast made him hungry, but he would have to be satisfied with a glass of fruit juice this morning.

Lee hated being late, he had a thing about being on time. He always tried to be at least a minute or two early for appointments if he could.

On this occasion though, what would it matter if he ended up being a little delayed? The day hadn't started well, and for once he didn't care about being on time.

Their newly fitted heating system had turned itself off an hour earlier than the timer had indicated, caused by the loss of power. The flat was now a lot colder than normal for this time of the morning. Even the new light green shag pile carpet felt chilly. To add to the misery, as Lee glanced towards the front door, rainwater was leaking in along the bottom edge. Driven in by the ferocious wind, it had left a wet patch by the doormat.

From the lounge window, he looked out onto the street. The road was partially flooded by the deluge, water spraying over the pavements to both sides as cars drove slowly past. Still, although it was difficult to see much through the streaked glass, the rain seemed to have eased off a little.

The thought of getting soaking wet this morning didn't add anything positive to Lee's already low mood. He searched for something warm to put on. He was so uncomfortable, and so cold. He pulled several woolly jumpers from a drawer before finding the one he wanted, the discarded items left in a heap on his side of the bed. Then the light flickered on as the power was restored. This was the second time in a week they had lost electricity for more than two hours.

As soon as he'd picked up his coat and keys, he could hear rain starting to hammer against the windows again. He swore silently to himself.

Lee ran out to his van, pulling his collar up tight around his neck, but the rain still trickled down inside.

It was a good thing the church was only a short distance away. In the cold air, the small van steamed up within thirty seconds. Lee tried to clear the moisture from the inside of the windscreen so he could see the road ahead of him, and stuffed a couple of tissues inside his collar at the same time.

Jim Hordram, Vicar of St Aidan's, had telephoned a day or two earlier in the week to ask if Lee would pop in this morning, on his way to work, to discuss replacing the church's ageing kitchen cupboards. The laminate was peeling away in places, and some of the lower doors looked as if they were about to fall off.

They appeared to have been handmade, were about fifteen or twenty years old and now in a pretty sorry state.

To replace them would be easy enough, but it needed to be done before the Health & Safety inspection, which was due sometime over the next month or two. The church would not receive much more than a day's notice, which gave the work a touch of urgency.

Lee wondered if the church's new parish secretary would be in today. After his discussion with Jim, he decided he would pop in for a cup of coffee with her, in an attempt to get himself warm.

Iwona Kolawaski had arrived in Tillshott in the spring and was currently in the process of helping to organise the church's accounts. She'd turned up, completely out of the blue, offering her services in the office. Jim and his wife Sue couldn't believe their luck.

Sitting at a desk doing paperwork was not Jim's idea of fun. The filing system and the church's finances were, putting it mildly, not in particularly good order. He'd thought the new recruit might be the answer to their prayers.

Iwona was an attractive young lady, about five foot four inches tall with long, curly, dark brown hair and a very slim figure. She always dressed smartly in colourful clothes and quickly became popular in the parish, with her infectious smile and a kind word for everyone.

Despite her excellent command of English, however, Lee sometimes found it a little hard to make out what she was saying.

He had liked Iwona from the first moment they met. He felt her outgoing and open personality made her a welcome addition to the community. As he walked into the office today, he thought of snatching an opportunity to have a chat with her before his official meeting, but realised it wouldn't look very polite. He wondered briefly where she'd learnt to speak English and why she had come to work here at St Aidan's – being Polish she was most likely Roman Catholic and could have gone to St Peter's, the Catholic church, near the railway station on the other side of town.

After taking a lot of measurements and discussing what needed to be done, Lee asked the vicar if he could have a hot drink.

"An excellent idea. Think we both need warming up."

Jim led the way back into the kitchen.

"No Iwona today?" asked Lee.

"Well, no. Sadly, she left us last week. The accounts were short of quite a lot of money… to put it bluntly, Iwona had her fingers in the till. We were about a hundred pounds down, and when I confronted her, she was forced into admitting she'd borrowed it, to buy a new dress. She begged me not to call the police and handed about half of it back to me, saying how sorry she was."

"Well, I'm amazed, Jim. I thought she was ideal for you. She seemed so nice."

"Yes, I know, we liked her too. I only hope Iwona has learnt the error of her ways and pray she doesn't do this again somewhere else. Things could be a little difficult if she asks for a reference…"

Reverend Hordram had a sneaking feeling he had not heard the last of this young lady.

"There must be plenty of other places in town that would employ her, Jim. There are adverts in several of the shop windows offering employment and the pubs are always in need of bar staff."

Lee sat with his cup warming his hands, thinking about Tillshott. It was a charming place, lively and friendly with plenty of things to do and see.

"How long have you lived here?" he asked the vicar.

"Oh, I was born here. My dad was the town librarian. My wife is the daughter of a senior magistrate. So I've come to know a lot of the people in town and most of its history over the years."

In fact, as a result of this, Jim had become rather too keen on local history. He relished relaying odd facts about the town to everyone he met, whether they were interested or not.

And today was no exception.

Lee instantly regretted having asked the question. For the next ten minutes he couldn't get a word in edgeways.

"The village was first built around an ancient crossroads – you know, where the traffic lights are in the High Street?

Over the last hundred years or so, what was originally only a few small houses, a church, a mill and a rather grand manor house… well, it grew into the small town we have today.

"In about 1890 the introduction of the railway and the automobile caused Tillshott to expand rapidly, attracting new businesses and shops to provide the supplies and services needed by the increasing population. By 1945, the war had ended and the numbers living here had almost doubled, bringing the need for a large modern school and a small industrial estate. The various pubs, hotels and cafés became popular, attracting more and more people.

"One of the strangest stories locally is about the pub in Tanners Lane, the Coal Scuttle. I expect you know it? From about 1911 until 1939, there was a coal supplier in

Tillshott Junction signal box

the lane. It was popular and busy, with four big bunkers for the storage of the large quantities of coal needed. The business supplied almost everyone in Tillshott, and other towns nearby. Then one night the owner was murdered and the place set alight. The fire raged for several days, and after the site was finally cleared they discovered two mysterious underground passages linking the coal merchant's offices to the next-door premises.

"To everyone's amazement, the place was revealed to be a secret brothel. Following an investigation, the building was closed down and boarded up, and several people were arrested, including the town's Mayor. All those involved ended up behind bars, though it appeared the murderer, whoever he or she was, escaped since they were never apprehended. After the war, the premises became vacant and reopened as a public house. It was aptly named the Coal Scuttle and quickly grew into a favourite pub in this part of town."

"Yes, we met in there the other day and…"

But Jim was on a roll now. Without pausing for breath, he continued,

"The old coal bunker area became the car park. Some locals were saying the site was haunted and swore to having seen ghostly images there at night. As a result, no one would build on it. Well, there you are, 'Tillshott in a nutshell'. Interesting, isn't it? Hmmm…"

As Jim finished his story he sat looking rather breathless. Lee quickly collected up his papers with the details of the new kitchen requirements, said goodbye and headed back to his office at Slater & Parkes, Joiners.

As he drove through the still-pouring rain, he thought, Heavens above! That man could talk for England.

8

Chapter 2:

The Fragrance of Lemons

1945 – 1950s

In the months following VE Day, Giovanni Stefano Agazzi met and took an immediate fancy to Maureen Summers. It was a mutual attraction. He was a typical Italian charmer, and she soon found herself infatuated with him.

Maureen worked in British military intelligence during the war, and at the beginning of September 1945 had been posted to a clerical job in the only usable part of a semi-derelict block of flats on the outskirts of Milan. At the weekends she and some girls in her office would drive up to Lake Garda, a beautiful area where they would have coffee and lunch before returning in the evening. Fuel was difficult to obtain, so they took a military Jeep and delivered "despatches" to an MOD office in a village a little north of Malcesine on the eastern shore of the lake.

One beautiful sunny afternoon when the girls were in a hotel bar having a glass of wine, Maureen first met Giovanni. The whole place seemed to be full of locals drinking coffee or wine, many of them dressed in various different military-style uniforms. Other than the smell of fresh coffee, a pleasant aroma wafted around.

This was the fragrance of lemons, which grew here in abundance. Giovanni was oblivious to their scent. Having lived here all his life, most of it in a farmhouse about two kilometres outside the town, he no longer noticed it.

Recent military activities had destroyed some of the trees, but this area still had an abundance of them. All along the water's edge there seemed to be lemon trees, some even growing among the ruins of damaged buildings.

The war between the Germans and the Allies, coupled with civil unrest among Italy's population, had disrupted the old ways of life in the north. Whole sections of the population from some villages in the area had simply vanished.

Some were imprisoned as Fascist sympathisers; others executed by the Germans during the Occupation and their reluctant retreat.

Against this unsettled background Giovanni and Maureen decided to marry, preferably in Malcesine in what was left of the local church. After that they would travel to England as soon as arrangements could be made.

Unbeknown to Maureen, her fiancé needed an excuse

to leave Italy and would prefer it to come about sooner rather than later.

After the Germans were driven out of the country and the war ended, there was a reckoning to be made between Italians who had found themselves on different sides during the conflict. Reprisals started to take place against supporters of the executed Fascist leader Benito Mussolini. As the weeks passed, these revenge attacks became more frequent. Many people Giovanni knew, including an uncle, disappeared, one after the other. He felt sure he knew why this was, but there were some things it was better not to query. He didn't want to draw attention to himself. He thought he could find work as an accountant in England. He had a natural flair for figures and accounting was his current occupation, working for the local mayor.

He also spoke excellent English.

Many years before, his father had been employed in the Italian diplomatic service.

This culminated in a prestigious posting to the Italian Embassy in London in the 1930s. English became Giovanni's second language, and he spoke it happily, wherever he happened to be.

His father had been only too pleased to be well away from the right-wing politics that were sweeping through his country at that time, not wishing to play any part in them. Giovanni himself became embroiled more from necessity than any deep-rooted ideology, but he realised that his position in post-war Italy would always be tainted by his association with the now reviled PNF.

Maureen suggested he could take the English version of his name, John, after they moved to England.

She felt that since Italians living in England had been interned there during the war, his Italian name might prevent him from getting work. In the end, that was what happened, and although he was upset by the change, he got used to it. Secretly, however, he hated being called John and over time this resentment festered.

The fact that he was now calling himself John and not Giovanni certainly did help him to find employment in England. After that, of course, the name stuck. He attained all the necessary paperwork, quickly found a position with an English bank and started to settle down to married life.

However, his quick temper still got him into scrapes until, with Maureen's help, he managed to amend his drinking habits, and things became a little more relaxed.

Their son, Stanleigh, was born in 1956 and the responsibility of becoming a parent produced a noticeable change in the young father, at least for a few years.

Family life suited both husband and wife at first. Maureen stayed at home to care for their young son and John, as head of the household, slowly advanced through various positions in the bank. He was well pleased with the life he'd built for them. They even had a small car.

Yes, John was well pleased.

Maureen, though, was not so happy.

She became more and more housebound; John was not a particularly outgoing person, and as a result she saw few of her former chums. John didn't seem to make many friends, and apart from one or two of his work colleagues they saw nobody. They went out infrequently, John making it plain he disliked most of Maureen's pals.

Over time she became mentally crushed. John gave her little freedom. Bluntly put, her husband was controlling and dominating.

Maureen thought perhaps this was how all Italian men behaved, but it didn't help, and she wondered if marrying him had been a big mistake. As a result, she became more and more unhappy.

Things brightened a little for her when the stray cat that had "adopted" them the year before gave birth to three gorgeous kittens in the spring. This gave them all a new interest. Maureen and Stanleigh loved the latest additions to the family. The surprise was that John also loved the kittens, and so life calmed down – for a while at least. They all played with the kittens during the evenings, one each. The soothing effect of stroking the furry little bundles on their laps worked wonders.

Pippy the cat

As more time passed, though, the arguments and bitterness started to re-emerge.

The kittens went to new homes. John's temper, never particularly good at the best of times, returned to its previous levels. This didn't do him any favours with their neighbours.

One evening there was a knock at the door. Two police officers stood on the doorstep. The lady from next door was so worried by all the shouting she was hearing coming from their house, she'd called the police, fearing the worst.

John answered the knock and almost punched the uniformed copper he found standing on the step. Luckily, his better judgement stopped him just in time.

Shaken by the experience, and by having to eat humble pie to the officers, he promised he would be quieter and more considerate in future.

For a few months things did calm down again until another row started — over some water spilt on the kitchen floor.

Most of John and Maureen's battles started over insignificant things like this.

One Sunday afternoon, Doug Hughes, a work colleague of John's, called at the house unexpectedly, to see how he was. The previous day he had been off work suffering from a bad chesty cough.

As they sat down for a cup of tea, Doug said he and his wife had been praying for John who had looked so unwell the day before. They were worried about him.

Surprised to hear this, John said he didn't know they were the religious type. In a distinctly cool tone of voice, he thanked them for the effort they had made on his behalf but said he didn't think prayer would make any difference to his life. It never had when he lived in Italy.

The Catholic Church, in his opinion, was overbearing and controlling. After arriving in England, he'd been only too glad to forget all about his former religion, run by allegedly pious priests with unquestioned domination over their flocks.

"…all a load of religious clap-trap," he denounced them to Doug. "It's a covert way of controlling the credulous, if you ask me."

So, religion was now off John's radar, he said. In fact, he put it like this:

"As you English say, it's all done and dusted for me."

Unpleasant memories of church-going during his youth still haunted him. Most particularly the way the strong-smelling incense used during services had made him feel. It had affected his breathing badly, often making him cough for hours afterwards.

Whether he believed in prayer or not, though, Maureen was annoyed by the way he'd dismissed Doug's observation about his friend being in his prayers. She considered this kind and thoughtful of their visitor, and thought John might have responded with a little more grace.

This was the first time Maureen herself had thought about God or religion in a very, very long time. She wondered if praying for someone made any difference to their life. Even the memories of her parents taking her to church functions during her childhood were somewhat vague.

Maureen's mum and dad had both passed away some years ago, and she had little recollection of there ever being discussions at home about God or religion, except in a purely historical context. Neither could she recall going to a religious service, even at Christmas. The only times she remembered entering a church was for the occasional wedding or funeral. Maureen hated funerals.

She decided to try and find the details of her parents' marriage and to look for her own birth certificate, to find out where she was born. After a few hours spent delving through drawers, cupboards and boxes, as well as in the little garage they'd put up by the side of the house, she gave up when nothing materialised.

But it made her think there could be more significance to this chance meeting with Doug than she'd previously considered.

Maureen decided when she next went shopping she might pop into the local Catholic church. She wasn't sure why exactly, and the whole business vaguely unsettled her. Over the following days, she withdrew into herself and tried to come to grips with the impact of Doug's words about prayer. They filled her thoughts and she found she could not dismiss them.

Chapter 3:

School Reports

1968 – 1973

It was 17 July 1968, a typically hot English summer's day. The sun streamed in through the large open windows. Not that John Agazzi noticed the weather in any way whatsoever. He was sitting at the kitchen table, feet resting on the wooden crossbar, a cup of coffee in one hand and his son's school report in the other. It had arrived in the morning post.

He wasn't too comfortable on the hard wooden chair and wondered who'd moved the seat pad. He shuffled his feet, so they were tucked right under him. He was uncertain how to react.

What should he do with this report on his son? He wasn't sure what to think. It wasn't exactly bad, but neither was it complimentary.

Comments made by some of the teachers compounded his paternal distress. Could do better… Lazy… Uncooperative. John focused on the negatives.

He began breathing deeply, and could feel a muscle twitching in his right eye. He shook his head to stop the irritating tic, but it didn't help. Neither did rubbing the eye with his hand.

In his agitated state, he grabbed hold of a pencil and started jabbing the tabletop with such ferocity that he snapped off the point, leaving a small hole in the pinewood surface.

The combination of his son's low marks and some of the derogatory comments made about him, had disturbed John. He considered that his son should be a reflection of himself. In his mind, the written criticisms of Stanleigh were indirect criticisms of his father.

Stanleigh's shortcomings would not be tolerated, John decided. He wouldn't let any son of his behave in this way in his house. Not now, not ever.

John's rage mounted inside him until he thumped his fist repeatedly on the table, causing his cup to bounce and rattle on its saucer. He would need to have a few sharp words with young Stanleigh. Something must be done about his attitude.

Noticing the empty cup, Maureen put a big mug of John's favourite Italian coffee out for him. She asked what he was studying and why he was getting so upset.

"Stanleigh's school report – it's not good enough. He's becoming delinquent, and such bad things they are saying. Not one good word anywhere."

At times like these, when John became annoyed, his

English always seemed to deteriorate. Sometimes he would even slip back into his native Italian.

"He's still very young – only twelve after all. Most children seem to go through ups and downs at his age."

"Not these things, Maureen. Bad things that make me ashamed to be his father. My son must be good at school or people will blame me. *I* will look bad." Maureen knew better than to say anything to John when he was in a bad mood like this, so she went upstairs to the bedroom, biting her lip nervously.

After Stanleigh came home from school, John took him into their rather austere dining room and told him to sit at the dining table. There was a moment of awkward silence. John could feel the nerve in his eye start to twitch again. Before Stanleigh got in from school, he had been pacing up and down the room, practising aloud what he wanted to say.

They now sat opposite each other, staring across the table for a while before John started to speak.

"I am going to read you, Stanleigh, what some teachers at your school say of you." He looked away from his son to steady himself and peered out of the large bay window instead.

After a few seconds, he took a deep breath and began to pass on the adverse comments.

"You are lazy… Uncooperative… Could do better… Not making any effort… and lots more."

This stream of accusations was relayed to his son in a voice that grew louder and louder.

Stanleigh just sat there, blinking at each point. The words felt like bricks being hurled at him, one after the other, hitting him on the head.

"What do you have to say to that, eh? No, don't answer, it's all here in the report. Nothing you can say will make any difference. You're failing at school and *I will not have it!*"

If the situation hadn't been so serious, the spectacle John presented would have been quite ludicrous. Having worked himself up into a wild fury, he was waving his arms about and pointing his finger repeatedly at his son with a stabbing motion. He stood up, report in hand, and smashed his chair into the table leg as he left the room, slamming the door hard behind him.

By now the boy was feeling tearful and afraid. He sat there, not knowing whether he should stay or go. He thought he must be stupid and useless, as his father said... Why else would his dad say these things?

He wanted to run to his mother and for her to hug him. In his miserable and confused state, he didn't know what to do, so he sat there getting more and more upset and depressed, trying to understand what he had done wrong. Fifteen or twenty minutes passed in this way as he sat staring down at the floor. A loud noise from somewhere in the house made him sit bolt upright. He glanced fearfully at the door, then aimlessly around the room.

The doorframe now had a small split on the lower edge, he saw. Some of the paint must have chipped off and left one or two white fragments on the carpet.

The clock on the mantelpiece seemed to have stopped, and on the sideboard, the EKCO radio was turned on, but there was no sound coming from it.

The boy looked down at the floor again, too afraid to move.

A tapping sound distracted him, and through the front window he noticed a robin settle on the sill, pecking at the putty holding the glass in place. It stopped for a short time and seemed to stare straight at him, cocking its head to one side before flying away. Stanleigh wished he could fly away too.

An overwhelming sensation of dark loneliness and insecurity began to consume him.

For Stanleigh, this scene with his father proved to be a defining moment. This one incident would mark the end of his childhood and the beginning of the next chapter in his life.

Never again would he think his father loved or felt any affection for him.

Neither would he have any feelings for his father apart from fear and hatred. He would have to live with this difficult situation every day.

It felt like the end of his little world and he started to worry about what might happen in the days and months ahead.

Still sitting with his elbows on the table, his head in his hands, the boy closed his eyes. Glimpses of events from previous years flashed through his mind. Some of the memories were happy ones. He could recall when he was about two or three years old, standing on the sofa looking out over railway sidings, watching and listening to the loud clatter as the massive engines shunted wagons about on the rail track.

Another memory flashed before him from one of the occasional long walks through the woods they took on sunny days: he sat perched high up on his father's

Tractor with gulls following

shoulders, watching and hearing the squawking gulls as they gathered behind a tractor ploughing the field they were passing.

Next he remembered laughter during snowball fights in their back garden in winter. One Christmas morning as they were out for a walk, he recalled his mother picking him up and wiping away his tears. He had tripped and fallen headlong into a stone wall, chipping a corner off one of his front teeth.

He visualised happier days spent making bamboo bows and arrows on hot sunny afternoons, and moving around barrows full of earth as his father tried to level the lawn, one day in early spring.

Not all his memories were so happy though. Once while playing with his toy steam engine, he cut his hand and was taken to the local hospital as the bleeding wouldn't stop. He didn't want to remember that at all.

His fear of hospitals stemmed from that day and would remain with him for the rest of his life.

Even happy memories now seemed tainted by an overwhelming sadness. These events seemed to belong to a different time.

He couldn't understand what had gone so wrong. Why did his father hate him so much?

His mum still loved him, Stanleigh was certain of that. And, oh, how he loved his mother! She was always loving and affectionate to him, and he felt safe and secure when he was with her.

Over the last few years, she'd struggled to protect him from the worst aspects of his father's bad temper and hysterical outbursts, which were becoming ever-more frequent.

From a young age, Stanleigh knew he could always go to her. In his early schooldays, when he had difficult homework questions or was upset about something, she was always able to calm him.

Maureen would put comforting arms around her son, soothing him with hugs and kisses. Sometimes she would sing to him. By the age of five or six, he recognised that this behaviour only seemed to occur when his father was working, or at times when they happened to be alone in the house.

None of it was of any significance to him then, but now, looking back...

Over the next few years, Stanleigh's problems with schoolwork, and predictably poor end-of-term reports, did nothing to improve his relationship with his father. The drawings and paintings the boy would do at home littered his bedroom. Sometimes his mum would collect some of them and show them to his dad.

"Look at these, John. Stanleigh is quite a good artist, isn't he? What do you think of this one?" She handed him a small painting of their house and garden.

"I suppose it's OK as a hobby. An utter waste of time, though. Can't he find something better to do?" John snatched the picture and tore it in two, dropping the pieces on the table.

Maureen, used to his outbursts, said nothing. She collected the pieces and went upstairs to the bedroom in tears.

As the reports kept dropping through the letterbox at the end of each term, John's dressing down of his son became a regular event. The ranting. The threats. On one occasion he threw the contents of his coffee mug at Stanleigh, missing his face by inches. On banging the mug back down on the table, the handle broke off, causing a brief pause in John's tirade. Stanleigh almost started to laugh. It was a rare moment of joy, which disappeared in the blink of an eye.

When he turned sixteen, the dreaded GCEs loomed and his sense of alienation increased. He became more miserable and depressed as time went by and developed a real fear and loathing of his father.

His dear mother also suffered from the outbursts, which became almost daily. John would shout at her, pushing her verbally into a corner with constant threats and accusations.

One morning, before breakfast, he asked Stanleigh to bring down an assortment of his drawings and paintings, telling him to leave them on the kitchen table before he left for school. Maureen believed at long last John was going to have a better look at them. He, though, calmly walked up to the table, picked up his son's work and, without even a second glance, tore every item to pieces.

"You can put these in bin, Maureen. His schoolwork is more important than this… this total waste of my time and money."

Her husband then picked up his coat and left the house for work without another word. Maureen stood there for a while in disbelief. Then she gathered up the pieces and carefully put them in an envelope, tucking this away carefully under the mattress in their bedroom.

Stanleigh reached the point where he even started to hate his own name. A bloody stupid one it was too, he thought, blaming his father. He can't even spell it properly – just Stanley would have been a bit better but it's so old fashioned!

On occasions, his schoolfriends called him Stan. He hated the name. Disliked this even more than the full version of Stanleigh, and for some unknown reason, it reinforced his feelings of remoteness and alienation.

One day, while looking into the bedroom mirror, he came up with an idea. He would call himself Lee. It sounded so much better, more modern, reminding him of one of the presenters on Radio Luxembourg.

Slowly, over the next few months, while away from home he would be known as Lee.

He knew this would annoy his father, and the thought of that brought a wry smile to the boy's face.

Hardly any of his schoolmates commented on the name change. Being addressed as Lee gave him an entirely new image of himself, which in turn made him a little more self-confident. At home, of course, nothing changed.

So he became both an "at home person" and an "anywhere else person". His alter ego of Lee seemed to create itself around him. Over a short time, with anyone apart from his parents, he was a different person.

Weeks and months dragged past.

Things at home didn't improve, and he kept out of his father's sight as much as possible.

There were occasional clashes over his homework, or what he was wearing, but nothing too alarming.

His father's behaviour seemed to be getting worse as time went by. There would be many rows. His treatment of Maureen was downright appalling most of the time although he always managed to stop short of actual physical violence, albeit coming close to it at times.

Even so, he would frequently reduce her to tears with his vicious, cutting remarks.

John Agazzi was a wretchedly unhappy man, often, quite falsely, raging about how he was forced to leave Italy against his will.

He threatened to return there… on his own.

Stanleigh hoped he would.

Chapter 4:

Repercussions

1973

Stanleigh's final school exams in June and July of 1973 arrived with a rush. In the middle of July he received his GCE 'O' level results.

These were somewhat predictable. Of the seven subjects sat, he passed only two, Art and Woodwork.

Stanleigh was in fact pleased with these results. The exam board gave him grade 'A' in both. These were the only two school subjects in which the teaching staff took an active interest in him. The two teachers concerned always encouraged him and tried to give help as needed – the direct result being, they were the only subjects at which Lee did well. The more academic disciplines didn't suit him at all.

The intense concentration needed to enable him to read and take in the various texts needed in other subjects made his eyes hurt, so that he would shut them for a moment or two every now and again. One day, thinking he was asleep, a teacher noticed this, and angrily threw a wooden blackboard duster at him. It hit Lee forcefully on his forehead, splitting his eyebrow and covering his face in blood. The boys at desks nearby started laughing – until they saw the blood.

Stanleigh would never forget sitting the first of his GCE 'O' level exam papers.

It was Mathematics, his worst subject. Even the simplest of mathematical questions drove him into a panic. He would look at the numbers and symbols, trying desperately to understand and make sense of them. He wrote and rewrote the various combinations on some spare paper, but whatever he did, it didn't help in the least. There seemed no logic to them. It was as if the figures were in a random meaningless state of disorder. The inner struggle to comprehend caused him so much stress, made him so agitated, his eyes became painful and he would feel physically sick.

After looking at the first two questions, which he didn't understand, he didn't even bother to look at the rest. He thought what an utter waste of time this was. Instead of working out answers, he started drawing in areas where the answers should be… he drew sketches of the teacher or one of the pupils instead. About twenty minutes passed in this way until Lee began to feel ill. He put his hand up to attract one of the invigilators but got no response. Then he threw up all over the desk. That got their attention quickly enough.

Stanleigh was rushed to the sick bay where he was put on a bed and covered with a blanket to doze until the school nurse arrived.

He couldn't comprehend how words and numbers worked. Every time he studied the figures, they looked different to him. Trying to read pages of text or understand mathematical questions caused him trauma. He tried, so many times, to explain this to his mum. She was always very kind, trying to calm him, but couldn't seem to understand his problem, and definitely couldn't help him.

One Saturday morning his father picked up one of Stanleigh's painting's, the study piece he did for his GCE in Art. He looked down his nose at it briefly, before disparagingly dropping it back onto the kitchen table.

"This painting nonsense won't get you anywhere. If you have any ideas about going to Art School, forget it. I'm not paying for that. I've seen these Art students. They're all the same – a bunch of drug-taking hippies."

Lee stood there, saying nothing. He wanted to punch his father in the mouth. Make him choke on and swallow his words. But instead he looked down at the floor, feeling useless. Exactly what his bullying father always said he was... useless.

In his head he could hear the parting words spoken by his Art teacher only a few weeks before.

"You can do it! You've got the talent, Lee. Look at your use of colour. Show them all what you can do. Get a degree in Fine Art..."

Lee never believed he could be capable of getting a degree... but it was his hidden dream. The reality was that there was no way on this planet he could ever get into a university without the right qualifications. And that would never be possible for him.

One thing his teacher had said was true, though: Lee was very precise about the colours he chose for his pictures. Every one of them needed to be correct. Each colour and its relative position in the composition was deliberate and purposeful. He didn't understand why or how this mattered so much, but the way the colours went together or merged was of great importance to him... they had to be right. It was the colour combinations and their positions to each other that gave his paintings structure and meaning, so he worked hard to make sure every tint and tone was in the right spot and of the correct strength. If his outline drawing was not perfect, this would be rather less important, so long as the colour was true.

On his last day at school, after saying goodbye to his Art teacher he left the school building. Stanleigh then took off his blazer, removing the nametag and rolling the hated uniform jacket into a ball. After placing it in the centre of the headmaster's private lawn, he proceeded to set it alight, using a small bottle of lighter fuel to get the flames going.

He could see the headmaster standing at his office window as the smoke started to drift across the grass. Stanleigh stuck up two fingers at him. The boy was laughing as he ran off with a couple of his admiring mates. He hated the headmaster with a passion, as did most of his friends. As far as they were concerned, the man was a nasty bully who never seemed to say a kind word to any of the pupils, or anyone else either.

The previous year, one of the fifth-form boys had tried to burn down the main school building. The blaze had been quickly extinguished and the offender been taken away by the police.

Then a week later, the Headmaster's car was vandalised with brake fluid and a sharp, heavily serrated knife. Over half the school was finger-printed by the police, but the culprit was never apprehended.

There followed a few weeks of relative peace until what turned out to be a tragedy for Stanleigh. His official GCE exam result sheet arrived in the post. This didn't show the number, or quality, of grades his father expected him to achieve. These, of course, according to John should have included English, Mathematics, Geography and History at a minimum. Stanleigh's two 'A' grade passes were ignored entirely, as if they didn't exist.

His father considered such qualifications useless for the job he'd already lined up for his son in the bank, where John was now a branch manager.

"With those results he'll be banging nails into coffins or else a drug-taking hippy!" he raged to himself, once again pacing up and down.

Another furious row broke out. John faced Stanleigh, grabbed his right sleeve and marched him into the dining room once again.

"*Che disgrazia!*" he began. "After all I've done for you and years of school fees, you – you produce no useful GCE exam result, not even one. *Nessuno! Mi spieghi* this worthless result." As he spoke he literally spat with fury.

Stanleigh sat there, becoming more and more uncomfortable, not knowing what to say.

31

"*Dimmi*, what good are these results?" his father raged.
Stanleigh started to speak.

"But I got the top grade, 'A', in Art and Woodwork.
They were the only subjects in which the teachers…"

"*Stai zitto!* I don't want your excuses, you are a useless
idiot. I say again, what use are these results – to me?"

John, screaming by now, stabbed his index finger into
his own chest at least ten times to emphasise the point.
He stood up abruptly, tipping his chair back onto the
floor where it landed with a thud, fractionally missing the
piano. Then he stormed out.

Stanleigh screwed up his eyes, waiting for the almighty
bang of the door slamming.

Instead, there was silence. The dining-room door
remained ajar. Everything went quiet. He heaved a sigh of
relief, thinking the worst was finally over. He hoped things
would now calm down, as they had in previous years.

But this time he'd got it so, so wrong.

A few days later, after seeming to be in a reflective
mood, John told his unsuspecting son to pack a bag and
get out of "his" house – the house that hitherto had been
known as home by the boy. John's attitude seemed to
change in a split second from being almost calm to manic.

Stanleigh couldn't believe what he was hearing. Surely
his father didn't mean it. Where was he supposed to go?
What was he going to do?

How would he live on his own? He had no money,
few clothes, almost nothing in fact.

Stanleigh could hear his mother crying in the kitchen.
He loved his mum and started to go to her, but his father
stood barring the way, arms tight at his sides, fists up and

clenched. The sight of his seething pitch-black eyes caused Stanleigh to take a step backwards in alarm.

He thought his father resembled a picture of Satan he remembered seeing in a Bible. There wasn't anything anyone could do to change things between them at this moment.

This was the lowest point in Stanleigh's life, and he didn't know what to do, or where he would go. At almost 6:30 in the evening, he was marched upstairs and told to throw a few things in a bag. Then he was ushered to the front door. "Go! Get out! You're a good-for-nothing, a disgrace, a useless lout… yes, a bloody useless good-for-nothing… go on, get out, get out! You… you take my money… I pay for your school, and you're just a bloody idiot. *Tu non sei figlio mio.*" John almost spat the last words at the boy he had decided was no longer worthy of being called his son.

Stanleigh, physically evicted from the family home, was shocked beyond belief.

How could his father do this? And why? What had he ever done to make his father hate him so much? Stanleigh was desperate to go to his mum, to hug her and try and protect her. He had never seen his father in a worse state. Maybe he would have a heart attack and drop dead… For a terrible moment, he considered the possibility that his raging father might kill his Mum.

His lasting memory was of hearing her in the kitchen, crying and screaming in protest at her husband's decision, and then the crash as the front door slammed shut in his face. The violence of it had cracked an edging piece, causing a panel of beading to become detached. The piece of wood was left dangling, held only by a thin nail.

33

Hearing his wonderful, loving mother in a tearful state would leave an indelible mark on Stanleigh. This would cause him more pain than anything else he had experienced in his short troubled life.

The memory of her distress, and his own feeling of absolute helplessness and inability to do anything to help her, would continue to haunt him for a very long time.

For a moment or two, he stood still, numb, staring at the damaged door. After a while, he started to back away.

The seriousness of his situation began to sink in then.

Where could he go? He now had no home, few clothes and only the coins in his pocket.

Stanleigh started walking away from the house.

He wandered in the general direction of the town centre for nearly an hour, not knowing which way to turn. He was wearing only his jeans, a T-shirt, a light blue rain jacket, and on his feet a pair of reasonably new black and white plimsolls.

He had no idea which way he should go. From their home in Cogg's Path, he wandered in both directions for a while, before arriving at a road junction and recognising the street name. Till Farm Road was where Georgie Slater lived, one of his few friends from school.

He thought Georgie's mum and dad might be able to help him or at least know what to do – although he'd accept help from almost any source at the moment.

He even considered going to the police station to try and have his father arrested, then changed his mind. Stanleigh was frightened of the police.

Feeing sad and weary, Stanleigh Agazzi, sports bag in hand, stumbled up the garden path to the front door of 12 Till Farm Road and rang the doorbell.

He wouldn't speak to or have any further contact with his father for the next thirteen years.

Chapter 5:

New Beginnings

1973

As Sarah Slater, Georgie's mother, opened the door to her son's friend, her usual warm friendly smile disappeared. She gasped at the sight before her.

"Lee, what on earth... Are you OK?" The tear-stained face and general appearance of the shivering young boy shocked her. Had someone attacked him? After a quick glance outside, she took hold of his arm and almost carried him into the house. They went through the wide hall and into the kitchen, where she sat him down, placing a blanket around the shaking boy before making him a cup of tea. Tea was Sarah's instant answer to every conceivable problem.

She pulled her chair up close to his and, putting an arm around his shoulders, rocked him gently like a young child.

Lee was now crying and spluttering, to such an extent he couldn't speak clearly, and what he did manage to say didn't make an awful lot of sense.

Slowly, over the next hour, Sarah managed to coax the whole sad story out of him.

When Lee had finished speaking, she told him her son Derek – the name by which Georgie was christened – had left with some schoolfriends two days previously for a camping holiday in Ireland.

"He won't be back for about two weeks," she explained. "That gives us a little while to see what we can do to help your situation. We'll get something arranged, Lee, don't worry. I'm sure this won't be as bad as you think."

Jim and Sarah's home was a four-bedroomed, detached house. They always kept a guest room in readiness and Sarah took Lee's small bag upstairs, placing it on a chair in front of the window. The large double room was bright and warm, with twin beds. As Lee looked around, he noticed it appeared to be much lighter and bigger than his bedroom at home.

"This will be your room for now, Lee, for as long as you need it."

"Thank you," was all he could manage to say.

Jim Slater arrived home late from work as usual and was dismayed to find Lee sitting in their dining room, looking upset and more than a little dishevelled.

"Are you OK, lad? What's going on here then?"

Before Lee could say anything, Sarah grabbed her husband by the arm, took him into the kitchen and closed the door behind them. Lee heard their muffled voices but was beyond trying to listen to the conversation. He sat in silence, almost numb, in his own black void.

After a few minutes, Jim came back with two tankards of beer and plonked himself down next to Lee.

"You look like you could do with one of these," he said, as he pushed a mug across the table. Lee was astonished to be offered beer, thinking this would never have happened at home.

"Thanks, Mr Slater." Nothing else was said until Sarah joined them a little later. The three of them sat talking at the circular dining table for quite a long time, or so it seemed to Jim. He was hungry and wanted some dinner after his long day at work. He wouldn't get much to eat except biscuits until much later on in the evening.

After the late dinner, Lee went to bed. He hadn't felt hungry and had hardly touched his food. He felt drained and exhausted. His eyes were red and sore. Sleep didn't come easily. But, after a few restless hours, he eventually drifted off.

Sarah pulled her chair close to Jim's and asked in a low voice if he thought they should contact Lee's parents. She thought his mother at least must be worried silly about him.

"What do you think we ought to do?"

"Having heard what Lee told us about his father, I suggest we leave things to simmer down for a day or two."

"He said his dad has a violent temper, Jim. I certainly don't want him coming round here. I think I'll phone them in a day or two. Probably during the morning as I think I'd be more likely to get Mrs Agazzi on her own at that time."

"Yes. OK. I think that may be an idea. Look, it's been a gruelling few hours. Sleep on it for now and see how we feel tomorrow."

The following day after Jim had left for work, Sarah woke Lee with a mug of tea. For an instant, he had no idea where he was. He jumped and almost knocked the hot drink over the bed. The realisation he wasn't at home in his own room made him upset again.

"What time is it?" he asked.

"A little after ten-thirty. I thought it would do you good to lie in for a while this morning. Sleep is a great healer, you know."

She felt so sorry for him. He was a young boy and to lose the security of normal home life was dreadful for him.

Later, alone with her husband, she spoke to him again about Lee.

"Do you realise he hardly has anything with him? He's got no money, and his bag contains only one change of clothing and a pair of shoes. The poor boy was so embarrassed when I asked about his clothes. He doesn't even have spare underwear. I can't believe any parent could do this to their child, whatever the reason. It's barbaric."

The following morning Sarah took Lee out to Marks & Spencer and they ended up with two trolley loads of new clothes, a completely new wardrobe. She also added a toothbrush, hairbrush and a shaver as he didn't seem to possess any of these either. Lee could feel himself getting flushed as Sarah talked about personal items, his lack of underwear and the toiletries he needed. He swallowed hard with embarrassment, looking down at the ground. In a weak voice, he told her he didn't have the money to pay her for any of it. Sarah told him not to worry about the money. She was only too pleased to be able to help out. He didn't know what to say, or how to thank her, so he just smiled. He opened his mouth to speak, but the words wouldn't come. Sarah put her arms around him, hugging him for a brief moment.

Slater and Parkes Ltd

Some years before this, Jim's sister Gina had married his best friend, Tom Parkes. And it was no surprise to anyone when Tom and Jim, who'd both worked as joiners since leaving school, started a business venture together. They opened a joinery, a short distance away on the local industrial estate. They were doing well and already expanding by employing four excellent and reliable workers. It was a small, happy and close-knit company, and they considered this would be a suitable time for them to take on a young apprentice.

Over a pint in the Coal Scuttle, their local pub, Jim talked at length with his brother-in-law about young Lee, to decide whether he might be the right candidate. He didn't know Lee overly well, but thought if he could prove himself reliable and work to a suitable standard, it might be a sensible move for the company. It would also give the boy some stability.

After discussing various options with Tom, they decided to ask Lee if he would like to come along for a chat, to see how he might feel about working for the company.

Jim wanted to ask what Sarah thought about the idea before saying anything to Lee. He always talked everything over with her first, and had done so ever since they married, most noticeably so since the company was created.

Her approval gave him more confidence and made Sarah feel involved. Sometimes she wished he would get on with things sooner, but secretly she liked her opinion being sought and appreciated. A couple of days later over breakfast, when she and Jim were alone, Sarah mentioned she was keeping a close eye on their guest and remarked on how polite and respectful Lee seemed.

He'd offered to help with the washing up and anything else that needed to be done. He'd gone to the local Co-op, to buy some groceries for her, the previous afternoon.

After dinner, though, Lee had become quiet again and gone off early to bed.

She related to Jim the stories Lee had told her about his troubled home situation, and how difficult his father made life for both him and his mum. She thought it would do no harm to suggest the apprentice's position to him as he certainly would need a job, and soon.

The position at Slater & Parkes would be an excellent opportunity for Lee. But would it prove to be to the long-term benefit of the company?

Only time would give them the answer to that question.

A couple of days later, after breakfast, Jim took Lee to the joinery to meet Tom. Lee was nervous, and during the short journey he hardly said a word. He hadn't met Tom before and had never been for an interview in his life.

As the morning progressed, he tried hard to appear interested and to say the right things.

Everything seemed to be going well. Lee even allowed himself to smile – and that made all the difference.

Tom took a liking to him and considered that, with careful training, this young man would do them very well. It could be a positive move for all of them.

Lee seemed like a sensible youngster. He was practical, loved woodwork, and Tom liked his mild, gentle nature. There was no belligerence in him. No negative attitude that Tom could detect, unlike one or two of the previous job seekers. Only maybe a slight touch of sadness and this was, in the circumstances, more than understandable.

Tom's instinct told him Lee would fit in well here. Before finalising the appointment, though, he wanted to talk it over in private with Jim.

He asked one of the machine technicians to show Lee around the premises, let him grasp at first-hand what the company made and the modern machinery they used.

Lee liked the idea of making things from wood, and some of the items awaiting finishing looked most impressive to him. He would love to achieve results of such high quality, he decided. Looking at a newly made high-backed Windsor chair, he thought, maybe one day... The positive side was that, with proper training, he believed this was achievable. Assuming he was offered the job, of course.

For the first time in years, Lee sensed a quiver of excitement run through him. This could give him a completely new life. His heart started racing at the very thought.

While he looked at the machinery, Jim and Tom took the opportunity to have a break and a chat.

Decision made, Jim invited the youngster to come back into the office and they offered him a position as a trainee on the spot. Lee seemed quite surprised and not sure how to respond at first.

"Oh... er, well, yes, please. I would love to work here, thank you very much."

Having only left school recently and never having worked before, not even at a Saturday job, Lee found the prospect exciting.

Tom worked out the details of his pay and hours.

It was decided the young man would start work the following Monday. This would give him a chance to get his thoughts together and, with Sarah's help, come to an arrangement about any extra clothes he might need. It would also give him the time to set up a bank account.

Sarah and Jim decided to let Lee stay with them, as a sort of unofficially adopted son, at least until his home situation improved to a point where he could go back to his parents.

When she approached Lee with their decision, he was lost for words. He was so grateful. The whole situation, though, made him feel rather awkward, and a bit of an intruder. After all, he had nothing to offer them. He wasn't in any position to pay his way as he still only possessed the few coins that were in his pocket when he'd left home. Sarah assured him his lack of money would not be a problem, and they were pleased to help in any way they could.

Anyway, he would be earning his own money soon. They certainly couldn't let him wander the streets until then, could they?

"Georgie will be home shortly, and you will be good company for each other," she reminded him.

Then the problematic bit Lee had dreaded and had almost forgotten, reared its ugly head.

Sarah wanted to call his parents to let them know he was safe and well.

"Lee poppet, I need to speak to them. You are still a minor. Not eighteen yet…"

He froze.

"No – oh, no. Please don't tell my dad where I am! Please, please, don't do that… I'll do anything you want, but please…"

Lee didn't want his father to know anything about him at all. Absolutely no way did he want contact to be made. Sarah tried to calm him as he stood up and sat down several times and then shuffled about on his chair.

After trying to wriggle his way out of any contact being made with his family, a mental image of his mum crying got the better of the boy and he caved in.

With tear-filled eyes, and by now shaking visibly, he wrote down the details in untidy handwriting and handed them to Sarah.

Was his new life going to end here? He didn't know.

Sarah had been so kind, but also so insistent, that there was no other option but to give her his full address and phone number. Although only a couple of days had passed since his arrival, it felt like weeks ago. Lee was happy and content for the first time in ages. Sarah was being a wonderful mum to him, and Jim was, in Lee's eyes, everything he considered a father should be.

His newfound security couldn't end now, could it?

Sarah tried to reassure him everything would be OK, and she and Jim would make sure there would be no problems – all the while keeping her fingers crossed under the table.

She wasn't looking forward in the least to making the call and decided to leave it until 10:30 the following morning, when hopefully Maureen would be on her own.

Lee had told her a fair amount about his home life, and this made Sarah nervous. She kept washing her hands, wiping them on her apron and continually fidgeting about in the kitchen, moving things around from place to place while staring out into the garden.

I wonder if a small sherry would be nice, she thought to herself before dialling. I need a little courage... Oh, well, here goes!

After a few rings the phone was picked up. A quiet but efficient-sounding voice said,

"Maureen Agazzi, can I help you?"

"Yes... My name is Sarah Slater, I'm phoning about Lee."

"Lee... Lee who?"

"Sorry, I mean Stanleigh."

Following a short pause, Maureen spluttered and coughed.

"Please... I mean, I'm sorry, oh... oh, dear. How is Stanleigh? Is he OK?"

"Yes, he's just fine."

After Sarah had explained what had happened, Maureen quickly grasped the situation, thanking her repeatedly for looking after the boy. She said she personally would pay any expenses incurred but would prefer to keep Stanleigh's whereabouts just between them for the time being as things at home were not good. Sarah told her to forget about the money and promised to give her a call soon, to let her know how her son was progressing. She said she hoped he might be able to return home in the future.

"I don't think that will happen for a long time, if ever. I don't think John... It's not something I can... Please can I have your phone number, Sarah?"

"Yes, of course."

"Tell Stanleigh I love him, please. And say to him also that I'm so sorry."

Then, as Sarah was about to say goodbye, Maureen broke in, saying,

"Oh, no! It's my…" And then hung up abruptly.

Well, I can't do any more, Sarah thought. At least Lee's mother knows where he is, and that he's OK and being cared for. Perhaps she will not worry so much now.

Sarah decided she would call again in the next week or two.

About two weeks later, she was sitting on her bed one afternoon, considering what to say to Maureen. As she started to dial the number she heard a lot of laughter and a bit of a commotion coming from the hallway downstairs, so went to see what was happening.

Georgie and his cousin Steven Parkes, Tom's boy, had arrived back home from their holiday in Ireland.

There was a lot of noise and loud chatter as two large rucksacks were dumped on the floor in the middle of the room and they started to take off a couple of the dirtiest anoraks Sarah had ever seen.

"You can't put those there! Drop your dirty clothes in the back of the garage by the washing machine. You're making a horrible mess in here and I've only just cleaned it."

"Hello, Mum. Aren't you pleased to see us?" said Georgie.

Of course she was, but the sight of two scruffy, dirty, tall young men in her nice clean hallway was a bit much.

Georgie's cousin Steven went off home after they'd had coffee, biscuits, cake and four or five slices of bread covered in butter and honey.

"Wow! That was great, Mum. We were starving. I could have eaten a horse! Think I'm going to have a shower now. I stink like horse poo because we haven't had a proper wash for nearly two weeks," Georgie laughed.

Sarah said she could tell that by looking at him and there was a noticeable musty sort of smell about him.

"OK, and don't forget to clean up afterwards, will you? Dump your dirty clothes outside as well. It will all have to go straight in the washing machine."

Honestly, teenage boys... what will they do next? Sarah thought. But in fact she was used to Georgie's outdoor pursuits. In addition, she was rather proud of him. He was always up to something, usually to do with sports or helping the local care home with any small jobs they needed doing. Most youngsters of his age seemed much less caring and helpful than he was, and she liked that. He was far better-adjusted than many of his friends, who wasted their time watching TV or boozing. Sarah's only son didn't smoke or drink because fortunately he didn't like the taste of cigarettes or alcohol, and she blessed the day he'd discovered that.

Later, after his shower, he appeared at the kitchen door in clean shirt and jeans.

Sarah said she needed to speak to him about something that had happened a couple of days after he went away on holiday. So mother and son sat at the kitchen table, with yet another cup of coffee.

Sarah started to tell Georgie the story of Lee arriving at their door and how it had come about that he was now living with them in their home. Georgie sat in silence and listened to every word. At a convenient point he said that, in a way, he wasn't too surprised Lee had left home. He knew he and his dad didn't get on well, but was surprised to hear about his friend being chucked out.

"How could his dad do that? Lee hadn't any money and nowhere else to go? I can't believe a father would do that to his own son."

Sarah felt Lee's story had shaken Georgie.

His demeanour changed after that, and for a teenage boy, he became unusually thoughtful and quiet. She wasn't used to seeing him like this. Usually her son was laughing loudly and telling jokes.

"We used to have a good time at school together, you know. Lee wasn't loud or pushy like some of the others. We'd have long talks on the way home sometimes. You would have been amazed if you'd been listening in. On second thoughts, maybe not!" he laughed.

It was getting late in the afternoon now and Sarah needed to get the dinner on. Lee would soon be home from work with Jim, and like most men, after a day's work, they would both be ravenous.

"Mum, I'm going to deal with the clothes in my backpack. There are also some books and maps I need to sort out and clean. I'm going to have a tidy up in the bathroom too. Can you give me a shout when Lee gets in, please?" said Georgie.

"Yes, of course, I will, but you may hear them arrive before I do."

It was well after 6:30 when Lee and Jim came in through the back door.

This afternoon Lee had been learning to use the routers with one of the more experienced machine operators, and this took considerably longer than they'd envisaged. Jim decided to do some paperwork while he waited for the boy so they could travel home in the car together via the local hospital where there was someone he needed to pick up. Sarah's face beamed as she noticed three people coming through the door. Tom's daughter Anna was with Jim and Lee since her parents were out that evening. They were deep in conversation about next door's cat who'd almost lost its tail under the front wheel of the car.

"That's one life gone… only eight left," said Anna.

Sarah had always had a soft spot for her niece. When Anna was a small child, Sarah would often babysit for Tom and Gina, so they'd formed a special bond. Sarah and Jim thought of Anna almost as their own daughter, and were very fond of her. They thought she had a sweet nature, and that her lovely blue eyes always seemed to smile.

"Dinner won't be a moment. Are you staying for something to eat, Anna? There's plenty for all of us – probably enough for twenty."

"Well, only if it's no trouble, Auntie. Thank you." Anna was starving as the day seemed to have been extra-long.

She'd been invited on a trial training day at the local hospital where she planned to become a student nurse. It had been hard physical work and now her back ached, but it hadn't changed her mind about her chosen profession.

Over dinner, they all listened with interest to stories about Georgie's exploits in Ireland. One such tale was of how the five of them got covered in elephant poo in Dublin Zoo.

Everyone was in stitches. Georgie was quite a comedian. Sarah noticed Lee wasn't fully participating though, and that he looked a little awkward and embarrassed.

She was sure he was finding it difficult to adjust to a different style of family life. After all, he had only been with them for a couple of weeks, and suddenly Sarah's son was home, and there were now five of them sitting at the table, eating, laughing and making quite a racket.

The two boys hadn't had a minute to sit and chat together yet. That concerned Sarah who glanced over at Lee, wondering what was going through his mind.

Between mouthfuls, he was looking at Anna, and Anna was looking at him.

That's interesting, Sarah thought and carried on with her meal.

After clearing all the plates off the table, the two boys went into the sitting room followed by Anna. The three of them sat together and the whole story of Lee's arrival in the Slater household was told. Sarah and Jim decided to leave the youngsters to it, with Jim helping out in the kitchen.

Later, Sarah took a tray with some biscuits and three mugs of coffee into the sitting room and then retreated to the kitchen where she and her husband sat quietly with their drinks.

"Think it's better to let Lee talk it through with Georgie, don't you?" Jim said.

Although this evening was probably the first time Anna had met Lee, Sarah felt certain her niece would be upset on hearing his story.

It was getting quite late when the three youngsters reappeared. They were unusually quiet. Sarah glanced at Lee and then at Anna. She did look upset, her eyes tinged with red. Sarah was sure she had either been crying or was on the verge of doing so. The two boys stood quietly. Jim broke the silence by saying he would run Anna home.

"Thank you, Uncle Jim," was all she could manage to say. Lee and Georgie moved to go upstairs as Anna went to get her coat. She came and gave Sarah a very long and deliberate hug. "Thanks for dinner, Auntie Sarah."

As she left the house, the girl gave a last lingering glance towards the stairs.

Chapter 6:

The Sight of Blood

July 1973

In July 1973, the same month and year as Lee was pushed out of his home, Tom Parkes' daughter Anna left her private girls' grammar school. Before she joined the next intake of student nurses at their local hospital, she decided to work for a while, part-time, at Slater & Parkes. She had done this on previous occasions during school holidays, to earn extra pocket money.

Tom needed extra help in the office since a clerical assistant had recently left, and Anna seemed to be in the right place at the right time.

So she was now going to be working in the same premises as the new recruit Lee Agazzi, the young man she'd met a few evenings ago at her aunt and uncle's house.

However, her first day at work would start in a manner no one could have imagined, and it was quite a shock to her system.

As Anna turned the corner and approached the Sidings Industrial Estate, she noticed there was an ambulance outside. As she drew nearer, two police cars with sirens and flashing lights arrived at the scene.

It was a couple of minutes before eight o'clock.

By the corner of the building, she could see two people receiving attention from the ambulance crew. One of them was Lee Agazzi.

The other was a man lying unconscious on the ground, his head covered in blood.

This morning Lee had decided to go to work early. As he rounded the side of the building, he'd discovered a man lying face down on the ground. Lee ran back to find a telephone box and phoned for an ambulance.

Before it arrived, he had returned to have a better look at the injured man. On seeing a lot of blood coming from a cut to his head, Lee began feeling dizzy. As he started walking away, he passed out.

This was not unusual for him, he didn't like blood or anything remotely medical, but it certainly added to the drama.

So instead of one injured man awaiting them, there were now two for the ambulance crew and police to deal with. The senior patrol officer thought there must have been a fight, or some altercation, between the two men and was going to arrest them both. But it soon became apparent this wasn't the case.

Anna was trying to distract Lee by placing herself

between him and the ambulance crew.

The injured person turned out to be an auto engineer who worked in one of the other factory units a few yards away. He too was on his way to work when he slipped on something, hit his head on the wall, and seeing all the blood on his hands when he put them up to the wound, passed out. The nasty cut to his head made him feel so unsteady he needed helping into the ambulance. Once in hospital he was quickly patched up before being allowed to leave.

Lee said he was a friendly guy, he thought his name was Harry something, having spoken briefly to him only a few days before.

While trying to explain all this to the police, Lee told them he was the one who'd dialled 999, after discovering Harry on the ground, then felt faint himself when he saw the blood. He was still very shaky when Anna took him into the office to sit him down. She made him a sweet drink and provided coffee for the police as they collected details of names and addresses, etc.

After they departed Lee was still feeling rather wobbly, so Anna sat talking quietly to him until some of the other staff started to arrive.

Tom appeared a little before nine.

He walked in to find Lee sitting in the reception area white as a sheet with Anna holding his hand, trying to calm him.

After a while, when all the rest of the staff were in, Tom thought he ought to take Lee home, as he didn't consider he was in a fit state to operate the machinery safely.

When Sarah saw them both coming up the garden path, she felt a surge of panic as it was only a short while ago Lee had left for work. Tom's explanations soon dispelled her worries.

He went back to the joinery, and Lee sat and talked to Sarah about the event, still feeling distinctly dizzy every time she mentioned blood.

Sarah was surprised to realise how fond of him she already was. She and Jim had become positively attached to their unofficially adopted son. She was almost as worried about him as she was about her own Derek – or Georgie as he always preferred to be known. She told Lee she was going into the kitchen to get them both something to drink.

In reality, she didn't want him to see how emotional and tearful she was becoming.

It was a little after 11 when Lee said he felt OK, and that he thought he should go back to work. As his colour had now returned to normal, Sarah agreed.

"A bit of fresh air will do you a world of good."

On his return, as he walked into the office, he got a round of applause. There was a lot of excited chatter for a few moments. Lee felt embarrassed and could feel his face reddening. Anna came up to him and gave him a big hug. The smile she gave him then was one he would never forget.

He stood there, blushing, trying not to stare into her eyes.

Work continued at an ever-increasing pace, and over the coming months, Lee proved that he was able to learn quickly and his confidence grew. He came up with various ideas to improve some manufacturing procedures and this added to the company's efficiency. It was not too long before he was sometimes asked to go out with Tom or Jim to meet the customers and discuss various job options with them.

Chapter 7:

A First Date

February 1974

Lee had arranged to meet up one Saturday with an old school pal called Mike Greenaway and his sister Tania, in a café near the traffic lights on the High Street.

It was late February, and the weather had been unseasonably warm for the last week or so. The café was a popular venue with most of the youngsters in the village. He thought they might be able to sit outside if it was warm enough. The place had an Italian-sounding name, but Lee couldn't remember it. He wanted to ask Anna if she would like to go with him so there would be four of them. Lee had never asked a girl out before. He was quite excited at the thought of it, and more than a bit nervous.

After work, seeing Anna walking out of her dad's office, Lee decided to ask her if she would like to join him, Mike and Tania. Anna smiled and said yes, she would love to, but she wouldn't be able to stay for too long as she was out later in the afternoon on a date with a bloke called William.

"That's OK, Anna. I just thought you... er, might enjoy it. I... er, wanted to ask you before but you haven't been around much lately," Lee faltered.

"OK then. I know the café. It's called Giulio's. See you about eleven."

Lee felt his stomach sink to his boots. He'd never considered the prospect of Anna already having a boyfriend. She'd never mentioned it before, and it had not occurred to him to ask. He hadn't expected that, and didn't know what to do next. He turned and shuffled home, feeling miserable.

The next day Lee felt a deep sense of isolation envelop him. He so wanted to go out with Anna. He dreamt about her all the time and had assumed she would think as he did.

While at school, he'd often felt alone, even in a class full of other pupils. Somehow, he felt unwanted. Lee did have some friends, and they would go off together occasionally and have a fun time, but he never considered himself to be a real part of the group.

At home, as a toddler, his mum would hold and cuddle him. Her actions and natural motherly warmth made him feel loved, safe and happy.

But as young Stanleigh became older, his already low self-confidence gradually diminished. He often felt he was "on the edge" of not being able to cope. Things had improved a little after he decided to call himself Lee, but any new or unexpected events caused a fearfulness in him that he seemed unable to shake off.

Anna's announcement that there was another boy in her life had shocked him, and reinforced his feelings of loneliness, inadequacy and worthlessness.

Above everything else, Lee wanted to be accepted and loved. Getting married was his dream, something he longed for. His greatest fear was that no one would ever want or love him enough to marry him. The sad part was, he didn't understand why he felt this way, or what caused his sense of isolation. Could it be because of his father's bullying of him over recent years? Or maybe it was his inability to do well at school or his failure to obtain the required GCE results. He didn't have any sensible explanation for any of it. He now had a good job, he was popular and more than capable, enjoying his work. The pleasure he gained from this diminished when he heard about Anna's boyfriend. His deep-rooted fears of rejection and of being thought useless, returned to dog him again.

The constant fear made him feel insecure, alone and unwanted. He knew it wasn't sensible or rational, but niggling voices continued to haunt him.

As Lee approached the café a few minutes before eleven, he could see through the window a smartly dressed Anna already chatting to Tania, who was in her normal attire, a dirty pair of tight jeans and old woolly jumper. There was a clang from the door's bell as he walked in.

"Hello, Anna – Tania. Am I a bit late? Where's Mike, is he coming?"

"No, he smashed his head on the garage door this morning and now has a big bruise and a terrible headache – the silly bugger!" Tania laughed.

"Oh, dear, never mind. I'm so please to see you, Anna. So pleased you came."

Tania jumped up, saying,

"I'll go and get us all some coffee and cake. Lee, do you want milk and sugar?"

"Er… yes, please. What do you want, Anna?"

"Oh, coffee, please, with milk, no sugar."

"OK, guys, back in a min…"

Lee sat there looking at Anna. He couldn't believe she was here with him.

"Have you been here before, Lee?" she asked.

"No… well, yes. I mean… not properly, you know… to sit down. I popped in to get a card from their stand. The one over there." He pointed to the display by the till.

"They have nice cards here, don't they? I got a lovely birthday card for my mum last year."

"Anna, I'm so pleased you could make it. I, er… I've wanted for so long to…"

Right on cue, Tania returned, with their coffee on a tray, interrupting the conversation.

"Here it is. They're bringing some cakes over in a min."

She then dominated the conversation, to such an extent Lee could hardly get a word in. He felt he was losing his chance of being with Anna. Inside he was upset that every time he tried to say something to her, Tania butted in and wouldn't stop talking. Lee's inexperience with girls made him embarrassed and he didn't know how to deal with the situation, so he fell quiet. He wanted to say things to Anna and hold her hand, but was too self-conscious. He wanted to hold her, to kiss her. He wished he could tell Tania to shut up.

After about an hour or so, Anna said thank you for the coffee and cake, saying she had to get off home to change. She was supposed to be meeting William at two o'clock.

Lee smiled at her. He felt he'd lost his chance, messed up what was supposed to be the first date of his life.

After Anna left, Lee also said he needed to get home. Tania was sitting back in her chair, legs akimbo, smiling and laughing a little at him.

"You were a bit slow there, weren't you, Lee? You obviously fancy Anna. Why didn't you say anything, do something… like give her a cuddle or a kiss?"

Lee felt himself becoming flustered. He stood up and muttered goodbye to Tania, almost through his teeth, as he left the café.

It would be several weeks before he would summon up enough courage to ask Anna out again.

Although Anna was not always in the office, over the next couple of months, she and Lee made a point of having a chat at some point on every day that she was there. Quite often, this would be during the afternoon tea break. As the day progressed Lee would keep looking at his watch and, as the time drew nearer to three, found it difficult to concentrate properly on his work, feeling his heart pounding. He would become hot and excited at the thought of being with her.

In her little office, Anna also looked forward to their time together and kept a careful eye on the movement of people wandering past the glass partition on their way to the kitchen, popping out as she saw Lee appear from the workshop.

He would long for these times when they would chat about everything and anything, with lots of laughter. He couldn't keep his eyes off her. Getting back to work was hard for him. One day Anna turned to replace her cup and bumped into Lee, who had to grab hold of her so as not to fall backwards. He could feel her warm body pressed to his and it inflamed his passion. He didn't want to let go. Anna didn't resist so they stood there for a brief second looking into each other's eyes. As Lee was about to kiss her, two of the machinists walked by. The magic of the moment was lost. It was the second day in May and he would not forget this day or the brief moment that might have been.

In a few days' time it would be Lee's birthday. He would be eighteen and wanted to celebrate it by going out for a curry.

There was an excellent Indian restaurant in Tanners Lane, which he thought would be ideal.

He wanted to invite Anna, and now at last felt more confident though still unsure of how to approach her, remembering that she already had a boyfriend.

On one particular evening Jim popped over to see Tom and Gina, leaving Sarah and Lee to have dinner together as Georgie, who would generally have been with them, was in Newcastle for the next few weeks doing some work experience with an electrical engineering company. So it was an ideal opportunity for Lee to ask Sarah how she thought he should approach the subject.

"Well, it can't do any harm to just ask her, can it? It's always nice to be asked. Why don't you give it a go?"

"OK, I will. Would you and Jim like to come too?"

"Well, let's wait and see what Anna says, shall we? If she accepts your invitation, which I think she probably will, you wouldn't want Jim and me along as well, would you?"

"Oh, yes, I would, Sarah. I owe everything to you and Jim. I don't know what would have happened to me if you hadn't been so kind. This would be a great birthday celebration. I can't think of anything I would prefer to do or anyone I would rather have with me."

"That's very sweet of you, Lee, thank you. Of course, we would both love to join you, but let's wait and see what Anna says…"

Sarah was secretly overjoyed at the thought of Lee and Anna being together. The notion of what might develop between them made her quite excited.

The next day Lee saw Anna sitting at her desk attacking a mound of files. As she was only there for a day or two every now and again, he thought this would be the right moment to ask her. He started to feel hot, clammy and nervous. Ignoring this, he walked straight in and asked if she would come and have a curry with him.

"It's for my birthday, to… er, well, sort of celebrate it… and I would love you to be with me."

"Yes. I would love to come, thanks for asking me." Anna's eyes were radiant, and she had a big smile on her face.

"I have rather been hoping we would go out again

ever since we met at Giulio's."

Lee spluttered with embarrassment.

"But you... you said you had a boyfriend then. So I wasn't sure you would want to come out with me."

"Oh, well... that bloke William was a real jerk. I only went out with him once or twice. He's the brother of one of my old schoolfriends. I only agreed to go out with him as a favour to her. I thought you might never ask me again, so I was going to ask you to take me out instead of waiting... But now you have. So, yes, of course, I'd love to have a curry with you. I love curry, but a pizza or anything else you fancy would do. I don't mind what it is, it will be nice to be together... on our own this time... won't it?"

Anna was beaming radiantly at him. Lee was so excited he thought he might explode.

He smiled back at her and was so pleased... and so relieved.

"Oh, that's great. I suppose I'd better book a table then."

"I know the owners of the restaurant you want to go to," Anna was saying. "I was at school with Sammi – she's their daughter.

I can speak to her and get us a table, if you like?"

"Well, OK, but I think it's something I ought to do," Lee said.

After being anxious about what Anna's reaction would be, he suddenly wasn't sure what to say. He was overjoyed, thrilled and excited.

Lee longed to make a good impression. He was happy but still unsure of himself.

Anna, on the other hand, always appeared so self-confident and capable. That did worry him a lot. He hoped she wouldn't get fed up with him.

A little thing he didn't know was that one of the other lads in the works had already asked Anna out, on at least two previous occasions, and she'd turned him down... both times.

After Lee invited her to the café a while ago, Anna was quite convinced he would ask her out again. For some reason, he hadn't; why, she hadn't known. But she wasn't about to give up on him. She had spent an emotional evening at her Aunt Sarah's house, listening to his story. She had also looked after him when he fainted outside the works, and often watched him surreptitiously while she was at work.

Although Lee seemed very shy and a bit sad sometimes, she liked his dark hazel eyes and his quiet, gentle character.

Anna was becoming fond of him and missed him on the days when she wasn't working at the joinery. Lee was head-over-heels in love with her.

His eighteenth birthday arrived, and he and Anna went for the curry on their own. Jim persuaded Sarah to think of a reason why they wouldn't be able to join the young couple. He didn't want to intrude on a romantic evening.

It was a great night out, and Lee was deliriously happy as they left the restaurant. They had each consumed several glasses of wine and he, unused to drinking, was feeling rather merry as he walked Anna home. It boosted his confidence and he pulled her into a shop doorway where he took her into his arms and kissed her passionately. Anna held on to him, pulled him closer to her, and they stayed in a tight embrace for a short while. Then, thinking she might have sensed how excited he had become and that maybe he had gone a bit too far, Lee released his hold on her and they stood looking at each other.

"Oh, Anna, I'm sorry. I hope I haven't, you know, put you off..."

"No – you haven't. It was lovely." And she put her arms around him and pulled him firmly in to her again. They stood there for a while before slowly moving on.

Lee was always fairly confident when talking to females for work purposes, but on a personal level he became awkward and always stumbled badly over his words. Embarrassment frequently prevented him from saying the right things, which made him feel uncomfortable and inadequate. Now sensing Anna hadn't rejected him, but rather the opposite, he hoped that would change and he felt happy – happier than he could ever remember.

Anna would occasionally talk to her mum about the people who worked at the joinery, and this included Lee.

Ever since the first time she'd met him, at her aunt Sarah's house, she'd liked Lee. She felt so sorry for him, being thrown out of his home, but there was also something about him that attracted her. She wasn't sure if it was his friendly smile or his kind nature. He reminded her, in many ways, of her father. Maybe that was part of it. Anna loved both her parents dearly. They rarely disagreed and were always very open about everything, including talking to her and her brother Steven about many of the household decisions. This had given them a lot of self-confidence.

She'd so hoped Lee would ask her out again at the coffee date, and after the curry outing was convinced he would. Anna glowed with anticipation. She was starting to fall in love with him.

Chapter 8:

Steven Parkes

August 1974

As Lee slowly got to know the family better, he became a little curious about Steven, Anna's brother, who seemed to have vanished off the face of the earth.

Anna explained the story to him one Sunday over a pub lunch.

Steven Parkes was the black sheep of the family, it seemed. He was a rebel in every sense of the word and over time had become a bit of an embarrassment.

Steven was unlike his parents and his sister in every respect. He had long unkempt hair, a plethora of tattoos, and was an extremely difficult and complicated character. He'd turned into what his mum Gina considered to be a 'hippy'.

Two years after he left school, when he turned nineteen, Steven's behaviour became disruptive. This resulted in several brushes with the law. Even though he hadn't been charged with an offence, he certainly was not in their good books.

One day he announced he was going to Australia to join a touring jazz band and might not come back. None of the family took this seriously as he'd made similar comments on several occasions during the previous year.

This time turned out to be different. After a few days, Steven packed a bag and, without saying another word to anyone, was gone.

Ten days later a two-line letter arrived from Australia with an address and not much else except the name of the jazz band he played with, Road to Ruin.

Gina was certainly upset by his departure but over the years had grown used to these antics and thought he would be home again in a month or two, or as soon as he ran out of money. They'd all considered the band's name to be rather appropriate.

After that, they didn't hear from him for almost a year.

Finally, he wrote a short letter to them saying he was coming home.

It seemed he'd been arrested at a gig for taking cocaine and a variety of other drugs… and this was not the first time.

The Australian authorities had notified him they were going to deport him back to the UK. The letter gave no date of arrival nor any specific detail about where he was currently so there was nothing either Tom or Gina could do. Tom contacted the Australian Embassy to see if they could give him any information, but they were not very helpful and only said they would look into it. That had been months ago.

While Steven was growing up, he was always reticent and reserved, even withdrawn. He had few friends and would often disappear for days on end, causing Tom and Gina a lot of worry.

He'd gone with Georgie and some chums to Ireland for a holiday after their 'O' levels.

That was the only time Lee could remember hearing Steven's name mentioned.

He was a typical rebel, everything his younger sister was not.

What worried Anna the most was a sneaking suspicion that her brother might suddenly return and end up wrecking all their lives. A well-founded worry as it turned out.

Chapter 9:

A Difference of Opinion and a Reunion

September 1974

Lee and Anna had been going out together almost every week since the night of his eighteenth birthday. On Saturdays they would regularly go to the Scuttle for a pub lunch and sometimes Lee would take Anna to the cinema in the evening. They would often sit in the back row, where they could kiss and cuddle without drawing attention. He, though, would be just as happy to hold her hand. He loved their embraces. They made him feel wanted.

On one occasion they spent a pleasant, jovial evening with one of Anna's nursing friends from the hospital, together with her boyfriend. As Lee was walking Anna home afterwards, it soon became obvious something was not right. She wouldn't look at him and snatched her hand away.

"What's the matter, Anna? Have I upset you?"

"Yes, you have. Whatever got into you?"

"What do you mean?"

"You told some smutty jokes that clearly didn't amuse them. Ddn't you notice how quiet they went? When you'd gone to the loo, I had to apologise for you since you obviously weren't going to bother! It was so embarrassing."

"Bloody hell! I didn't mean any harm. I thought I was being humorous, that's all. They were jokes I'd heard on the radio today. I just didn't think..."

"No, you didn't! And that's the problem. Don't do it again."

"I'm really sorry, Anna. I won't – I promise."

They walked the last few yards to her house in silence and Anna went inside after a curt goodbye, leaving Lee feeling stunned.

The following day at the office she came looking for him. She gently pulled him aside and, a little red-faced and tearful, fumbled for his hand. Holding it tightly, she apologised for what she'd said to him.

"I'm very sorry. I vastly overreacted. Can we forget the whole thing?"

"Yes, OK."

Lee put his arms around her and held her for a while. He felt almost overwhelmed with relief. He kissed her hands briefly before he was called away and asked if she'd go to the cinema with him that night.

As they sat in their usual place in the back row, torchlight shone briefly over them, making Anna jump. An usherette was showing another couple to their seats nearby. Anna quickly adjusted the buttons on her jumper and sat upright, going red in the face. Lee looked the other way and tried not to laugh. They didn't go to the cinema again for several weeks but he didn't care. He was just glad that Anna was still with him.

By the end of September, Lee felt as though he had been living with Sarah and Jim for absolutely ages. In reality, it was about thirteen months, and in that time Lee, at least in his opinion, had become a changed person. So much had happened in such a short period, he couldn't quite believe his good fortune. He was doing well in the joinery and was so much happier than he'd ever imagined he could be. He felt safe, secure, comfortable and contented, for the first time in his adult life. He was holding down a good job, earning reasonable money, and only a few days ago had received a very handy pay rise, but the real bonus was… Anna.

When their local vicar Jim Hordram told him a small flat was available for rent at 3a Tanners Lane – the flat above The Sweet Shop – Lee thought maybe this would be a good time to consider getting a place of his own. The flat and the shop below belonged to the vicar's wife, Susan. She offered it to Lee at a special rate. Susan's parents had owned and run the shop for many years, buying the freehold when it came up for sale about twenty years previously. They'd both died some time ago, and the Hordrams decided to keep the property and let it out for rent as this would give them a small extra income.

Tanners Lane – The houses and shops

Reverend Jim Hordram knew Slater & Parkes well and had met Lee on several occasions. The joinery was engaged by the vicar several times to carry out a variety of repair jobs in the church, mainly to the pews and the front door. Various other smaller maintenance jobs had also been carried out by Lee and one of the other lads. Jim trusted his gut instinct. He liked Lee, felt he was a decent, honest young man.

It was a bright Saturday morning, and as lunchtime approached, Lee decided to go and have a look at the flat. He was unsure how he would feel about living over The Sweet Shop, which he'd visited many times when he was a small boy. The shop was on the main road, and Lee was undecided about it as he set out to climb the stairs to the front door of the flat above the little shop he knew so well. He didn't know quite what to expect.

He had always lived in a house where he was used to having everything done for him. This would be a completely new ball game, doing his own cooking, washing up, cleaning, etc. Jim Hordram gave him the key and said he should go and have a good look around on his own. As he let himself in, Lee's eyes lit up. He was thinking to himself, Oh, wow, it's really great! It wasn't too big, but not small either. This place could be his new home.

There were two bedrooms, an excellent modern kitchen, large enough to accommodate a small table at one end, a smallish lounge and a surprisingly large bathroom. It seemed to be an excellent flat. It was clean, well maintained and nicely decorated. Almost as if no one had lived there for a while.

Lee was so excited he felt he would burst. Wow! A place of his own. He could feel his heart pounding… He could bring Anna here and they would be completely alone. His mind started racing ahead. He was getting a little overexcited at the thought of it.

His mum would be so proud of him… Well, she would have been. With that thought hanging in the air, sadness came over him as he realised he wouldn't be able to tell her about the flat or anything else. He would have to find a way to let her know in secret. He stood silently in the small entrance, his initial excitement evaporating.

Lee closed the front door, locking it carefully, and walked back to Sarah and Jim's home.

Ever since he'd arrived on their doorstep all those months ago, Lee had been happy and content here. Sarah made him so welcome, and both she and Jim made him feel like one of the family. He didn't want to upset them or make them think he was ungrateful for all they had done for him. Nobody could have been kinder or done more. He didn't know how to approach the subject of the flat. Maybe he would say nothing for a day or two.

Lee also wasn't certain he would be happy living on his own.

Should he give up his newfound security, living with the Slaters? Would he be lonely? How would he feel if Anna dumped him?

It didn't take long to walk back, and by the time he opened the front door some of his excitement was returning. He was desperate to tell Sarah his news and wanted her to go and see the little flat with him. He needed her approval of the idea. Lee was sure it would work out if only Sarah and Jim would help him and give him their support.

"Lee, is that you?" she called from the hallway. "Jim Hordram called to see if you have looked at his flat yet. He has someone else enquiring about it."

"Er... well, actually, I've just been to have a look around, Sarah. It's, er, well... it's pretty good really. I'd just like to... Would you come and see it with me, please? I don't know what to do."

Phew, he thought. That's made life a whole lot easier. He was excited and terrified at the same time. This was a massive step for him.

After a few moments, Sarah appeared with her coat on, saying, "Come on then, young man, let's go and do a proper viewing."

Bubbling with excitement and trepidation, he took her back to the flat. Later in the evening, Lee sat down with Sarah and Jim Slater plus Sue Hordram, and while eating Sarah's delicious homemade cake, most of the details were sorted out. Jim thought Lee was rather young to sign the contract, so he and his wife offered to stand surety for Lee by agreeing to rent the flat in their names.

It all seemed rather too easy and informal. There were no complicated documents, more of an all-friends-together arrangement.

So, Lee was now set to move out of the Slater household and into a place of his own. Over the next month, with Sarah and Jim's help, he put together some furniture, a bed and all the things necessary to set up home for the first time.

According to Sarah the flat's kitchen was quite well equipped. It came complete with a fridge and a brand new electric cooker, with four cooking rings, a grill and a good-sized oven. There was even a washing machine under the worktop.

Lee started collecting things from all over the place. Cups and saucers, plates, knives and forks, cooking utensils, dishcloths, drying up towels... the list seemed endless. Even things like bigger bath towels, a toothbrush and toilet rolls. Those things had been provided for him all his life, he'd never thought about the cost of household goods or where everything came from.

This was going to be a massive change in his life, and although he was looking forward to it, he was frightened of failure too.

Lee finally moved into his flat at the end of September. It was a big day for him. Sarah came with him to help make up his bed, check he had some food in the fridge and make sure the curtains all pulled in the correct way. She also gave him her old Hoover as Jim suddenly decided they needed a new one. Anna turned up mid morning to help as well. Lee was so pleased, excited and surprised she was there. He hadn't been expecting her. Around 11:45 Sarah considered it was about time for a break – oh, heck, he didn't have a kettle. How could they have forgotten the kettle?

A smiling Anna retrieved a gift-wrapped box from the floor by the kitchen door and handed it to Lee. Inside was a brand new Russell Hobbs electric kettle. He looked at her in amazement, his eyes starting to well up.

"How did you know...?" He put his arms around her and would not let go until Sarah said, "Hey, you guys, how about a drink for the workers?" Anna looked a bit embarrassed.

Lee hadn't looked at the attached label saying it was from Gina and Tom as a First Day in Your New Home present. Now it was his turn to be embarrassed.

The new kettle was filled with water, plugged in, and soon they were holding three of the sweetest cups of tea Lee had ever made.

It was only after Sarah and Anna left and he was finally on his own that his inner fears started to grip him. Looking around, he began to shake. He thought he was getting a stomach ache. What would he do if he fell ill here on his own?

He wanted to go back to Sarah and Jim's house, but his pride wouldn't let him.

So, feeling unwell and miserable, he curled up in his new bed and went to sleep.

This was something he would do many times over the coming months.

As soon as he was settled into his flat Lee decided he would try and contact his mother. He hadn't spoken to her since the dreadful day he was forced out of the family home. There were so many times when he'd oh-so-nearly called her, but had always backed out. He was fearful his father might pick up the phone and worried as to the reaction he might get from his mum. It upset him, making him feel guilty, so he tried to put these thoughts to the back of his mind.

Sarah had telephoned Maureen several times during the previous months, to let her know how Lee was, and tell her he was happy and doing well at work. Over several long conversations, she filled in a lot of detail about Lee's work for Maureen and also answered many of her questions, and concerns.

Sarah commented on what a very nice young man Lee was. She said he was polite and considerate and Maureen should feel proud of the way she'd brought up her son.

About four months after moving in, Lee thought he would take a day's holiday and invite his mum over for tea.

He had hardly taken a day off since joining Slater & Parkes, and was sure it wouldn't be a problem. Nor was it. Lee spoke to Tom and explained what he wanted to do. Tom actively encouraged him to go ahead with his blessing, adding he needn't take a day's holiday. The company would be only too happy to grant him time off to see his mother.

Lee took several days to screw up his courage to make that first phone call. He waited until about eleven one morning, while sipping a strong coffee, and nervously dialled the still familiar, home phone number.

He hadn't spoken to his mother for almost two years and wasn't sure what she might say. He was very nervous when the 'phone started ringing.

After what seemed like ages it was answered, and Lee heard his mother's voice, hardly recognising it.

Maureen had suffered badly after he left the house and was now nervy. Her strained voice reflected how bad things had become for her.

"Hello, Mum, it's me, Lee... Stanleigh. How are you?"

There was a short silence followed by a strange gurgling sound.

"Hello," Lee said again.

"Hel...lo, Stanleigh, I'm so pleased to hear you," she spluttered into the mouthpiece.

"I thought I might never hear your voice again."

"I would have rung before, Mum, but I was frightened, in case *he* was there."

"John has gone to Manchester today for a banking seminar. He won't be back, I think, until late this evening." Her voice was getting a bit stronger.

"I wondered if, when you go shopping one day, you might like to come and see me in my new home. We could have some time together and..."

Now Lee's voice was starting to break from the emotion he was trying so hard to suppress. It was getting the better of him. He couldn't hold it in much longer. He couldn't believe he was talking to his mum.

"Yes, Stanleigh, I would like that very much. I will be going to the shops on Thursday morning. Won't you be at work though?"

"Don't worry about it, Mum. I've got a day off. My address is 3a Tanners Lane, over The Sweet Shop. You know it. I'll be there all day. Please come. I love you, Mum, and I've missed you so much, and I... er... got to go now. 'Bye, Mum. See you Thursday, 'bout eleven."

Lee put the receiver down. He couldn't speak anymore; his eyes felt sore. He sat there shaking with the emotion and wondered whether she would really come.

Oh, how Lee loved his mum and how he'd missed her. He wanted her to meet Anna. Lee was certain his mum would love her too.

Knowing Sarah was in touch with his mother was a comfort, but it wasn't the same as seeing her himself. He wanted to put his arms around her and hug her like he used to do. Would she pull away from him? He hoped she would still love him as she always used to.

Well, he'd done it now. He had actually phoned his mother, after all this time.

He wished he had found the courage sooner. He felt drained.

Then the phone rang and he slipped back into work mode.

During the evening Lee went to see Sarah, to tell her his mother was going to come and visit him in his new flat.

She was delighted as she'd often felt like suggesting something similar to him, but for some reason had decided it was better not to interfere. She was especially pleased the idea had come from Lee himself, a sure sign his self-confidence was improving, if only slightly. She hadn't seen him so excited since Jim first offered him the job at the joinery.

"Do you think I should get cakes or something else, Sarah?" Lee was aware he hadn't ever entertained anyone before, and wanted her reassurance he was doing the right things.

"I think a nice piece of cake and a cup of tea will be just great. I suspect your mother won't even notice. She will be so pleased to see you."

On Thursday morning Lee was up early, even earlier than for a workday. He got a duster and went around everywhere he could think of, then ran the Hoover over all the floors – then did it all again. Finally, he remembered to clean the loo. He wanted it all to be perfect when his mum arrived.

It was still only a little after 9 in the morning. Lee couldn't concentrate on anything, so he sat and waited. Ten o'clock came, then 11. He was so stressed he felt he might explode.

At ten-past there was a tap on the front door. Maureen hadn't seen the bell button so knocked instead.

Lee jumped up like a startled rabbit. He wasn't expecting a knock.

Nearly tripping over his own feet, he rushed and opened the door.

"Hello, Stanleigh, can I come in?"

"Of course you can, Mum. I'm so pleased you have..."

Both Lee and his mother were in tears as they hugged each other. No words were spoken for several minutes.

She then asked how he was doing, living on his own, and Lee just shook his head. He couldn't speak. Not yet...

A while later as he was in the kitchen preparing the refreshments, Maureen commented on how much taller and more grown-up he looked. He was a man now. She felt so proud of him.

They talked for what seemed ages and Lee showed her the rest of the flat. It wasn't massive and didn't take long, but he was proud of it, and he wanted his mum to feel happy to visit him here; moreover, he wanted her to see he was coping well in his life.

It was after one o'clock when Maureen said she had better get on with her shopping or she might be late getting back home.

So Lee and his mum stood by the front door, hugging and saying their goodbyes.

"I'm so pleased I came today, Stanleigh, and so relieved you are doing well. Sarah has kept me informed with regular phone calls. Please will you thank her for me? I think I would have gone mad without her kind updates."

"Next time, Mum, I'll ask her to come as well if she can, so you can meet her. She and Jim have been very kind to me."

"Oh, I know she has, but I'm not sure..."

"Mum, you would like her, she's very kind and nice, and I would love you to meet her... and Anna too. She's my girlfriend – you'll love her, Mum, I know you will."

"So you have a girlfriend too? That's nice. OK, I'd love to meet her. Now I have your address and phone number, at least we can talk sometimes, can't we?"

"Of course we can," Lee said as he waved goodbye. He couldn't help noticing how much older and more nervous his mother seemed since he last saw her. He was quite shaken and saddened by the realisation.

The stress of the last few hours had left him exhausted.

Lee left the cups and plates where they were and flopped onto the sofa, lying there, staring into space.

Chapter 10:

The Right Decision

April 1975

Lee was sure Anna was the only girl for him. It was almost a year now since he had asked her on that first date. One warm evening after work they went for a short walk along the path running alongside Tillers Stream.

As they walked down from the small bridge by the allotments and came in sight of Tillers Mill, Lee took her hand and pulled her down onto the grass beside him.

He kissed her passionately. Holding her in his arms, he could feel her body pressing against his as he looked straight into her soft blue eyes.

"Can I ask you something, Anna?"

"Yes, of course, what is it?"

"Please will you marry me?"

The bridge over Tillers Stream

Anna sat bolt upright with a jolt, placing both hands firmly on the grass. She turned her face to look at the water instead of at Lee.

There was a moment or two in which she didn't say anything.

Lee panicked. He certainly hadn't expected that reaction.

Anna seemed to have been surprised, even shocked, by his proposal.

After a few moments she turned back to face him. Her face was clearly flushed, eyes were swollen with tears, which started running down her cheeks.

She was quivering with emotion as she looked at him.

"Yes, of course I will. Someone has to look after you."

She pulled him to her, hugging him and gripping him tightly as if her whole life depended on it.

"Oh, Lee, I would love us to be married, more than anything else in the world."

They lay back on the damp grass, locked together in pure delight.

Arms wrapped around each other, they were oblivious to anything else around them.

Lee felt overwhelmingly happy… and profoundly relieved.

He'd been terrified Anna might have turned him down. He didn't believe anyone would ever want to marry him.

But did she love him enough to go through with this and say yes on the day?

Anna too had some niggling doubts. She wasn't certain Lee felt the same way as she did. She loved him dearly, and was wonderfully happy that he had proposed to her.

The sudden awareness this was now for real hit them both, and they huddled together in the cool afternoon sun and fell asleep on the grassy bank.

Lee's surprise at seeing Anna looking shocked when he asked her to marry him caused him, for a brief moment, to feel physically sick. Even though she'd said yes, she did want to marry him, it had left him with a queasy feeling that wouldn't go away.

A little later Anna woke up, shivering. Even though they had only been there a short while it was becoming dark and getting chilly. The sudden movement woke Lee.

"Think it's got a bit cold here. I'm shivering – look at the goosebumps on my arms. What on earth is the time? Are you hungry, 'cos I'm ravenous?"

"Think we ought to get something to eat and then see what your parents feel about it, don't you?"

Would Tom and Gina consider him good enough to marry their precious daughter?

"Yes. But I know Mum will be pleased," Anna reassured him.

Lee took her hands in his, kissing them several times before they set off. Then hand in hand, swinging their arms in the air with elation, they retraced their steps up the pathway. They were blissfully happy.

But by the time they approached Grove Chase, Lee was becoming decidedly jittery. His moment of self-confidence was dwindling. What had he done? What on earth would Tom and Gina think... and say?

He had little to offer Anna. He had no money or qualifications and wasn't at all sure her parents would think he was a right or suitable person for their only daughter, whom they clearly loved to bits.

Tom and Gina were watching the news on TV, as Anna and a nervous Lee, arrived at the family home.

"Mum, Dad – there's something we want to tell you... Think you had better sit down, Mum... Lee has asked me to marry him."

He was standing nervously behind Anna, holding her hand tightly. Gina jumped up, almost squealing in excitement.

"We wondered how long it might take you two to get around to discussing your future together. We are delighted. You might not believe it... but we've been waiting for this moment to happen and have already put some champagne in the fridge. It's been there for a couple of months. Tom, will you open it? I'll get some glasses."

Tom got the bottle of chilled wine, popped the cork and poured out the cold bubbly wine. He raised his glass.

"Here's to you both. We wish you every happiness. Welcome to the Parkes family Lee." Tom was as pleased or even more so than Gina. They were overjoyed.

"You certainly kept us waiting though, didn't you! We couldn't wish for a nicer son to add to our family."

"We are so, so happy and delighted…" Gina said before speaking became impossible for her.

She moved towards them, putting her arms around the pair of them.

"I'm so pleased and happy – I don't know what else to say."

About an hour later and before it got too late, they went to see Jim and Sarah, to give them the news. They too were delighted. In fact, Sarah almost exploded with excitement.

"This is like a dream come true! It's the most wonderful news…"

On the first available Saturday, Lee took Anna to London, found some excellent jewellers in a side street near Holborn and there, glowing with pride, bought her the engagement ring of her dreams. Ever since she was a young teenager, as most daughters do, she would chat to her mum about jewellery now and again. Earrings, engagement and wedding rings of course cropped up in these conversations. An element of anticipation of what the future might hold for Anna was always evident. Gina's engagement ring was a large ruby and diamond cluster, which she called her "knuckle-duster". The colour suited her bright hazel eyes perfectly. She suggested Anna should look for gemstones to complement her eyes, which were a beautiful blue.

So it was no surprise when Anna chose a white gold ring with a single large bright blue topaz, surrounded by seven smaller, water-clear white diamonds. These reflected the topaz, making the whole appearance of the ring stunning.

Anna couldn't believe they'd managed to find the perfect ring in one of the first jeweller's they went into. She fell in love with it immediately and was excited when it fitted her exactly.

There was a problem, of course, and this was the price. It was over double the cost of their original budget. Anna looked up at Lee. Her eyes said it all. Without saying a word, she was pleading with him.

Lee put his arms around her, kissing her gently on the lips.

He held her for a moment as they spoke in hushed voices.

"You really want this one, don't you? OK then, there is no price for love, is there?"

The jeweller, an attractive woman in her thirties, watched and realised why they might be hesitating.

"I can give you a small discount if it would help you decide…"

Lee, pretending to be the big businessman, looked at her and in a deepening voice asked how much they were talking about.

"If I could give you… let's see. Yes, seven per cent. Would that discount help?"

Lee looked at Anna and, after they'd whispered a few words together, agreed to the reduced price.

"Would you like me to pack it for you, madam?"

"Oh, no... NO. I want to wear it now." Anna looked up at Lee, smiling widely.

"Yes, that would be best. It looks so sparkly and it makes your eyes look even bluer-er... I don't think blue-er's a real word though, is it?"

The ring box and receipt went into Anna's handbag, and the ring stayed firmly where it was, on her finger.

The business of the day made them hungry so, seeing a small restaurant a little off the Strand, they decided to go for a celebratory meal before catching the train back home. It was a wonderful and happy day, and they were both dead tired on getting back to Tillshott.

On arriving at Lee's flat they prepared a snack, opened the bottle of champagne he'd placed in the fridge the day before, and between them proceeded to drink the lot.

Feeling rather woozy and more than a bit amorous, Lee coaxed Anna toward the sofa and pulled her down next to him. They were both giggling like schoolkids.

"I don't think... hic... we should be doing this. We've had too much to drink... hic..."

"Why not? We're getting married soon, aren't we? Come on, let's have a cuddle."

Anna was feeling happy and constantly glancing at her new ring. She always enjoyed a cuddle, but didn't want it to go further, not yet anyway.

"Don't you love me anymore?" Lee was laughing as he pulled her nearer to him.

"Yes, of course I do, but..."

"But what?"

"I want our wedding day to be special. I don't... well, you know, I don't think we should have sex before we are married. I know its old fashioned, but it's what I think."

"We can still have a cuddle though, can't we?"

"Yes, but please don't, well, you know..."

"OK, OK." Lee dismissed her words in his head, and let his excitement continue to grow.

He eased Anna closer to him, kissing her passionately at the same time. She responded warmly to his advances, and Lee slowly slid his hand up under her jumper. Anna started to relax, enjoying his fondling, but after a while, as he managed to unclasp her bra strap, realised things might be going a bit too far, and asked him to stop. Lee, though, was now in a high state of arousal and did not want to remove his hand.

Anna gently, but firmly pushed him off her and sat up. He was none too pleased at this and tried to ignore her protestations. But she was insistent and after a bit of push and shove, killed the moment.

"I'm... I'm sorry, Anna. I was getting a bit, er... well... carried away. I'm not trying to force you. Honestly, I'm not. It's just, I love you. You make me feel randy, and I want to..."

"Oh, yes. I know what you want to do... so do I. But please can we wait till we are married?"

Lee, feeling frustrated, looked down at the floor and mumbled,

"Yes. OK."

Anna flopped back on the cushions grabbing and holding his hands tightly in hers. Her head was spinning from the effects of the alcohol.

"I do love you, you know. It won't be long now, love, will it?"

"No, s'pose not."

They were tired from their day out and feeling the effects of the wine they had consumed a short while ago. They sat quietly together, hand in hand. Within a few minutes, they were both fast asleep in each other's arms.

It was after 1:30 in the morning when Lee delivered Anna home.

Jim Slater was having a working lunch with Tom on Friday, and one of the topics for discussion was to consider organising some driving lessons for Lee. It would make him more productive as he could take their van to see customers and deal with some of the smaller jobs, which they found him extremely capable of doing. They also thought they would start to prepare him for a more sales-oriented position at the same time, as he had shown, a little to their surprise, a real flare in dealing with customer's enquiries.

One evening Lee was having dinner with the Slaters when Jim put the company's proposals to him.

He was overjoyed. This would indeed be a big step up for him – all he needed was the self-confidence to pull it off. Jim was now suggesting part of his time would be spent in sales. He was thrilled and terrified, not of meeting the customers, but of failing to come up to Jim's and Tom's expectations.

To start with, Jim suggested he should learn to drive. "How does that sound to you, Lee?"

"It sounds great, Mr Slater. I can't believe you have so much confidence in me. I promise I won't let you down."

Chapter 11:

A Wedding to Remember

19 September 1975

The morning of 19 September finally arrived, and the usual last-minute nerves had set in.

Gina tried to put all distractions out of her mind as she was sorting out the last details on Anna's wedding dress. Almost at the same time she was checking the catering at the Five Horseshoes, where the reception was to be held. Gina was in a state of panic.

"Anna, please keep still or this needle will stick in you. You don't want blood on your dress, today of all days."

"OK, Mum, sorry."

The Five Horseshoes

"Tom, for heaven's sake, don't bring your tea near here. It might get spilt on Anna's clothes."

"I wish you'd stop fussing. I won't spill anything."

Tom decided it would be more peaceful in the kitchen, so he went downstairs again.

Some months ago, he'd asked Anna and Lee what kind of wedding they would like: a large plush wedding with a short honeymoon, or a much smaller wedding with a fantastic honeymoon instead. Lee and Anna opted for the latter. The thought of a luxury holiday greatly appealed to both of them.

A large blue car with white ribbons on the bonnet turned up exactly on time to the Parkes' drive and Anna, who looked radiant in her beautiful white tight-fitting dress, was ready and waiting at the front door, all set to go. Gina was still rushing around like a thing demented, checking Tom's tie was straight, his shoes were clean, and a million other things.

Finally, Anna's mum was ready. She was wearing a beautiful pale peach outfit with matching accessories, which she and Anna had chosen on a special shopping trip to London's Oxford Street. The driver helped her into the front passenger seat of the car with Tom and Anna in the back.

At the same time, Lee was leaving with Sarah and Jim from their house in Till Farm Road. Lee was shaking like a leaf and Sarah was fussing like a mother hen, which didn't help calm Lee down one bit. Jim kept telling her to relax and everything would be fine... and even if it wasn't, it was too late to do anything about it now.

Lee was panicking. Would the car they'd sent to collect his mum have arrived on time? Would his dad let her come to the wedding at all?

Lee had originally asked Georgie, his closest friend, to be his best man. But Georgie was away on a training course in Germany, so Lee had decided to ask Mike Greenaway instead. Mike and his sister Tania were waiting to greet him outside the church. The pair of them stood there grinning like Cheshire Cats.

They exchanged greetings and a few moments of humorous banter before going into the church to sit down.

In the end, everyone turned up on time. The weather stayed gloriously sunny and warm, even though the forecast had suggested rain.

Jim Hordram, who was conducting the marriage service, was standing just inside the church doorway to greet the bride and her parents as they arrived.

Lee made a point of making a fuss of his mum and made sure she was well looked after.

As they were signing the register after the traditional ceremony, Anna made a mistake and started to get the giggles. Her loud laughter was highly infectious and Lee, Jim Hordram and the witnesses all started laughing so much, and so loudly, they could be heard in the main church. The entire congregation started laughing too.

Following the signing of the paperwork, as the service came to its conclusion, Anna and a very proud-looking Lee walked down the aisle to be welcomed by a shower of confetti as they stepped out through the church doors.

After all the official photos had been taken, the newly weds made the short journey to the Five Horseshoes for the reception. Lee looked among the guests for his mum, but couldn't see her. She had been in the front row of the church and had given him a big hug as the ceremony proper was about to begin. Now she was nowhere to be seen.

A moment or two later Jim Hordram told him his mother had been taken home in one of the cars as she had developed a severe migraine.

Lee was upset, disappointed and worried as to what the real reason for her absence might be.

Everyone was standing around with glasses of wine and chatting happily to each other as Tom banged on the table and called for the guests to sit down as the main part of the reception was about to commence. Some people were getting their written notes ready. They'd decided to go against tradition and have the speeches before the meal, so that it would be more relaxed.

After Tom had given his speech, Mike Greenaway, as best man, was about to stand up and deliver what he considered a comedy speech, when there was a scuffle at the door to the dining room. Raised voices were coming from the bar beyond. Everyone started to turn their heads to see what was going on and who was shouting.

The pub manager came in and spoke quietly to Tom.

Steven Parkes had chosen today to return.

He'd arrived at the family home and found no one in, so had called in to see one of the neighbours who'd told him where they all were.

He bellowed from the bar,

"Where's my bloody invitation then?"

Tom got up to greet his son and tried to calm things down.

"Steven, we couldn't contact you. You gave us no address or phone number. Where have you been? Please come in and sit down with us."

"Oh, yeah? Well, fuck you lot."

"Please sit down, Steven."

"I'm not sitting anywhere near you…"

He swung a punch at his father, missing him by a mile. Tom dodged the blow, slipped, fell backwards and hit his head hard on the edge of a table.

Three of the other male guests tried to grab Steven as he was about to put the boot in. Tom was now half lying on the floor, hanging on to one of the table legs.

Steven, swearing loudly, then turned and had a go at one of the younger waiters, launching a vicious attack on the poor unsuspecting fellow. He smashed a tray of drinks out of the waiter's hands and, before the lad could regain his balance, punched him hard in the face. The youngster staggered backwards, landing on top of Tom, both of them spread out on the floor in a heap.

His face covered in blood, the waiter had been knocked out cold. The manager called the police and within what seemed to be only a few seconds, three large police officers arrived and grabbed the struggling young man, wrestling him to the ground before they cuffed him.

He continued swearing at everyone and trying to lash out with his feet before one of the officers put him into a tight headlock until he became calm.

Steven Parkes was driven swiftly away in a patrol car. The ambulance crew started to deal with Tom, who had a nasty cut on his head. The poor waiter, who was still out for the count, was taken away on a stretcher. That left only one of the female guests to deal with, who had passed out.

While all this was unfolding, Lee was standing frozen to the spot, holding Anna tightly to him. He had been keeping a very close eye on Steven. Anna was crying her eyes out, hanging on to Lee, her head buried in his shoulder. Several of the male guests, who had grouped together to protect Sarah and Gina from Steven's kicks and punches by forming a human shield, were now straightening their ties and wiping spilt drinks off their clothes.

Some of the waiters were coming round with moist cloths and bowls of water to help clean up the mess. One of the long tables had been pushed over and its contents strewn all over the floor.

Everything seemed to have happened so quickly.

Gina was then sick all down her new outfit. Sarah, who was trying to help, soon realised there was little she could do. She stood there, tears running down her face, looking from Gina to Jim and back. Jim, standing with his arm around his sister, was rigid in astonishment.

After Steven's departure and the ambulance had left with the injured waiter, everything became rather quiet.

The guests were moving around nervously, treading on fragments of glass and murmuring to each other. The broken glasses and other wreckage were being hastily cleaned up by the staff, and the giant industrial Hoover was the only loud noise to disturb the gathering.

Mike Greenaway asked the manager if they could play some music as the area was rearranged and the tables reset.

He grabbed a microphone and asked all the guests to join with him in singing the songs coming over the PA system. Poor Mike was tone deaf, but no one seemed to care and some of the guests, with a lot of encouragement from Jim, started to join in.

He then asked if the hotel could provide some extra drinks and nibbles to cheer everyone up, while the tables and chairs were being reorganised.

The hotel staff, trying hard to be helpful, went out of their way to make up for the trauma that had taken place.

Several of the younger female waitresses even tried to get the event going by offering to dance with some of the guests.

Twenty minutes or so later Jim announced everything was about to be restarted and they would all be able to have the wedding breakfast as soon as the tables were ready.

About fifteen minutes later Tom reappeared, with a thumping headache and a bandaged head, to a great round of applause. He politely asked everyone to sit down as the food was about to be served. Taking the microphone, he stood up to apologise for the shambles, all caused by his son, and hoped, in spite of what had just happened, Lee and Anna would now be able to enjoy the rest of their day.

Of course, the magic of it was shattered for them, but it certainly would be a day they would always remember… even if not for all the right reasons.

Tom, although in quite a lot of pain, quietly tried to comfort Gina, who was still terribly upset and now dressed in an outfit she'd borrowed from a wedding guest who was staying at the hotel.

"His eyes were glazed, Gina. I'm pretty certain he's on some kind of drug. Steve would never behave like this. He's not been violent before. I know this is hard to deal with, but for Anna's sake… and we don't want you making yourself ill, do we?"

At the same time Lee was trying to comfort Anna, who was as white as her wedding dress.

Her mascara had run down her face and he was gently trying to clean her up when Tom came over to them, putting his arms around the young couple.

"You certainly won't ever forget your wedding day, will you? I hope and pray the difficulties you have faced today will make the bond between you even stronger. You have many happy years ahead of you. Please don't let these sad events spoil that."

Never in a million years had they anticipated anything like this would happen. Steven had always been a problematic and self-willed boy, even when young. But he was never aggressive and throughout his younger life was fond, if not a tad over-protective, of his little sister Anna.

Now he would certainly be facing criminal proceedings after being detained in custody by the police.

Lee and Anna had booked to spend their wedding night in the bridal suite of the Five Horseshoes.

By ten o'clock the last of the guests had left the hotel. Anna hugged her mum and dad, thanking them for everything, and then she and Lee went to their room.

Despite the earlier trauma Lee was still excited. He couldn't wait to get Anna to himself. He had been thinking of little else for ages. Sometimes on narrow paths, he would walk behind her and stare at her lovely round bottom and her sexy legs. At times in the middle of the night, he would wake, heart racing and sweating in panic, terrified she didn't want to marry him anymore.

Anna was, in her own way, a little apprehensive about the coming night, but chatted happily with her new husband as they went to their room.

The light was on and everything looked smart enough apart from the buzz of dozens of large flies surrounding the central light and on the walls.

"Ugh… what are those horrible things?"

Lee phoned reception to explain the problem. The young receptionist who answered was less than helpful. A few minutes later a young man arrived with a can of fly spray. He closed the windows and sprayed the contents all around the room.

"We can't stay in here. It's full of flies and this stuff stinks!" Lee said.

"They're only clegs, sir, horse flies – quite common in these parts. The spray will soon get rid of them for you. I'm afraid we haven't any other rooms available. We're fully booked." He left them to sort out the problem.

"Not exactly helpful, was he?" said Anna.

About half an hour later the floor was covered in dying and dead insects. Many were still buzzing, going round in circles. This time Lee went down to the reception desk and asked for a torch to scan the floor area as they couldn't see where the flies were. The smell of the fly spray was still unpleasant, but it was diminishing. Crawling around on the floor trying to catch the insects provided some much-needed amusement. Lee asked Anna to shine the torch across the carpet surface as he, with handfuls of tissues, pounced on the little critters.

"Quick, Lee… there's one."

"Got the bugger… "

"…and there's another one."

"Got him too."

This went on for a while as they crawled about on the floor together. By now Anna was laughing so much at the ridiculousness of the scene she could hardly hold the torch still. Eventually, when they thought they had them all, Lee accidentally backed into her while she was still giggling like a schoolchild. He could feel her body warmth against him, inflaming his ardour to fever pitch. He started running his hands under her dress and tried to pull at her panties, at the same time attempting to undress himself.

Anna was letting him do whatever he wanted and kissing him passionately at the same time, until there was a resounding ripping noise.

Anna immediately pushed him off her.

"Oh, heck... Mum made this dress for me. She'll be so upset... look, it's torn all down the side by the zip."

For a few moments they both froze, looking at the damage, mouths open in surprise.

There was a short silence.

"Let's get rid of these dead flies, Lee. They give me the creeps," Anna said in a small voice.

"OK."

Lee flushed down the toilet the fifty or so dead insects he'd retrieved from the waste bin, hoping there were no more. He carefully helped Anna to remove her torn dress, followed by the rest of her clothes. He had some difficulty as by now a combination of tiredness and the alcohol he'd drunk at the reception was affecting him. As Lee started to undress himself, he fell backwards and landed with a dull thud on the floor, his legs in the air. Anna laughed loudly and grabbed at his trousers, trying to pull them off. They giggled non-stop as they scrabbled about.

Lee looked around and was disappointed to find the room not as spacious as he'd at first thought. The rather small bed, which sagged noticeably in the centre, also left a lot to be desired.

Once fully undressed he got up and turned the main light off, leaving on only the dim sidelights. Immediately the atmosphere became more romantic.

Sitting there without a stitch on gave Anna an idea. She jumped up.

"Let's have a bit of fun and get in the shower together..."

The shower stall, though, was far too small for them both to get in together, so that plan was abandoned.

Lee then decided to turn off the bedside lamps and partially open the curtains, letting in the moonlight to lend some romance to the scene.

In happy anticipation, he sat down on the end of the bed in the semi-darkness, becoming more excited by the second.

When Anna appeared from the shower dressed in only a white fluffy bath towel, Lee thought she resembled a goddess. He pulled her down on top of him. Wrenching the towel away, his hands started to wander all over her body, starting at her lovely round bottom and working upwards.

"Hey, you... slow down, we have all night!"

Lee, however, was too excited to stop, and as Anna kissed him fervently, she could feel him pressing against her.

Within a few seconds, the intensity of his passion got the better of him.

They lay locked together, trembling in the moonlight as Lee's desire dissipated. This wasn't exactly what he'd had in mind for their wedding night. He was embarrassed and felt awkward. He had failed yet again. Too much champagne, he thought, seeking an excuse as they hugged each other tightly. Anna had planned to wear a sexy nightdress, which she'd chosen specially for tonight, but now thought it would be pointless. After a while, they got into bed and started to cuddle each other affectionately. Within a few moments Lee fell asleep in her arms, his head resting on her shoulder.

Anna looked lovingly at the peaceful smile on his face.

"Sleep well, my darling," she whispered to him. It was shortly after midnight when Anna lay back on her pillow with a deepening sense of disappointment. This evening's experience didn't fit at all with her romantic idea of how a wedding night should be. She closed her eyes and tried to put these thoughts out of her mind. After the disaster at the reception, nothing seemed to have gone as she'd hoped. She was restless, and sleep didn't come easily.

About two o'clock in the morning, Anna was in the middle of a strange dream. She was floating in a warm sea when she was accosted by a large octopus. She could feel the creature's tentacles on her skin, exploring every inch of her. Startled, she woke to find Lee's hands all over her body. He was kissing her lovingly.

Later, as the early dawn light started to creep in through the window, they lay quietly in the middle of the bed, hand in hand.

"Are you OK, Anna?"

"Yes. You were wonderfully gentle. I love you so much…"

Anna became tearful then and turned to Lee, clinging to him. Once again he began to caress her tenderly. But the emotional strain of the day was taking its toll. With their arms and legs intertwined they fell into a deep contented sleep.

An unplanned alarm call from reception awoke them at 8:30.

With a struggle, they managed to squeeze themselves into the tiny shower together. They could hardly move then so, giggling and laughing at the amusing situation, gave up.

Anna pushed Lee out of the cubicle when he wouldn't let go of her.

He was still laughing as he sank down on the wet floor. Lee stayed there, watching her shower. He couldn't believe that he, Lee Agazzi, would ever in his wildest dreams be looking at such a sexy, beautiful, kind and loving girl as Anna, who was now his wife… his wife. He thought he must be the luckiest man alive. He watched her as she moved around in the cubicle; he couldn't take his eyes off her, his fervour and passion building again.

It would be almost 10:00 a.m. before they appeared for breakfast.

While eating bacon and eggs in the main dining room, Anna was sure some of the other guests in the hotel were looking at her. She felt something was different this morning, making her unsettled and self-conscious. Lee on the other hand was having a great time, eating his full English breakfast with gusto, and beaming from ear to ear.

They were to set off the following day for their two-week honeymoon trip of a lifetime to Iceland. They had chosen this destination as they considered it somewhere a bit different and potentially exciting. Lee, in particular, wanted to see its geological features, all of volcanic origin as Iceland sits right across the Mid Atlantic Ridge.

The plan was to fly from Heathrow to Reykjavik late in the afternoon.

After the unexpected and upsetting events of their wedding day, neither of them felt in the right mood for going anywhere and suggested cancelling, but Tom wasn't having any of it, insisting they should go.

He was due to be their chauffeur, but his injury had given him a dreadful headache and it wouldn't go away, making it impossible for him to drive anywhere safely. So a taxi was arranged, and after an early lunch, Lee and Anna were whisked away to the airport. Neither of them had ever flown before and they were distinctly nervous as they approached the terminal buildings.

Luckily for them the flight was smooth and uneventful, and after a good night's sleep in a smart hotel in Reykjavik, they felt excited and keen to explore. The tour company arranged for them to have a trip around the capital before moving to a few other major towns around the country, returning to the UK by ferry. It was to be a grand adventure.

After leaving Reykjavik, they first set off to see the famous geyser area, where Strokkur erupted every five to ten minutes, spouting boiling water a hundred feet into the air. Lee in particular wanted to see this, and went on and on about it for hours. Poor Anna wasn't interested in the geology, but she didn't try to stop him rabbiting on.

"I can't believe it's so high or so hot. It's boiling water, you know..."

Strokkur erupting – Central North Iceland

To prove the point to Anna, he dipped his little finger in the edge of the water and instantly regretted it.

"Ouch! Bloody hell, that's hot." Anna had to turn away, she was laughing so much. Lee's finger had become quite red and tingled for several hours.

"Told you to listen to the guide, didn't I?" Anna couldn't stop giggling.

"It's not funny, it bloody well hurt."

After lunch they travelled on to Gullfoss, a fantastic set of waterfalls, before returning to their hotel in the capital.

The following day was to be another busy one as they went to see the volcano Snaefellsjokull. This was the pathway into the abyss as described in Jules Verne's novel *Journey to the Centre of the Earth*. The scenery here was amazing and Anna wanted to stand still and take it all in before they left for another hotel a few miles further north. Lee took photographs from every conceivable angle.

"Wow! No one will ever believe this when they see it…"

After having a fabulous meal with champagne, they turned in for the night. Lee said he couldn't ever remember feeling so tired, the excitement and the wine they'd consumed knocked him out. At least there wouldn't be a rush in the morning. They were to spend a couple of days in Akureyri. The hotel room was large, warm and comfortable and came with a wonderful shower with multiple water jets, so they got in together…

After a late lazy breakfast, they headed to another spectacular waterfall, Godafoss (Waterfall of the Gods). The weather was again superb, the bright blue sky and tiny white clouds reflected in the shimmering water.

"I wish Mum could see this, she would love it." Anna couldn't believe how beautiful it was.

Anna in Iceland

Their next stop, Myvatn, was not too far away. Myvatn or Midge Lake was a fantastic area of shallow water formed by yet more volcanic action.

Unfortunately, the place without a doubt lived up to its name. Poor Anna had so many midge bites she was scratching all night long and the itching continued well into the following day. Also nearby were the amazing mud pools of Hverir where the boiling mud gave off an evil toxic-smelling gas. The midges didn't seem to mind the terrible smell, though, they were out in force there as well.

Their last memorable moment in Iceland was seeing a large colony of puffins on the coast near their port of departure, Seydisfjördur in the south-east of the country. They sailed to Torshavn in the Faroe Islands and then on to northern Denmark from where they took another ferry home.

The trip was delightful. Other passengers and staff on board the ship treated them like royalty. Everyone seemed to know it was their honeymoon and they were awash with free champagne for the entire journey.

Lee was so pleased they did not have to drive. Later, during the long taxi ride back to Tillshott, Anna, lying in her husband's arms in the back seat, said she didn't want to see another bottle of champagne ever again.

By the time they were approaching Tillshott she was asleep with her head tucked into Lee's shoulder.

Ten days after returning from honeymoon Anna received an unexpected late-evening call from her dad.

"Hello, Anna, sorry it's a bit late. I thought you should know that Steven has been released from custody and he's out on bail. He's apologised for what happened at your wedding and has asked if he can live at home for a while. Naturally Mum is pleased to see him. She hasn't said a lot but I know she's really worried about him. I can see it in her face. I'm trying to keep a low profile for now… He's said he would like to see you. I don't know how you'd feel about that."

Anna hesitated.

"I, um… I don't know, Dad. Not sure it would be a good idea. It might make things worse. I'll have to think about it."

"OK, love. I won't mention it anymore, unless he asks again."

Steven's court appearance should have taken place two weeks later. Tom drove him to the court building, leaving his son to wait for him inside the main entrance while he went to park the car. On entering, Tom couldn't find him anywhere and when Steven failed to appear at the hearing, sat there with his head in his hands not knowing what to do next. His son seemed to have vanished into thin air.

Tom spoke to everyone he could see near the entrance where he had left Steven but no one could recall having seen him. Later that day he went to the local police station to report Steven as missing.

Three weeks later, as Gina was clearing away the breakfast things, there was a knock at the door. She was shocked and alarmed to find a tall police officer and a WPC on the doorstep.

"Good morning, madam. Are you Mrs Parkes?"

"Yes, I'm Gina Parkes," she said in a cheerful voice.

"I am Constable Nigel Standish and this is WPC Anita Morris. We are from the Metropolitan Police in Brentford. May we please come in?"

Gina invited them to take a seat in the lounge.

"I believe your husband reported your son Steven missing a few weeks ago. I'm very sorry to have to tell you this, but a person answering his description, and whom we believe to be your son, has been found on the towpath of the Grand Union Canal just north of Brentford Town."

Gina gulped audibly.

The glass of water she had been holding slipped from her hand and landed with a crash on the floor. She started crying with shock, as she tried to speak. The WPC gently put her hand on her shoulder.

"What... I mean... How did he... Oh, no, no. Is he...?"

"I'm afraid there is no easy way to say this, Mrs Parkes, but Steven was pronounced dead at the scene by the emergency services. It appears that he may have suffered a heart attack. There is no evidence of foul play. A full post-mortem will have to be carried out by the local coroner. Until that has been completed we cannot give you any further explanation. I'm very sorry."

The two police officers stayed with her for a short time as she phoned Tom.

Within a few days of the formalities being completed, the cause of death was confirmed as heart failure, almost certainly caused by the high level of drugs that were found in Steven's bloodstream.

At the funeral Anna was distraught and in tears, blaming herself for refusing to see him. Lee tried hard to comfort her without much success.

"I caused him to go, didn't I? If I'd come to see him when he asked, maybe he'd still be alive."

Her father, who was usually so positive, looked downcast and tearful as he held her in his arms.

"I don't think it would have made any difference. Sadly, I'm of the opinion Steven was on a course of self-destruction. I don't know why or what we did wrong while bringing him up, but somehow we failed him. It certainly is not your fault Anna, so please don't think that."

The death of Steven cast a long shadow over them all for many months.

Chapter 12:

The Greenaways

October 1975

Lee had known Mike Greenaway for many years. They were in the same class at school and became friends over time. The friendship deepened after the sad death of Mike and Tania's mum and dad, who were killed in a tragic road accident while on a motoring holiday in Spain about eighteen months before Lee's wedding to Anna.

The information sent by the Spanish authorities hadn't given many details. The accident report stated that while the Greenaways were travelling in the mountains of Northern Spain and on their way back to Santander to catch the car ferry home, there had been a landslip on a major road. This cut through a narrow gorge and several vehicles became caught up in the mayhem.

Their car ended up on the valley floor with a heavy goods vehicle on top of it. The scene was one of total devastation.

Seven people were found to have died when the emergency services eventually cleared the wreckage.

The sad aftermath was not only that Mike and his sister lost their parents, but it also put at risk the future of the Greenaways' lifelong dream, their garden centre.

Both the siblings worked at the nursery and had done so since leaving school. But it was by no means certain if they would now be able, or would even want, to take over and run the business on their own. They were both still very young to take on such a daunting task.

They still lived at the family home, so at least they would still have a roof over their heads.

It took a few very upsetting months for them to arrange the funeral and their parents' financial affairs.

But as the dust settled, the contingency plans Mr and Mrs Greenaway had put in place some years before kicked into play. They had made excellent provision for their two children in the event of any unforeseen circumstances.

After a lot of discussion with their solicitor and members of the extended family, Mike said he would like to continue running the nursery if Tania wanted to do the same, which she did.

The centre was given two years to achieve financial stability by the bank that had financed it.

They also required additional monetary surety, and this would be provided by Mr Greenaway's two brothers.

They had been heavily involved with the finance and running of the nursery from the beginning.

Mike and Tania were determined to make a go of the business, and came up with several new ideas to help achieve that aim.

They considered the buildings needed extending and modernising and Mike felt they should include a café area. He was confident this would encourage the customers to stay longer and spend more money. Now, with his uncles' blessing for the drawings of the expanded premises that he had produced, Mike needed to get an accurate price for the proposal.

With drawings in hand, he popped over to see Lee at the joinery and showed him the plans for the new timber-framed greenhouses and a Scandinavian-style log cabin, which would become the café. If Slater & Parkes managed to obtain the order for these new buildings, it would be a big project with the potential to be the most substantial single order in the history of the company.

Mike asked Lee if he would provide them with a quote for the construction of the buildings, which were to go on solid concrete foundations with low supporting walls. At the back of the already existing structures would go the café and the revamped shopping area.

The new premises would give them about fifty per cent more space for growing and displaying plants in a sheltered environment plus the coffee shop and a new retail outlet. Careful planning and a full surveyor's report would be required before starting the final quotation.

A local builder would also need to be engaged regarding the initial foundation work. The site, partially obscured by a small piece of woodland, sloped slightly downhill towards the railway line. Many of the trees here were beech, but there were also quite a few ancient oaks and elms, and several of the oldest had preservation orders on them. If this area could be avoided, it would make things much more accessible and a lot cheaper.

Over the coming weeks Mike and Lee would often meet after work for the odd pint when time permitted, to go over aspects of the plans.

The two of them always enjoyed getting together in the pub, apart from one thing: Mike couldn't hold his drink.

He would sometimes get out of hand and could become quite outrageous. Once or twice Lee managed to get him away before any trouble started. Over the last year, though, he'd insisted Mike should only have one pint during an evening, and this seemed to calm him down.

Tania was another matter altogether. She was a beautiful girl with an amazing figure, though she liked to conceal this under baggy unattractive clothes. Despite this she was, in Lee's words, quite a stunner. At least she didn't have a drink problem. She never touched alcohol.

She managed the office and purchasing side of the nursery.

Right back in their school days, Lee had fancied Tania, even though she could be quite volatile at times and would sometimes go into a sulk for days at a time. However, although she had never showed the slightest interest in him, the three of them got on well, most of the time.

Lee often felt there was a hidden side to Tania. She was rather quiet at times and rarely gave much of an opinion on, well, pretty much anything, other than work.

So the Greenaway's job, if he managed to pull it off, was going to be a real coup for Lee and he was getting excited at the thought of it. This would be one heck of an achievement for him.

Anna had to put up with his excited chatter about it for hours, but was delighted to see him so happy. Life had been exciting and pleasant for them both this year. Lee would chat to her all the time, often over dinner, about how he, Georgie and Mike used sometimes to skip off school and go up into the woods behind Grove Farm, for a crafty fag. Sometimes they found pieces of aircraft wreckage from the spot where a German bomber crashed during the war.

It was a Heinkel He 111, shot down by RAF Spitfires from the nearby air base, killing the aircrew. There were often men wandering around the crash site with metal detectors. Mike and Lee would play about with the bits of metal, wiring, fabric and other parts that sometimes turned up.

Lee had found and kept, in a drawer in his childhood bedroom, a chunk of something he thought might have been from the bomber. The metal bodywork showed evidence of green camouflage paint. He wondered what had become of it now.

Lee's next evening with Mike got off to a bad start.

For no apparent reason, he'd developed a headache earlier in the afternoon and it persisted into the evening.

The Coal Scuttle

As he was setting off to meet his friend at the 'Scuttle', Lee noticed a flat tyre on his van. So after uttering a few silent (and some not so silent) expletives, he changed the wheel while keeping one eye on his watch. He was supposed to be going over some important details for the garden centre.

Lee arrived, rather flustered, at the pub about an hour later than arranged and it was quite apparent Mike had been there for a while and already consumed more than his usual single pint!

Oh, hell, this wasn't a good omen. He was sitting with two other blokes, one of whom was Tania's "sometimes-boyfriend", as she called him, and the other chap was someone Lee didn't recognise at all. About ten minutes passed and then Mike started talking, in rather a loud voice, about the goings on at home the night before.

Apparently he had gone to bed early when Tania walked into his room, as she often did, dressed in only her bra and a pair of skimpy panties, got into his bed and started larking around, tickling him and causing him to wriggle about.

"Mike, I think that's enough, mate. You're drunk. Come with me," Lee told him, slightly alarmed by the direction the story was going in. Mike, though, brushed Lee's arm away and seemed anxious to continue his story. After yet more embarrassing detail, things took a decided turn for the worse.

"I just couldn't... keep her... off me," Mike giggled. "I was beginning to get horny..."

Then, unexpectedly, Tania appeared at the pub door. Walking straight up to her brother, she shouted something abusive at him, and proceeded to punch, kick and generally lay into him. Then the "sometimes-boyfriend" joined in. Other people were moving away, and one or two left the pub to avoid the affray.

At some point, Tania and the boyfriend started to have a go at each other.

Mike by now was lying on the floor. His nose was bleeding and his face was covered in blood. Lee dragged him to his feet and almost carried him out of the pub, pushing him into the van.

As they drove off, Lee noticed in the rear-view mirror a police car complete with flashing blue lights. It arrived at the scene and blocked the car park entrance, preventing anyone else from pulling in or leaving.

Lee thought he ought to take Mike back home to clean him up. Anna wouldn't be too pleased, as she wasn't a great fan of Mike or his sister. It would appear there was some history there.

Mike, now almost incoherent, could hardly walk, so Lee half hauled him up the stairs and into their flat.

Once Lee and Anna had finished cleaning Mike up, he curled himself on the sofa like a child and seemed to go to sleep.

Anna put a warm blanket over him as he was shivering.

Lee was exhausted. Since they'd left the pub, Mike had hardly spoken a word, other than to mumble that he wanted more beer. So when he seemed to be asleep, Lee and Anna went into the kitchen for a chat. He started telling her what had taken place and what Mike had been saying. Anna let him talk awhile, didn't say much apart from,

"This is nothing new, you know. Something has been going on there for some time. I'm surprised you didn't suspect."

Lee certainly didn't know anything about it, he assured his wife.

"It appears Mike and Tania have been fooling around together, running about the house in the evenings with little or no clothes on. It seems to have been going on for a while. No one really knows, but there's been a rumour going around at the hospital ever since one of the district nurses saw them through the window when she was passing the house some time back. I think it would be best for all concerned to get him out of here as soon as he is able to walk."

Then the doorbell rang. Anna got up quickly, to see who it was, putting her hand on Lee's arm and telling him to stay where he was.

It was the police.

Oh, heck, thought Lee. He had never been in trouble with the law in his life. This was the last thing he wanted.

A police sergeant came into the small hallway followed by a female police officer. While she stood talking to Anna, the burly policeman was trying to get some sense out of Mike.

"We will have to take you down to the station, Mr Greenaway. The publican has made a complaint," he said.

Mike got up unsteadily and was taken away by the policeman.

"We would like you, Mr Agazzi, to come to the station tomorrow to make a statement, please," the WPC continued.

"It will only be a formality, I think," she reassured Anna. "Apparently, there was a bit of an affray at the Scuttle earlier this evening, and some furniture has been damaged. Your husband isn't implicated, but we need his statement nevertheless."

"OK, Lee will pop down in the morning."

He felt like a naughty boy caught in the headlights. He just stood there while Anna and the policewoman, Louise, talked about "it" and "him". He felt very embarrassed, and this brought back a whole rash of unwanted memories.

After the police left, taking Mike with them, Anna explained that she found Louise to be friendly, helpful, and liked her a lot. They met on occasion in the hospital canteen, while Louise attended RTAs or other incidents.

"Oh, I wondered how she seemed to know you so well," Lee said as he poured himself a glass of water.

"Think I'm off to bed now, I'm exhausted," Anna told him. "That's enough excitement for one day. Got to be up early tomorrow, there's a training course starting in the morning and I'd better not be late. Don't stay up too long, you look tired."

"OK, love. I'll deal with the crockery and be with you shortly."

Alone in the kitchen, Lee sat staring at the wall. He couldn't believe any of what had happened over the last few hours. He'd always known Tania could be belligerent and stroppy at times, but this… Well, this was unbelievable. As far as Lee could remember, Mike had never said anything about his sister that in any way would have led anyone to suppose something of a personal nature was going on between them. Quite the opposite, in fact. Instead Lee had always thought Mike didn't like Tania much. They often argued, shouting at each other while he was with them. But this was always at the garden centre and about work-related things, like plant choice or greenhouse temperatures.

Lee couldn't remember ever seeing them together, other than at work. At least, not since they were all at school together.

Then as if a lightning bolt had struck him, he remembered why he'd been meeting up with Mike… The new building contract. Oh, no. He had been working on this for some time and had hoped it would become a firm order this week.

I suppose that's not going to happen now, Lee thought to himself.

"You stupid, idiot Mike…" he said aloud.

Then he remembered he was to go to the police station in the morning and make a statement. He sat there at the table, head in his hands, his mind blank.

There was a sudden bang and Lee jumped. A cup had fallen off the table and onto the floor. He must have nodded off and knocked it by accident. As he looked down he was surprised to see it was still in one piece and only a tiny amount of liquid had spilt on the floor.

A lucky escape, he thought to himself, wiped up the mess and went to bed at 1 a.m.

Chapter 13:

Georgie's Bombshell

November 1975

Derek Slater, as Georgie had been christened, asked his mum and dad if they could have a chat over their evening meal about how he wanted his career to progress in the future.

Tonight was going to be his opportunity to tell his parents of his plans, and it wasn't going to be easy. Neither of them would want to hear this.

"I know you won't like my idea, but I've been dreaming about this for a long time and it is what I really want to do. I want to join the army, the Royal Engineers if possible, and train as an electrician with them. In years to come, when I leave the forces, I will have a fantastic qualification and can start up my own business, which is my grand plan. There's always work in the electrics industry, and I should be able to earn a good living. I've wanted to do this for a while and now while I'm young and fit is the ideal time. What do you think?"

Jim looked at Sarah and thought she was about to faint. She had gone as white as a sheet. Jim didn't like the idea either, it worried him a lot.

But Sarah was mortified.

"I think I'm going to be sick..."

She got up and went into the kitchen, closing the door behind her. She grabbed hold of the sink and stayed there till the feeling subsided. The thought of losing her only child to the army was something she just couldn't handle. She felt her whole world was about to cave in on top of her. What if Georgie was injured? Or killed even?

How on earth would she cope with that?

Jim wanted to make sure his son fully understood the implications of his decision.

"Are you sure you know what you are taking on? You won't have any control over your own life in the forces, you know. You have to do what you are told."

"Yes, I know. I have thought it all through. I've been to see the recruitment people, and they've explained exactly what's involved and what the risks are. This is still is a great opportunity. I want to learn how to train others as I progress. I might be able to travel the world too. This is something I've always wanted to do."

Sarah came back and sat down at the dining table again. She was still very white. This news had shaken her to the core.

"We will never stand in the way of whatever you want to do, you know that, but please will you reconsider this before you do something you might regret? The army, air force and navy are all combat-oriented. You will become a trained killer, you know."

"I think of it more as a trained defender, Mum. I don't want to kill anyone. I want to be an electrical engineer. Of course, it's military as well, I'm well aware of that. I know I could be killed if things got difficult. But you can be killed crossing the road, can't you? I've been thinking about this for about two years now but, Mum, I promise I will go over it all again before I sign up for anything. And I will get a lot more information for you, so you won't be too worried. Life in the forces can be pretty exciting too, you know. And I like exciting things, don't I?"

"Yes, I know you do, but…" Sarah's voice trailed away. She was so upset. The thought of losing her son was quite unbearable to her. She'd always known he would fly the nest one day, of course, but not like this. Definitely not this way.

Six weeks later Georgie signed up with the RAF to be trained as an electrician.

Sarah was heartbroken but had come to terms with his decision. The exact date was to be advised shortly after the medical and other checks were completed.

For the next few weeks, a dark cloud descended over the Slater household. Neither Jim nor Sarah spoke much about Georgie's departure. Life went on as usual, but it wasn't the same for any of them. Sarah felt all the joy had gone from her life, for good.

She sank into a state of deep depression.

Not even Lee or her beloved Anna could lift her spirits for more than a few moments at a time. Jim was becoming worried about her state of mind, but didn't know how to resolve it. He was pretty upset himself.

It wouldn't be until Sarah had been to see her doctor about an unrelated matter that things started to come to a head. In the surgery she had broken down and after a lengthy appointment was prescribed a course of antidepressants. Over the next few weeks her mood slowly lifted and a little of her former self started to reappear.

Chapter 14:

High as a Kite

Mid-November 1975

It was now almost a month since the pub incident and Lee decided to find out how matters had progressed with the nursery project.

He couldn't afford to let the contract for Greenaway's new greenhouses and outbuildings slip through his fingers, so decided to see if he could get it sewn up.

He needed this order. Lee felt it would do his credibility at Slater & Parkes a lot of good.

He left a note on his desk saying where he was going. After collecting the latest costing and plans from a cabinet in Tom's office, he headed off to the garden centre.

Approaching the nursery car park, Lee could see it was empty.

There was a prominent CLOSED notice by the entrance on the main road, which he considered strange.

Greenaway's was always open six days a week. This was a Tuesday, not the day they would usually be closed. Lee avoided the main customer entrance, so missed seeing the notice about the change in opening hours for the current week. He walked straight to the side staff-only gate, which he had used before, but found it locked. Puzzled, he then decided to go to the rear door of the office. As he rounded the corner, Lee noticed there was a light on, so he knocked on the door. Before he had even removed his hand, the door was snatched open by Tania.

She looked flustered; her eyes were radiant, sparkling and staring. She wasn't dressed in her usual attire of jeans, a jumper and wellies. Instead, she was barefoot and wearing a fashionably short bright yellow and white dress with a zipper all the way down the front.

Lee was astonished. He was a lot more than that, in fact. He was gob-smacked. Even in their schooldays, Lee had never seen Tania dressed like this.

She looked amazing, stunning – apart from the expression on her face.

Oh, dear, it looked like Mike's little sister was in one of her moods. Lee knew this would not be a good start to the meeting.

There seemed to be no sign of Mike and other than Tania the whole place was deserted.

"What *do you* want?" she asked in an aggressive and sarcastic tone.

"Actually, I was hoping to speak to Mike, is he around?"

"No, he isn't. He's pissed off to London to see a financial bloke. Does that answer your question?"

"Well, yes and er… no. Sort of. I was hoping to discuss the building contract, but as he's not here…"

"No, he isn't, and as for the contract, you were supposed to sort it out with him weeks ago in the pub, instead of causing so much trouble."

"*I* didn't cause any trouble, it was you who hit your brother, remember?"

"Well, you could have fooled me."

Ignoring Lee entirely, she paced left then right, flapping her arms up and down.

"You were in there with the others, all having a good laugh, weren't you?"

"Actually, no. It wasn't funny. I was trying to stop Mike from making an ass of himself. He was drunk."

"Oh, really… I don't think that's what you were doing at all. I think you wanted a bit of the action, didn't you?"

Without pausing for breath, Tania unzipped her dress from the neck to the bottom hem in a single movement. It fell loosely to her sides, and she shook it off her shoulders, letting it fall to the floor.

She was wearing nothing at all under it.

Lee stood there with his mouth half-open as if to speak, but no words would come. He froze, staring at her naked body.

He started to breathe deeply. Found he couldn't move.

Tania was less than eighteen inches away – completely nude.

Lee didn't know what to do or say. This was too much for any man.

She smirked at him.

"Well, come on then, here I am."

With her sparkling eyes fixed on his, she grabbed Lee's left wrist in a vice-like grip and, almost pulling him off balance, thrust his hand between her legs, holding him there, pressing and rubbing him hard against her.

All the time she stared at him with a seductive expression and in a low husky voice said,

"This is what you want, Lee... isn't it?" Her eyes closed and she muttered something he couldn't make out.

After what seemed to be an eternity, she relaxed and released her grip. Lee snatched his hand back.

He could feel his face was flushed, his legs felt like jelly. He was almost exploding with sexual tension. She was gorgeous!

The sight, touch and fragrance of Tania's body created a dramatic reaction in him.

Other than Anna, Lee had never seen another female totally naked except in girlie magazines.

He passionately wanted, more than anything, to grab hold of Tania and...

"Tania, I... Bloody hell, *mio dio*! Oh, no. Tania... NO – that's not what I want."

He spoke in a stifled croaky voice, struggling to control himself and trying to sound sincere.

"Please put your dress back on. This isn't the way to... er... do things, and it won't help anything, will it? I've only come to discuss the quote for extending the buildings, nothing else. Certainly not this."

Feeling awkward, he coughed a couple of times. His mouth was dry, plus he was shaking and sweating profusely.

Tania stared at him defiantly, hands on hips, her glazed eyes fixed on his.

After a few moments she calmed down, and with a casual gesture rubbed her hands over her firm breasts, as if to wipe away dust. She crouched down and retrieved her dress, never taking her eyes off Lee as she started to put it back on.

In deliberate slow motion, she pulled the zipper up until it reached her neck. She then faced him brazenly and with a sugary-sweet smile blew him a kiss.

Shrugging her shoulders and still in bare feet, Tania flounced out without saying another word, leaving the door wide open.

Lee was left standing there, shocked and still shaking. He couldn't believe what had happened and felt so screwed up he couldn't think straight. What on earth would she do next?

There was a deafening silence about the place.

Lee wasn't aware of any sound around him at all, not even the ticking of a clock. All he could hear was the steady, rather fast thumping of his own heart.

After a short while, he walked back to his van, got in and locked the doors. He shifted about in the driver's seat for quite a while, until he felt more relaxed and comfortable. He muttered to himself. "Bloody hell, what the heck is she on? She's high as a kite." He looked at his wrist and there was already a big dark bruise forming where Tania had gripped him.

Where did she get such incredible strength?

What would he say to Anna or to Mike about this morning's events?

No one would ever believe him.

For a short while, Lee sat in the van staring into space. He couldn't get the vision of Tania's beautiful firm body out of his mind and began to wish he had pushed her over the desk and had sex with her. He wondered if, ridiculous as it might seem now, this was what she'd wanted all along, then tried to dismiss the thought.

He had no idea what effect today's events would have on the contract and all the plans he had drawn up with the Greenaways.

Would either of them speak to him again?

Lee had never experienced anything of this nature before. He couldn't see any possibility of a way forward at this moment. He was in shock.

On his return to the joinery, a message left on his desk made him feel even more uptight.

It was from Mike, asking him to visit him on-site the following day.

Lee felt sick and faint at the thought of meeting him there after today's events.

What would he say?

How could he even begin to explain?

Would Tania have said anything to her brother, and if she had, what might she have said?

What if Mike didn't know?

Worries about the possible ramifications of Tania's bizarre behaviour made Lee feel ill.

Why had she been dressed the way she was? In all the years he had known the Greenaways he had never seen Tania in such a seductive dress. And what made her eyes appear so large, bright and sparkle so much? He was convinced she must have taken some sort of drug.

Why was the garden centre closed?

He became aware of how painful his wrist felt. He couldn't believe Tania would have the strength to be able to grip and then hold his arm with such incredible force.

He was so preoccupied with his thoughts he failed to notice the office door opening.

Lee was jolted out of his nightmare when Tom walked in, wanting information about an urgent job.

"Are you feeling alright, Lee? You're looking very pale."

"Yes, thanks, Tom, I'm fine. I'm rather tired, that's all."

"How did you get on at the garden centre?"

"Mike wasn't there, but he wants to see me tomorrow to discuss the job. I, er… just got a message a few minutes ago."

"Well, never mind. You can't win 'em all. Better luck tomorrow."

Tom collected his papers and left.

Then Lee's work took over and some normality returned to the rest of the day.

It was almost 6:15 before he prepared to go home, about half an hour later than usual, happy to be on his way at last. This had been an extraordinary day, to say the least.

As he left, he shared a couple of jokes with two of his workmates. They were making a staircase for the Five Horseshoes. This was urgently needed as the result of fire damage caused by some old wiring, so they were working overtime.

Lee waved goodbye as he turned to go, reminding them to lock up when they left. He felt brain dead and drained, and couldn't get the image of Tania's breasts out of his mind. He could feel his heart pounding and his whole body becoming tense at the very thought of her.

Lee hoped Anna would be at home. He needed her to be there. He craved her love and reassurance, and needed to make love to her. He wanted her to hug and hold him tight until he calmed down.

Flashes from the past reappeared in his mind: the times when, as a small boy, he would run to his mother and hug her legs if he became upset. She would put her arms around him, sing little songs, smooth his hair and wipe his eyes.

He fumbled with his keys, hands shaking, looking for the correct one. He couldn't get it into the lock. Eventually he managed to open the door and it was obvious Anna was not home.

He dropped the keys by the phone and in the kitchen found the note she'd left for him on the worktop.

Just popping round to see Mum as she is feeling unwell.
Dinner in the oven.
Back soon.
Love you, Anna XX

Lee's heart sank. He wandered into the lounge, switched on the TV, dropped onto the sofa and within a few minutes was asleep.

An hour later he was awakened by the sound of the front door opening.

Anna was home. Lee sprang up and rushed to her, kissing her passionately while pulling her onto the sofa as he tried to remove her clothes.

Within a couple of minutes they lay still, Lee sprawled on top of her motionless. Anna tried to push him to one side.

"Lee, what's got into you? You're not normally like this… in such a hurry. What's the matter, has something happened?" She looked at him, puzzled by a large dark and yellowing bruise around his left wrist.

"No… No, not really, I just want… needed to make love to you. I was feeling randy, that's all. Maybe it was because you weren't at home when I got in."

"OK. So there's nothing wrong?"

"No, nothing… nothing at all. Have you eaten at Mum's? How is she? You said the dinner is in the oven."

"I only had a cup of tea with Mum and she's OK. Yes, the dinner must be ready by now. It won't take me a minute to finish the veg."

"Great. I could eat a horse." Lee smiled at Anna, who stood up and attempted to straighten her dishevelled clothing. She looked at him with her head a little to one side, not believing a word he'd said. She knew him too well. She was convinced his wrist injury was something to do with today's unusual behaviour. She hoped after a while he would open up.

Lee put his arms around her, hugging her tightly to him. He wanted desperately to tell her about what had happened at the Greenaways' but was too embarrassed and ashamed. He could have stopped it – couldn't he?

He felt so guilty about the whole business. He didn't

know what to say and was terrified Anna wouldn't believe him and would walk out, leaving him.

Later, during the night, he woke up about 4 a.m. The problems of the day now reappeared, in his head, and in more exaggerated detail, as is often the case in the middle of the night. Lee was in a distressed state as he turned over to lie on his stomach. He gently touched Anna, startling her. He started to tell her the whole story of what had taken place the day before.

"Why didn't you explain this last night? What did you think I would do?"

Lee could hear his father's voice shouting at him, over and over again: "You're nothing but a useless idiot!"

"Didn't... think you or anyone else... would ever believe me. I thought you... you would leave me... I'm sorry. I'm so sorry."

"Oh, Lee, honey – I would never leave you. You don't have to be sorry. You haven't done anything wrong, have you?"

"No... No, but I couldn't... I couldn't stop her, and I couldn't bloody move!"

Anna pulled him to her like a small child. Her mind was in turmoil. She realised she had never fully understood Lee's deep sense of insecurity. To see him this upset worried her.

What could she do to comfort him and calm his inner demons? She cuddled him lovingly; rocking him with a soothing motion until he finally went to sleep.

After that Anna lay wondering what the coming days would bring.

Chapter 15:

The Contract

November 1975

The following morning, feeling tired and more than a little apprehensive, Lee arrived at work a little later than usual. He dug out the relevant paperwork for the Greenaway's quote and started going through it carefully, making sure everything was there and it was all in order.

Any mistakes at this point could be disastrous.

He was relieved to have told Anna about the events of the previous day. He now thought it best to put the whole incident behind them.

But try as he might, he found he could not dismiss memories of yesterday from his mind. The constant torment of the image of a naked Tania standing before him made him shake involuntarily and his pulse race.

At last, satisfied the paperwork was correct and trying hard to sound cheerful, he popped into Tom's office to let him know where he was going.

"Morning, Tom, I'm off to Greenaway's now. I have all the paperwork and hope to come back with the order. It's been going on for too long, I want them to commit today. I hope I can persuade them to sign on the dotted line."

"Good luck. I'll speak to you later then, OK?"

"Hope so."

Mike's blue BMW was parked by the office door, right next to Tania's little red Fiat.

Oh, well… here goes, thought Lee.

He knocked on the office door and let himself straight in, as he always did.

"Hi, Mike, how did you get on in London?"

"It went really well. I've got all the finance agreed, and we've been told we can go ahead with the project, subject to one or two small changes."

"Wow! That's great. Pleased to hear it. We've all worked hard on the planning and it will be good to see it start to materialise at last."

"Lee, can you hang on a moment, please? I need Tania to agree to the changes the bank's solicitors have asked for. Give me a moment…"

"OK."

Lee was on his own in the office for a while when Mike went to find Tania.

He was feeling nervous, hearing their voices as they returned together.

Mike pulled up a couple more chairs for the three of them.

Tania said hello to Lee, giving no hint of what had taken place the day before.

The changes required were minor legal matters in connection with council building regulations, and these could be easily resolved. There was only one outstanding problem left to deal with, preserving an old oak tree – but it would be easy to fix, one way or the other.

Tania got up and made each of them a drink, handing one to Lee and putting the other two mugs on the desk together with some chocolate biscuits.

"Well, if you are happy with the contract, Lee, we will sign it. Then you can start organising the groundwork. If it's at all possible, we would like it completed before the New Year."

"I'll have to check with the factory and the company doing the foundations. But I don't think it's beyond the realms of possibility. It's always better not to be doing groundwork when it's too cold, so the sooner, the better."

"Great. You OK with that, Tan?"

Mike had always called her that ever since they were children.

"Yes, of course. It will be nice to have more space and a proper café."

Mike, Tania and Lee signed the contracts and Lee hurried to collect the completed documents, placing then into a folder.

"I'll prepare copies for each of you and send them off later in the coming week."

"I'm so pleased we've been able to give you this contract, Lee. I know it's taken longer than we wanted, but we got there in the end, didn't we?"

"Yes, it has taken a lot longer than I expected. It's been hard work, but I'm sure you will think it was all worth it. Thanks for the order."

He shook hands with them both, trying to avoid eye contact with Tania. Mike said goodbye and announced the excitement (and the coffee) had got to him. He was going to have to dash to the toilet.

Tania smiled at Lee, saying goodbye. When he turned to leave she quite deliberately rubbed her body against his.

"Oops, so sorry! I must have slipped…" She gave him a sly smile as he left.

Lee, though, wasn't smiling in the least. He turned away, sweating, and could feel his whole body become tense. He made his mind up to ensure he would never be left alone with Tania again.

Getting swiftly into his van, he returned to the joinery.

By the time he arrived back in the office he was nonetheless feeling pretty elated. He was bubbling with excitement and grinning like a Cheshire Cat, waving the contract in the air as he entered Tom's office. It was the single most significant order the company had secured since Lee had joined, and it was all his own work.

Tom was overjoyed, patting him on the back.

"I think I'm going to take you to lunch today, my boy," he said. "You've done a superb job of winning over both the Greenaways."

Lee could feel his face reddening with embarrassment.

Chapter 16:

A Chat with the Vicar

March 1977

Two police officers sat in Jim Hordram's office. They both knew him well. One was a regular at the church for Sunday services, and the other had got married at Saint Aidan's two months ago.

This visit, though, was not a social one. The officers were there to investigate and deal with an allegation of attempted sexual assault on Iwona Kolawaski, a previous employee of Reverend Hordram's. They claimed he had initiated the assault but been forced to stop when someone walked in on the scene.

Iwona was now working behind the bar in the Coal Scuttle pub. They had been looking for additional bar staff for some months, and Iwona seemed to fit the position well. Being an attractive young lady, with an outgoing personality, she appealed to the majority of their male clientele.

The pub's owners wrote to Jim requesting a reference. Iwona had given St Aidan's Church as her last place of employment. He declined to provide one, saying he'd been obliged to ask her to leave. It was a short time after this refusal that her complaint was made to the police. When questioned in detail at the police station, Iwona said she knew someone who would vouch for her. She told the police officers it was Lee Agazzi who had walked into the room when Jim had been making advances to her, causing him to stop molesting her.

Unbeknown to Iwona, though, the day she claimed the offence had taken place, Jim was away attending a three-day church seminar in Bristol, arriving back at least forty-eight hours after the alleged assault.

The local police also checked with Slater & Parkes as to Lee's whereabouts on the date Iwona had given them. Jim Slater told the police that, according to their records, Lee was at the works all day and remained there apart from popping out for a sandwich at lunchtime.

When confronted with these conflicting statements, Iwona was calm and unemotional, saying she might have got the date wrong.

Lee, when questioned by the police, said he didn't know what she was talking about. He remembered going into the church office one day a few months before, and Jim telling him about some missing money, adding that the vicar had explained then he had offered Iwona the option of resigning as he didn't want to have to dismiss her.

Lee had thought no more about it and forgotten about the incident until the police turned up at his office. He was astonished by the whole business as he'd thought Iwona was a genuine, respectable girl.

A few weeks after leaving the job at the Scuttle for reasons that were not made public, Iwona applied for a job at Greenaway's Nursery, which was always advertising for sales staff.

By pure chance, Lee was at the nursery when Mike started opening the day's post. He was standing chatting to his friend in the office as he opened an envelope containing a job application.

"Well, I'll be… Look who's applying for a job here. It's that pretty Polish girl, Iwona. I quite fancy her. You know, the girl who worked at the Scuttle recently. She's very sexy, isn't she?"

"And she's married," Lee told his friend firmly. "If I were you, before you reply to her, I'd go and have a chat with Reverend Jim Hordram at St Aidan's. She worked there for a bit a while ago. Seriously, you need to talk to Jim before you consider employing her."

Mike looked at him and started laughing aloud.

"What, me? Speak to a man of the cloth? Have you taken leave of your senses?"

"No, I'm not joking. I'm deadly serious. If you value your business, you need to see Jim or at least speak to him. Forget he's a vicar. He is also an employer, the same as you are. You need to be careful. Look, we have been friends for a long time, and I wouldn't want you to get caught out by taking on the wrong person. Please be sensible about this."

"Can't you at least tell me what the problem is? She seems nice enough and she's got gorgeous tits."

"I don't really think it's my place to comment on what happened. For once do yourself a favour, speak to Jim Hordram."

Lee heard no more about the problem with Iwona and Jim for a week or two.

Then, one morning while he was in the office at work, he received a call from the clergyman to tell him no further action was to take place regarding Iwona's allegation. The police said there was no evidence to back up her story and told Jim they thought Mrs Kolawaski had probably made it all up, out of spite.

Mike did call Jim Hordram, despite his misgivings, and they talked at some length about the young lady in question. As a result the Greenaways would not be employing Iwona to work at the nursery.

Mike also phoned Lee to let him know of his conversation with Jim and offered to take him and Anna out for a meal one evening as a thank you.

Chapter 17:

Railway Cottages

April 1978

One day while Anna was driving home from work her car started playing up. She stopped and discovered the left front tyre was almost flat. Although she was only a short distance away from the flat, the car was unsafe to drive, the tyre being in a bad way. She could hear a hissing sound. Anna parked the car and locked it. As she was about to start walking home she noticed, out of the corner of her eye, a For Sale notice in an adjacent shop window for a two-bedroomed house in Woodstock Rise. For some reason the sound of it appealed to her, and she decided to go in and make a note of the details.

Later in the evening, after the AA had arrived to change the wheel, she decided to mention the little house to Lee.

"By the way, guess what I saw today? An advert for a house... you'll know the ones, Railway Cottages. It's an end property. A small piece of paper was stuck in the greengrocer's shop window and I popped in and spoke to them about it. Odd place to advertise a house... oh, well. It wasn't in the estate agent's window – I looked in there after I'd left the shop. I thought we could go and have a look. We've been living here for almost two years now, and we could do with a bit more space. What do you think?"

Anna was starting to get excited about the house but was unsure how Lee would react to the thought of leaving the flat. He started to feel uneasy.

"I thought you liked it here."

"I do. But it would be nice to own our own house rather than renting, wouldn't it?"

"I don't think we could afford it," Lee said, hoping that would put an end to the discussion.

"We could still go and look at it, couldn't we?"

Anna was full of it, and wasn't going to be put off.

Lee was reluctant to move out of the flat, the first place he'd had to call his own. Although it had taken him a while to settle in, now he felt safe and secure there. The thought of moving away from this cosy refuge, to any other flat or house, worried him greatly.

How could he explain to his wife the sheer terror that the prospect of leaving his home instilled in him? It gave him the same sinking feeling he'd experienced when he first left Sarah and Jim's and moved into the flat. It was a dreadful hollow acid pain in the pit of his stomach. It came in waves and took away all his joy in life.

"Well, OK then," he said reluctantly. "I don't mind having a look at the house. Do you know if anyone is living there at the moment?"

"Not sure. The lady in the shop said her mum lived there till she died. Then she and her husband emptied it, redecorated, and have now decided to sell it. As far as I know, it's empty."

At the weekend they popped in to collect the keys and found out the property was indeed empty, as Anna believed. They drove around, straight away, to have a look at it.

Lee, though, had made his mind up. He wasn't going to like it.

He would try and put every obstacle possible in the way of them going there. He didn't want to move, there or anywhere else.

All sorts of things that most people carried out unthinkingly stressed and frightened Lee, and he couldn't understand why he got himself into such a state over comparatively normal events. The thought of the paperwork involved in a house purchase made him feel faint. Shortly after arriving at Sarah and Jim's he'd had to fill in a bank account application form. He found it so confusing he sat there staring at it for ages, having only filled in his name and address. His hand shook so much he couldn't focus on it, or anything else. His eyes started to ache. The turmoil in his head produced a sensation of panic and he didn't react well to that, getting annoyed.

"Bloody stupid bank! Why do they need all this filled

in? I can't do it." He threw the pen across the table in frustration.

Sarah, seeing how distressed he had become, sat next to him and helped him to complete the form. It would be one of many similar incidents over the following months. She didn't know why Lee got so stressed over certain things, but she always managed to calm him down and help him get the tasks completed.

A strip of land running parallel to the railway was used to build accommodation for the workers who maintained the track. A row of terraced houses was constructed there in 1931. Railway Cottages had attractive tile-hung frontages. Their small front gardens featured six wide steps leading up to the front doors, each of which contained a small square stained-glass window with a different-coloured train motif. The back gardens were narrow, and a bit flatter than the front. Some of them were 150 feet long before they reached the high fence blocking off access to the track. Shrubs soon grew up around the fencing, which helped to obscure the passing trains from view.

As they stood there in the front garden, a train went by.

"I wouldn't want to live with that dreadful noise all the time," grumbled Lee.

"It wasn't loud, Lee. The sound of lorries and cars in Tanners Lane is a lot louder than that train, and there's traffic throughout the day."

He made no comment to this.

On reaching the front door, they went inside and as the front door closed everything seemed to become quiet. The house's new double glazing not only looked good but made the interior better insulated for warmth and against noise. There was a new kitchen and two living rooms downstairs, although one was rather small.

Everything looked new, even the carpets, and it seemed the whole place had indeed been redecorated. Upstairs were two good-sized bedrooms and a new fitted bathroom with a shower.

"Wow! This is nice. Look, Lee, it's got a proper shower."

He didn't say anything as he wandered from room to room. Try as he might, he couldn't think of anything negative to say about the house.

Anna put her arms around him and gave him a loving kiss.

"I know you don't want to leave the flat. I do understand why, but this is a lot bigger, much more modern and it's all new…"

"Yes. I have to admit, that's true. The decor is much lighter and newer than the flat's. It's very nice, isn't it? I don't think we could ever afford it, though."

"Last night after you had gone to sleep, I worked out that if the price was a little lower than they are asking, we could afford it. The mortgage would only be about twenty pounds a month more than we pay now including insurance."

The more Lee thought about the house, the more he liked the idea of living there.

"I have to admit, it's a lot nicer than I thought it would be and a lot bigger, so it might be possible. It would be pretty exciting, I suppose, as long as we can afford it. Do you know how much they want for it?"

"They're asking ten thousand pounds for the house."

"WHAT... ten thousand? We haven't got that sort of money. I think we'd better go home."

Lee was shocked by the cost. Admittedly he never looked at house prices, but this seemed to him a tremendous amount of money.

"Look, you know my gran left me some money. We can use that as a deposit and between us we can get a mortgage for the balance over twenty-five years. It would be a good idea to buy now before prices go even higher."

"I s'pose that's true. I still don't think we could ever afford the repayments though."

"If I can prove to you we can do it, what would you say then?"

"If we could afford it... it would be, er... well... great, but..."

Anna interrupted him.

"Would you agree to it?"

"Well, I suppose so, yes. As long as you can prove it, well, yes. Bloody hell Anna, what are we getting into?"

Lee was hesitant and too frightened to get excited at the thought of being able to buy a house. He'd never dreamt this would happen. In fact, had never considered it at all.

Anna, over the following days, agreed a price of nine thousand five hundred pounds with the owners. She sorted out the finance, a mortgage, and even arranged for a solicitor to act on their behalf.

"This is one of the good parts of doing shiftwork. It's surprising what I can do in a morning," she said.

Over the next few months everything was put in

place, and at lunchtime on Wednesday 12 April 1978, Lee and Anna were handed the keys to 7 Railway Cottages in Woodstock Rise.

They were both bubbling with excitement when they opened the front door and walked into their first real house.

"It's our new home! I can't believe it." Anna was jumping up and down. Lee caught hold of her, hugged and kissed her.

"I would never have done this if you hadn't pushed me, you know."

"That's 'cos you are an old worry guts!" Anna laughed, still jumping about.

After a moment or two, they stood with arms tight around each other, staring out of the front window to the street below.

Lee pulled her to him and looked into her eyes, saying,

"I love you so much, Mrs Agazzi." He leant his head towards her and ran his hands up her back, holding her face between his hands until their lips lightly touched. Then he gave her a long loving kiss.

Lee was getting excited, and with the sudden realisation they were alone and owned this house, he knew exactly what he wanted to do...

He pulled Anna down onto the lounge floor. Despite her initial protests, Lee carefully removed all her clothes one by one, folding them into a neat pile by the window as he did so. Slowly and lovingly, he started to kiss her from head to toe while Anna lay wriggling on the floor.

"No… no, stop it! You're tickling me," she giggled as he nibbled at her toes.

Then Lee quickly undressed and they made love right there, on the lounge floor, out of sight of the window.

Later, leaning against the windowsill, Anna was doing up her jeans. She looked down at Lee with amusement. He was still sprawled out on the floor and staring up at her. His clothes were scattered all about him.

"What would Mum say if she could see us now? I wish I had a camera."

"I'm bloody glad you haven't…"

They burst out laughing. Anna knelt on the floor and started tickling Lee as he pulled a T-shirt over his head. The pair of them giggled as he squirmed about on the floor trying to put the rest of his clothes on. They continued fooling about for a while until the sound of the postman, knocking at the door, brought their frolics to an abrupt end. This loving and tender moment in their lives was one they would both always remember and cherish.

Over the next few evenings, having the use of one of the company's vans, they moved all their furniture and other belongings from the flat to the new house. Anna laughed when she started making up the bed there so they could spend their first night in the cottage.

"There doesn't seem to be much furniture here, does there? We'll have to buy some more soon…"

"I'm too tired to care at the moment, Anna."

Neither of them could quite believe they had bought a house. It was exciting, even scary, and they were exhausted. It had been a busy couple of days.

As he drifted off to sleep, Lee hoped his mum would

be as pleased as he was with their new home. Ever since Maureen had first visited Lee in the flat in Tanners Lane they'd met on a fairly regular basis every month, sometimes at the flat but more often in one of the local cafés for lunch. Lee looked forward to bringing her to the new house. He was sure she would love it.

He was right, she did.

Chapter 18:

Explosion

February 1979

Maureen decided during her next major shopping trip, she was going to pop into the local church, St Aidan's, on her way back home, to have a word with the local C of E vicar.

She'd met Jim Hordram only a couple of weeks before at a friend's coffee morning, which Jim and his wife Sue attended. Maureen enjoyed her time there, and although she only spoke to Sue for a few minutes, she had taken a liking to her. She felt comfortable speaking with Jim and his wife, thought he would be kind and listen to her. This was not something she would typically have done, and she was surprised at herself for even considering such a course of action.

However, her well thought out plans for the day did not turn out as expected.

As she was approaching Barclays Bank, she noticed some building work taking place in the shops across the road. There was some scaffolding along one side extending to the roof. At the exact moment Maureen waved to an acquaintance standing on the other side of the road there was a massive explosion. The buildings on the far side of the street seemed to erupt. The shock wave knocked her backwards and she fell hard against the wall behind her. Then everything went black.

Maureen was taken, with several others caught up in the event, to the nearby military hospital a few miles away, where she remained drifting in and out of consciousness for a couple of days. She was indeed lucky to have survived.

Her first recollection was of a light shining in her eyes and someone speaking to her, asking lots of questions. She couldn't make out what they meant and didn't know what to reply. How did she get here? And where did she live? Her mind was in turmoil as she struggled to remember anything.

Maureen suffered a severe concussion, and afterwards had a terrible headache and a severely bruised shoulder. Others, though, were less lucky.

The explosion killed five people: the three workers on the construction site plus an elderly couple, who were unlucky enough to be walking on the pavement at the exact moment of the blast.

Several others were seriously injured, including the shop owner who was buried for some hours in the wreckage where she remained until it was deemed safe enough to get her out.

The local papers were full of it. It was even reported on the national news.

The reporters thought one of the site workers most likely had triggered the explosion. Police cars, fire rescue vehicles, a whole fleet of ambulances plus a bomb disposal crew, all turned up. The police were only with difficulty keeping onlookers away from the site. Adding to the confusion were local journalists and a TV crew, who seemed to appear out of thin air.

The general opinion seemed to be the sudden explosion could have been caused by a ruptured gas main, or an unexploded bomb left undiscovered since the war. There was now a large hole in place of the shopfront, plus a heap of glass, bricks and wood extending into the roadway. The shop that had been undergoing renovations was reduced to a pile of rubble.

The whole area was sealed off, as the bomb disposal squad searched the area for any further devices but without success.

It remained unclear what had caused the explosion.

Maureen stayed in hospital for several days before she was allowed home.

After a couple of weeks, John was more than a little concerned that his wife was not recovering as well as expected; she was not reacting as she had done before the incident. Nevertheless he was sitting down for his evening meal at precisely 6:30 p.m. as usual, expecting her to look after him.

Maureen knew in her heart things were not right. She

didn't seem to remember where things were in the house or what she was supposed to be doing while preparing the meals. She hoped that over the coming weeks everything would return to normal.

John found the situation difficult to comprehend and did not know how to respond to it. So he said nothing. Most evenings he got up after eating and walked down to the local pub. Although he was upset by his wife's slow recovery, he didn't know what to do or say – couldn't handle the situation at all.

Ever since Stanleigh left the household, years before, Maureen and John had slowly drifted apart. The current state of affairs emphasised how bad the situation had become.

John realised he was at least partly to blame, but felt unable to resolve things or even discuss them without getting agitated or angry.

He couldn't deal with stressful situations at all. The reality of it was, he didn't know what to do. It bothered him, that was all he could think.

Maureen's world became increasingly quiet. The blast had damaged her eardrums and made her slightly deaf. This made things worse at home, as she kept asking John to repeat things.

It wasn't so much she couldn't hear what was being said, but the words didn't seem to register in her brain. Nothing made much sense anymore. The constant headaches, the flashing lights before her eyes and her state of mental confusion, resulted in her not eating properly. So she started to lose a lot of weight, making her appear gaunt.

John became ever-more stressed, worried and annoyed with the situation. He was now spending more time in the pub more than he had for quite some years.

He often returned late and not in a good humour. He never seemed drunk but he wasn't sober either. He was, in polite parlance, a bit "the worse for wear".

So as not to cause Maureen any extra stress, he moved into the spare bedroom. He knew his coming home late was disturbing her and hoped this might help a little. He thought he was being kind and thoughtful, but in reality it was having the opposite effect. It was driving an even bigger wedge between them as communication, never good at the best of times, now became almost non-existent. He was trying, so he thought, to be more attentive, but wasn't able to explain this to Maureen, who became even more depressed as a result.

"Bloody hell. What a mess!" the borough surveyor said as he looked at the state of the wrecked road and the building beside it. The local council closed the area for two days before fencing half of it off with bollards so the traffic could start to flow again.

"What d'you reckon then? A wartime bomb?" he asked the workmen who were making good the area.

"It doesn't look big enough for a bomb, does it?" the guy on the digger said.

"I saw loads of bomb holes in The Smoke after the war. We were fillin' 'em in like ninepins. I was only a lad then, but I remember it like yesterday. Not something you forget easy, is it? Whatever this was, it must have been laying there ever since the war – unless they hit a gas pipe, of course.

"Everywhere they was then, bomb 'oles. Honest, though – they was all bigger than this'en. I don't reckon this was a Gerry bomb. The 'ole just ain't big enough."

A local councillor decided to have a word with the bomb squad official who'd attended the scene and asked to see the initial written report.

A few days later, the police and an officer from the squad came to have another thorough look at the damage and to re-examine the area, in particular, part of the basement below the wrecked shop.

Shortly after the war, this basement flat had been rented out. The lack of suitable housing meant every habitable building was needed to shelter those who were either homeless or waiting for repair work to be completed on their properties. This was one such place, and a young man had taken the small flat on a short lease. He was a bit of an oddball, very quiet and kept himself to himself. Often out till the early hours, he'd always carried a small cardboard suitcase. There were many people with similar-looking cases after the war, so no one took too much notice of him.

A member of the bomb squad sifted through the rubble and discovered some pieces of metal, which looked like the fins of a type of military mortar or stick grenade. They were small, twisted sections, but he was certain these were not bomb fragments. As he was scraping some dust away with his foot, in the rubble he saw a hand grenade and froze… The pin was in place, thank goodness, and he heaved a sigh of relief. Everyone on the site was ordered to leave at once. He recalled the bomb disposal unit to remove the grenade and check for any other ordnance.

Then, out of the corner of his eye, he saw protruding out of the debris the edge of a military-looking steel ammunition case. The top was bent back, he could see inside. There looked to be shiny new .303 rifle rounds – loads of them. What on earth were they doing here?

The police managed to track down the man who had rented the small flat and after questioning him for some time and showing him the items they'd found, arrested him on suspicion of stealing ammunition and other military hardware from a local army depot. The depot commanders were reluctant to confirm what was missing but said the ammunition case certainly came from there. Difficult to deny as the reference marks in white, stamped on the side, were clear enough.

This resulted in a confession from the accused, who presented a long list of the stolen items he'd stored there – at least the ones he could remember.

It seemed that on several occasions he'd broken in through the outer perimeter fencing of the depot and stolen all sorts of military hardware, including grenades, rifle ammunition, several mortar bombs and other items.

These things were initially hidden under his bed and in the bottom of his wardrobe. Later, he put most of the stolen items under the floorboards. They remained there and over time were forgotten.

When the building work was being done, something must have hit or pierced one of the explosive devices and then the whole lot, or most of it, blew up. Whatever the truth was, it made a damn' good story, and the local press had a field day!

No Gerry bomb. A madman hoarding munitions was the headline.

But this didn't help those killed or poor Maureen who was suffering real physical and mental trauma as a direct result of the blast.

She was just at the point of phoning her doctor to get an appointment when the doorbell rang. It was Doug Hughes's wife, Alice. Ever since the explosion they had become anxious about her, and Doug had suggested it might be a kind gesture for his wife to pop round with some flowers and see how Maureen was doing.

"Oh, hello, Alice, do come in – I'm so pleased to see…"

As they were walking through to the kitchen, Maureen turned around, burst into tears, and fell into her visitor's arms. She was so distraught she couldn't speak. Alice guided her to some chairs where she managed to sit them both down. After a few minutes, she said she thought a cup of tea might be a good idea and Maureen agreed.

"Yes, please."

For the next couple of hours, she poured out all the pent-up pain and agony of the past years, going right back to the time when Stanleigh was just a schoolboy in short trousers.

Except for several very tearful moments, her account didn't stop. By now Alice was becoming upset too. She couldn't ever have imagined the sadness of the story her friend was pouring out to her.

She knew Maureen and John had had some problems, but this was far worse than anything she had expected to hear. Alice had always thought John seemed to be a rather pleasant, if somewhat quiet and reserved, man, although she was aware he did have a bit of a bad temper at times. Bloody hell, she thought, it just goes to show you never know what goes on behind closed doors.

"Maureen, my dear… Why have you never spoken to anyone about this before? Could you not have spoken to your doctor?" Alice asked.

"No, I couldn't, because he is also John's doctor and it was all too awkward and embarrassing. He might have spoken to John and… and then…" Maureen started crying again and said between sobs,

"I just can't take any more." She reached forward, dropping her cup on the floor where it smashed to pieces, spraying the contents all over their shoes.

Maureen seemed to flop back in her chair in an unusual way, all the time staring at Alice through red, swollen eyes.

She thought something dreadful was about to take place and grabbed the phone to dial 999, requesting an ambulance. Then Alice rushed to one of the bedrooms, grabbed a blanket and wrapped it around Maureen. It was only then she began to notice how cold it was. There was no heating on anywhere in the house.

She remembered Maureen saying something about John not letting her have the heating on during the daytime.

Within what seemed to be only a few minutes the flashing lights of the emergency vehicle were reflecting on the kitchen wall. The front doorbell rang and Alice rushed to let the medics in. They assessed the situation and gave Maureen oxygen after which she was taken on a stretcher to the waiting ambulance.

Alice rummaged around in Maureen's bedroom, collecting a few things she might need. She grabbed her handbag and some clothes and rushed this out to the ambulance before it left for the hospital. Alice followed in her little car.

At the hospital, she talked with one of the doctors dealing with Maureen, who thanked her for her prompt action in calling the ambulance.

"It looks as though Mrs Agazzi may have suffered a heart attack. We are waiting for some tests to be completed. She is calm now and under sedation. Please can you tell us how to contact her husband?"

Alice gave the doctor the information he needed and left the hospital. There was nothing more she could do. She was pretty upset and wanted only to be home sharing the story with Doug.

Her husband was a mild-mannered man but she thought she knew how he'd react to an account of everything Maureen had told her.

Chapter 19:

A Chance Encounter

May 1981

Late on a hot and muggy evening in the middle of May, Ted Manner and his wife Ellie were setting off home after visiting friends. It had been a boozy affair and they left the car on the drive, deciding to walk instead.

A little black and white dog ran up to them, jumping around, barking and whining. The dog kept running away about ten feet and then coming back to them. This happened time after time.

"I think he's trying to tell us something, Ted."

"Yeah, I reckon he is. Let's follow him and see where he goes."

Ted followed the little dog, which led him right up Raven Close, past two houses and disappeared into the front garden of a bungalow at the end of the street. Here they found a lady lying on the ground, half in and half out of a front door. The dog sat dutifully next to her, licking her face.

"Ellie, quick… get some help from the house next door."

A few moments later she reappeared with the neighbour.

"My husband has called an ambulance, and he's going to stay by the phone. I'm afraid we don't know anybody around here yet as we only moved in yesterday. I think this lady said her name was Margaret. She said hello over the garden fence this morning. I'm sure she called her dog Scruffy," said the woman, adding under her breath, "He does look scruffy…" Her facial expression left them in no doubt, she most certainly didn't like dogs.

"I'll pop back and get something to keep her warm."

Fifteen minutes later an ambulance arrived and the crew took over.

Margaret Sanders-North had started feeling ill as she returned from a walk with Scruffy. As the key turned in the lock of her front door, she collapsed, pushing the door half open as she fell across the sill.

Margaret was still breathing when the ambulance arrived, but not very responsive. The medics got her aboard as soon as they could. A short while later, they left for the Casualty department with lights flashing.

The couple from next door, who'd tried to help their neighbour, agreed with great reluctance to take care of the small dog overnight.

Ted and Ellie then walked home discussing the merits of the loyal little dog, who had, without a doubt, saved his owner's life. Ted Manner ran the local newspaper, the *Tillshott Echo*, and thought it might make a good front page story: **Pet dog saves life of local woman**. He made a mental note to get a photograph taken of Scruffy.

Anna, as senior nurse on the women's medical ward, received a message that a Mrs Margaret North was being admitted to the hospital, and would be brought onto the ward in the next hour or so. Two hours later she was wheeled in. Anna and her team helped to get her into a bed and tried their best to make her comfortable. Anna pulled the screens around her, and with another, younger nurse, started checking the patient over and filling in forms, ready for the ward doctor.

The new patient, who seemed to have suffered a minor stroke, was agitated and confused. She kept asking, "Where's Scruffy? I can't see him. Please help me. Please, can you help me…"

Anna checked her name on the chart. It read "Mrs Margaret North".

"Margaret… can you hear me, Margaret?

You had a nasty turn, and you are now in hospital. Who's Scruffy?"

"Dog… he's my dog. Is he alright? He's all I have."

"Please don't worry, Margaret. We will get someone to make sure he's OK. Just you relax." Anna's soothing words calmed the patient and she closed her eyes.

"Thank you, my dear, thank you."

Later the same evening, Anna asked Lee if he would come with her and go round to Margaret North's bungalow in Raven Close. They must try to locate Scruffy and make sure he was cared for adequately.

As they approached the bungalow, they could hear barking coming from her neighbour's house, and assuming this might be the dog called Scruffy, knocked on the door.

The house was piled high with crates and boxes. The owners explained they'd moved in only the day before, and how they'd helped out last night by calling the ambulance and taking in the dog. They wouldn't be able to keep him, though, as the husband seemed to have an allergy to fur and had come out in a rash.

The wife then asked Anna and Lee to kindly take Scruffy away and find someone else to care for him until their neighbour could return home.

With this, she handed the lead to Lee, saying, "Here you are. Please take him away... Thank you."

They were ushered towards the front door, which was then slammed shut with a thud, almost before their feet had cleared the step.

As they walked away from the house with Scruffy in tow, Lee said in a soft voice to his wife,

"I'm glad we don't live next door to them. What on earth are we going to do now?"

"I don't know. We seem to have inherited a dog to care for. I promised I would make sure he was OK but didn't expect we would have to care for him ourselves."

An hour or so later, after they'd got home, Anna phoned her mum and asked if she would take care of Scruffy for a few days.

Gina had always wanted to have a dog but somehow never got around to doing anything about getting one. She seemed quite pleased to help out and welcomed the small dog into the family home when Anna delivered him about thirty minutes later.

The next day was her day off, but so that Mrs North wouldn't worry about her dog, Anna decided to go and tell her little Scruffy was in good hands.

To her surprise, Margaret North was sitting up in bed and reading a newspaper. Anna went and sat down next to her.

"Hello, Margaret. How are you feeling? You're looking a lot better, a vast improvement on yesterday. I'm not on duty today, but I thought you would like to know that I went with my husband to your house last night. We found Scruffy, who was with your new neighbours, and to cut a long story short, he's now with my mum. So there's no need for you to worry at all. He will be loved and cared for there until you are able to go home again."

"Oh, thank you, Anna… may I call you Anna?"

"Of course."

"You have an unusual surname, my dear – Agazzi. I knew the name the instant I saw it. A nice lady I met while shopping the other day has the same one. Her name was Maureen. Do you know her by any chance?"

"Yes, she's my mother-in-law. My husband's father is from Italy."

"Ah-ha, yes. I know it's an Italian name, my dear. I know this name so very well, you see. Even though I've only come across it once before, a long time ago, it brought back a lot of old memories for me."

"That's amazing. What a strange coincidence."

"I'm not so sure it's a coincidence, Anna. I think the chance of…"

The ward doctor arrived then and interrupted the conversation. Anna said it was about time for her to go home.

"Anna, before you leave, could you please tell the hospital authorities my name is given incorrectly on the forms? It's Margaret Sanders-North, not North as they have written it. It's important to me that it's correct. I hope you understand."

"Yes, Margaret, of course I do. I'll get it put right, please don't fret about it."

"Thank you, my dear."

Margaret was starting to look tired. Her head sank into the pillow and her eyes closed as Anna left.

When Lee came home from work, Anna was excited. She started telling him about the extraordinary conversation she'd had with the lady in the hospital whose dog they'd helped to rehome.

"It's rather strange, but she must have bumped into your mum while shopping in the town. I wonder how the family name came up."

"I can't imagine. You don't go up to a stranger and say your name, just like that, do you? Something must have happened to prompt it."

Over the next few days, Anna found out Maureen had dropped her chequebook while paying for some shopping and Margaret had picked it up, noticing the name upon it. It was quite a surprise to her. She hadn't seen or heard the name Agazzi for about forty years. Of all the people in Tillshott... Agazzi. She could not believe it.

A week or two went by and Margaret was not

progressing well enough to return home, as she lived alone and would have no one to look after her.

The doctors considered the best course of action would be for her to go to a local care home to regain her strength. Her state of health was to be reassessed later.

Margaret proved to be a very independent and rather stubborn lady. She wanted to go home straight away. Anna tried to convince her the stay in the care home would only be for a short while until she could walk normally and care for herself, as she had previously.

But Margaret refused, and after a lengthy and difficult discussion, the hospital, against their better judgement, decided to take her back to her own home the following Monday morning, with specific provisos.

The local district nurse was waiting for her when the hospital transport arrived, to see her settle back in. All seemed well for the next day or two. Then Anna decided to pay her a visit and take Scruffy with her, hoping she might be able to reunite them.

As Anna arrived, it was pretty evident Margaret was in no fit state to care for a dog. She wasn't walking too well, and even opening the front door to them was proving to be a bit of a problem.

"Hello, Margaret. I've brought Scruffy to see you."

The little dog went wild with excitement for a few moments, jumping up and down and running rings around them both. Finally, he sat at Margaret's feet, looking up at her, panting and wagging his tail in excitement.

Although she was delighted to see him it quickly became obvious she was not going to be able to take him back, at least for a while. Margaret bent down to fuss him and lost her balance, falling onto Anna's shoulder. Visibly upset by this, she kept apologising.

"Oh, dear, do you think your mother would look after him a little bit longer? You know, just for a short while, until I get back on my feet."

"Of course she will. I thought you would like to see he was OK. I hadn't planned on leaving him with you for a while yet," Anna reassured her.

Two weeks later, during a routine visit, the district nurse found Margaret on the floor. She had fallen and couldn't get up, so the nurse called for an ambulance to take her back to the hospital.

A clear decision was made to place her in the Sands House Care Home, and this time Margaret agreed, saying she hoped it would not be for very long, only until she could walk about easily on her own.

The weeks slowly lengthened into months. Although she grew mentally stronger, her physical strength did not improve enough to enable her to return home. It was at the end of the second month that Margaret finally realised she was not going to be fit enough to return to her bungalow.

Following several meetings with her solicitor, it was decided that selling her home in Raven Close would be the best course of action.

She needed to pay the care home fees after all.

The proceeds from the sale should take care of everything. It was decided to put all her belongings into storage, to enable the sale to go ahead as quickly as possible. Anna and Lee offered to help pack up the house and take care of any other little things that might crop up, including looking after her almost-new car.

"Would you like to have it, my dear?" she asked Anna. "It's no good to me and you could make good use of it for getting to and from work, couldn't you?"

"Well… yes, I could, Margaret. Are you really sure that's what you want? We could arrange for it to be sold if you like?"

"Absolutely not, my dear. I would love you to be able to use it. I like the idea of you being able to drive it. It doesn't do motor cars any good if they are not driven. They seize up and go rusty."

"Well, alright then, but we will have to fix a price and I'll buy it from you."

"Don't be ridiculous, my dear. Let's just say you can borrow it… at least until I'm fit enough to drive again. How does that sound?"

"Margaret, your car is only a few months old, I don't…"

"Anna," she interrupted, putting on a stern expression. "I need someone to look after it for me, someone who will care for it, and it will help make your life easier, so that's the end of the matter. Here is the key."

After some further discussion, including Anna offering to pay the car insurance, it was agreed.

Margaret's room at the care home needed a comfortable chair near the window so she could sit and look out over the nearby woods. As a small thank you for the car, Lee said he would make her a nice high-backed rocking chair with a soft padded seat and arms.

The task kept him quite busy in the evenings for the following two weeks. About three weeks later the chair arrived at the home from the upholsterer's and Lee and Anna were with Margaret when it was brought in to her.

She was delighted.

"It's so nice and comfortable. my dears. Thank you so much. I'll be able to snooze in peace now during the afternoons. Some of those old people downstairs can be very annoying, you know."

They all laughed and then Lee and Anna turned to each other and smiled.

Over the following few months, Gina, Anna or Lee would take Scruffy to visit Margaret most days while they were taking him for his walks. It became part of their daily routine.

On one occasion when Anna arrived with the dog, Margaret seemed to be flustered and upset.

"I don't know how I'm going to pay the home, Anna. Now the bungalow is being sold… I don't know if it will be in time. You know, in case the money runs out."

"I wouldn't worry about it, Margaret. You said your solicitor didn't seem too concerned and he was here only a week ago. I'm sure he will sort things out for you, whatever happens."

"Maybe, my dear. He is very good, but it does worry me." Margaret looked around her and in a low voice said,

"Yesterday, the bossy lady who owns this place told me some of the residents have left the home lots of money, in their Wills, to help keep it going. She suggested I might like to do the same or the home might have to close. In fact, she has said it to me several times. Joe calls her a greedy old cow and says she's rolling in money."

"Who is Joe?"

"Oh, he is my solicitor, the one you met the other day. I've known him for years. He goes to the same church as I do, you know. He said she has a Rolls-Royce parked on the driveway at her home. She bought it last year, so he said."

"He's obviously a good judge of character, Margaret. Please don't worry about it anymore. Everything will be fine."

By the following day, Margaret was back in good spirits again when Lee popped in to see her with Scruffy, who made a huge fuss of her as he always did.

Margaret, a devout Catholic, received weekly visits in the home from Father Shaun O'Malley of St Peter's Church. And every time Lee or Anna visited her, she encouraged them to go to church.

"God loves you both, and He has so much to give you."

Father O'Malley always spoke very highly of his parishioner.

One evening Lee was on his way back from the home bound for Gina's after taking Scruffy for one of his daily walks when he saw Father O'Malley coming towards him. He grinned at Lee as they met outside the home. "A very kind and caring lady is our dear Margaret. I could tell you many little stories about her. Maybe one day…"

A few weeks later as Anna and Scruffy arrived at the home, she was stopped by one of the young carers who told her Mrs Sanders-North had been taken ill during the night and transferred to the hospital at about four o'clock in the morning.

Margaret had suffered another stroke, and this time she was in the Intensive Care Unit when Anna arrived to see her. She was only able to sit with her for a short while. Margaret opened her eyes once, mouthed a few words and squeezed Anna's hand.

The following evening Margaret deteriorated considerably, eventually slipping into a coma. Father Shaun O'Malley was called. He stayed with her for a few hours, holding her hand.

Two days later, on 4 December 1981, Margaret Sanders-North passed away peacefully in her sleep. She was seventy-one years old.

Her funeral at St Peter's was to be organised by Father O'Malley, according to Margaret's wishes, with the help of Joe Parson, her solicitor and only other long-time friend.

The funeral was to be held the following Thursday at 11 a.m. at Saint Peter's. Margaret had commented several times over the last few weeks that she would, when her time came, wish to be laid to rest next to her husband Jack. This was now going to be arranged according to her wishes.

The weather for Margaret's funeral could not have been better. It was a glorious sunny day. With only an hour to go, Lee realised he didn't have a suitable black tie, so dashed off into town to get one. He had never needed one before and hoped he wouldn't need it again for a long time. Lee hated wearing ties. He didn't like anything he considered restricting around, or anywhere near, his neck.

Finally, he and Anna were ready and made their way to the church to ensure they were in good time for the funeral.

They had both taken time off work for the occasion.

The church looked great. There were white flowers at the entrance and in pots beside the front pews.

As they arrived, they noticed Gina walking up the path with Scruffy, who as soon as he saw them started pulling in their direction with his tail wagging wildly in excitement.

They all walked inside the church together.

Margaret's coffin was already in place near the altar. It was draped with a Union Jack and covered in white lilies from end to end.

"Why do you think there's a flag over her coffin? It's a bit unusual, isn't it?" Lee whispered to Anna.

"I don't know."

Then Father O'Malley started the service by greeting everyone present.

There were not many there to pay their last respects.

A couple of staff members from the care home together with Ann the owner, a few parishioners who had known Margaret for many years, and then sitting a little towards the back were a man and woman who were strangers to everyone except Joe Parson. He went and greeted them and asked them to join him in a pew near the front of the church. They were then introduced to Father O'Malley as Josette and Marcel Leroux.

Their flight from France for the funeral was at the specific request (and expense) of Margaret's solicitor Joe, who'd arranged everything for them, right down to the last detail.

As the service proceeded, the eulogy given by Joe Parson astounded all those present, even Shaun O'Malley who'd thought he knew everything there was to know about his dear friend Margaret.

"I would like to start by saying I feel very honoured to be talking to you today about a very remarkable lady, Margaret Sanders-North. Now that dear Margaret has passed to a better place, I can finally tell you a bit about her," Joe began. "These are things she discussed with very few people as far as I know.

"In her younger days, Margaret trained as a pilot. She'd always loved flying, but it was most unusual in those days for young ladies to be trained and qualify as pilots. It was considered to be a man's job. That didn't stop Margaret though.

"Shortly before the outbreak of hostilities in 1939, she applied to join the RAF. She spent the first years of the war as part of the ATA, ferrying new planes from factories to the many air bases around the country. Then, on one occasion, a pilot was suddenly taken ill. He was due to fly a Westland Lysander on a special mission.

"Margaret said she would fly the plane as there were no other pilots available. Two 'passengers' needed to be flown into France and dropped behind enemy lines as part of an SOE operation. Following this first successful mission, Margaret flew five more times behind enemy lines before being shot down and caught by the Gestapo in Northern France, near Tours, in October 1943.

"She suffered a brutal interrogation, was sentenced to death and was awaiting execution when a British bombing raid on a nearby town destroyed the building in which she was being held.

"None of the German military personnel survived the raid and Margaret, although seriously injured, was dragged out of the burning building by a French couple, Sofia and Marc Leroux.

At significant personal risk, they took her to their farmhouse and with the help of a sympathetic local doctor nursed her back to health.

They managed to keep Margaret hidden until well after the Germans were driven out of France and she remained there, in secret, until the war ended in September 1945. Only then did she return home.

She was honoured for her bravery as were her rescuers.

"Sofia and Marc sadly passed away some time ago, but their son and daughter are here today at my invitation.

"Margaret owed her life to the Leroux family. They and she performed acts of true heroism and devotion to their respective countries. After the war she kept in touch with the Leroux family for many years until Sofia and Marc passed away.

"I want to thank Josette and Marcel for coming here today all the way from the family farm in France."

Joe continued his account of Margaret's life for a while longer then sat down.

Total silence had fallen over the church.

It was difficult to take in, or quite believe, what they had just heard. Margaret's story was astonishing. To say the small congregation felt stunned was an understatement.

Father O'Malley stood up and continued with the service up to the point where the coffin was about to be taken to the churchyard for burial.

As they all got to their feet, Scruffy began whimpering and pulled away from Gina's grip. With his lead trailing behind him, he trotted up to the coffin. Then, sitting down before one end of it, he threw back his head, uttering a soft howl before lying on the floor with his head resting on his front paws.

No one moved for a minute or two.

Finally Anna stood up and lifted Scruffy, cradled him in her arms and carried him back to her mother. She'd tried so hard not to get upset, but couldn't help it. She was crying openly by now, as were some of the others. Anna placed the dog gently back on Gina's lap. Her mother looked up at her, tried to smile, but was too upset to say anything.

Joe Parson arranged for refreshments to be served to everyone attending the funeral in a room at the Old Manor House Restaurant. It was only a short walk from the church and set in beautiful surroundings.

While drinking coffee there Anna was accosted by Ann, the lady who owned the care home.

"Margaret was such a nice, kind lady. She's leaving the home a handsome legacy in her Will, you know. So very good of her, wasn't it?" Without waiting for any response, she turned away to broach the matter with Joe Parson.

Father O'Malley overheard the one-way conversation. Seeing Anna looking somewhat shocked by Ann's behaviour, he walked over and spoke quietly to her.

"I wouldn't take too much notice of her, my dear, she has made similar comments at funerals many times over the last few years. It's in bad taste and may not even be true. She has caused quite a few upsets with relatives before – in this very room too."

Half an hour or so later, Lee said he needed to get back to work. Anna decided to stay and talk to the couple from France.

Josette was talking to Father O'Malley and as Marcel was standing on his own, looking a little lost, she decided to speak to him. Sadly it appeared he only spoke a little English. This made proper conversation rather difficult, and it didn't last too long. Anna was delighted and relieved when Joe Parson stepped in. Speaking in perfect French, he took over the conversation.

About a week later, when life had started to return to normal, Lee and Anna received a letter from Parson's Solicitors asking them to attend his office for the reading of Margaret's Will.

"I can't keep taking time off work. It's been happening too often of late, what with one thing and another," Lee said.

"Yes, I know. It's getting difficult at the hospital too."

Lee studied the letter again, turning it over to see if there was any more information on the other side.

"This sounds more like a command than an invitation though. I think I'll phone Joe Parson from work tomorrow morning and see if we need to be there for any specific reason."

"OK, that sounds like a good idea."

Lee phoned the solicitor's office and tried to explain the timing was going to be rather difficult, only to be told that both he and Anna needed to attend the reading of Margaret's Will as they were significant beneficiaries.

Lee was rather surprised. "Oh… er, well, in that case, I suppose we really ought to come then, although to be honest I can't imagine why on earth we would be mentioned in her Will."

Over dinner, Lee and Anna chatted about what they thought might be in Margaret's Will that made it so vital for them to be at the reading.

Lee didn't know much about Wills, and was puzzled about the whole thing.

"I'm wondering why we are mentioned at all. We hadn't known her very long. It's not as if we have been lifelong friends or family members, is it?"

Anna agreed, saying,

"I don't think it will be anything important. I remember one day Margaret was in a bit of a panic about the care home fees, which, if I remember rightly, was why we helped Joe Parson to pack up her belongings to go into storage. It was so the bungalow could be put up for a quick sale. But surely if she wanted us to have an item from her house, she would have said something about it then. I can't imagine what else would make it so important for us to be at this reading."

At the appointed day and time, Lee and Anna arrived at Joe Parson's office for the reading. They were surprised to find only Father O'Malley there apart from Joe and themselves.

"Good day to you all," Joe began. "Well, let's get on with this then. As you all know, I have dealt with Margaret's affairs for many years, and one of my duties was administering her Will."

Joe coughed, shuffled a pile of papers about on his desk, found what he wanted and started to read aloud.

"I, Margaret Amy Sanders-North of Sands House Care Home, Maple Close, Tillshott, hereby revoke all testamentary dispositions previously made by me and declare this to be my last Will and Testament...

"I appoint as sole executor and Trustee, Mr Joseph Parson of Parson's Solicitors, 25 High Street, Tillshott.

"I having no heirs do bequeath all my personal chattels that were placed in storage from my previous home at 15 Raven Close, Tillshott, to Mr Lee Agazzi and Mrs Anna Agazzi, both of 7 Railway Cottages, Woodstock Rise, Tillshott.

"I specifically leave my Blue Ford Fiesta Ghia to Mrs Anna Agazzi..."

Here Joe stopped reading and looked over the top of his glasses at Anna.

"This is already in your possession, I believe."

"Yes, it's parked outside our house."

He continued, "My residuary estate after all death duties..."

The rest of her Will was formally read out to the three beneficiaries present. In essence it stated that Margaret wished her estate to be split and distributed in four equal parts.

Twenty-five per cent was to be given to Saint Peter's Church in the form of a trust to help provide a drop-in centre for the elderly of Tillshott parish. She wished this trust to be administered by Father Shaun O'Malley and Mr Joseph Parson.

Twenty-five per cent was left to Battersea Dogs' Home, as this was where Scruffy came from.

The balance was to be given in equal parts to Anna and Lee Agazzi.

Joe, looking at a rather shocked Anna and Lee, added, "There is also a letter and a sealed package addressed to you both."

Having handed over the items to Lee and Anna, Joe said that was pretty much all that was needed, and he would send each of them a letter in due course with final details on completion of probate.

"Although I don't have the exact figures yet, I can tell you it is quite a substantial sum. After the various deductions have been dealt with, Margaret has left about one point eight million pounds."

At this point Joe allowed a few moments' silence to let this information sink in. They looked at each other in astonishment. Then, with a big smile on his face, he added,

"I hope you are pleased. Over the last months, I spent a lot of time with her and this is exactly what she wanted, I assure you. Please be in no doubt about the validity of this Will. It was properly witnessed by two of the care home staff and there are absolutely no mistakes in it." He continued smiling, looking from one to the other of them.

"You look shocked, Lee," he said.

"To be honest, I am. I don't know what to think."

"In that case, shall we have some coffee now? My mouth is rather dry." And Joe added, with a twinkle in his eye,

"Or if you wish, you can have something a bit stronger."

The short drive back home passed in almost complete silence. Neither Anna nor Lee could think of anything to say — they glanced at each other with mouths half open.

Anna started to speak first as Lee reversed into their parking place,

"I can't believe what he just said... Why us?"

"I don't know. It's like an incredible dream and I'm still in it. I feel like I'm floating in space."

Lee was unnerved but also excited to think of the vast amount of money they would soon receive. It was more than he could imagine possessing, even in his wildest dreams.

Once they were back home he handed the dusty brown paper-wrapped package Joe had given them to Anna. It was tied up with yellowing string and sealed with red sealing wax, which also looked rather ancient.

And then there was the small matter of the envelope Margaret had left for them. Lee had kept hold of this in his hand while Anna examined the package. Now he handed this to her as well.

"I don't think I... er, will you read the letter that's in here... please?"

"Yes, of course. OK, Let's have a look then." Anna's hand was shaking a little as she opened the envelope, trying hard not to tear it.

Inside was a four-page handwritten letter signed by Margaret. It was not dated.

Anna started to read it.

Dear Anna and Lee,

By the time you read this letter, I will be at peace with Our Lord Jesus Christ.

You will by now have spoken to Joe Parson, the man who has given you this letter. He has been my family solicitor for the past umpteen years. Please talk to him if you need to, regarding my Will or anything else. He is a lovely man and entirely trustworthy.

Jack (my husband) and I asked him to deal with our financial affairs ages ago and Joe has loyally been doing so ever since.

You may not have realised that I have no living relatives. I do not know who my parents were.

While only a few days old, I was left in a cardboard box, outside a church in Swindon. I was taken in and brought up by the local vicar and his wife. They were so very kind to me over the years.

Later on, I married Jack, and sadly we had no children. So when he died, I was suddenly on my own again.

I do not wish to go into detail about my life, but I do want you to know I would not be here now were it not for a kind and courageous French couple, Sofia and Marc Leroux.

I only mention this at all because dear Sofia's maiden name was Agazzi.

Her parents lived in Malcesine on Lake Garda in Italy.

It was for this reason, Lee, that I asked you whereabouts in Italy your father was from. Agazzi is not a very common name, and I am certain your father must be a relative of Sofia's. He may even have known her when he was a youngster. It feels almost divinely ordained, after all these years, that while in my greatest need I am once again being cared for by members of the Agazzi family. For certain this cannot be a coincidence. I hope and pray you may get to meet and talk with the Leroux family one day.

I have asked Joe Parson to notify them should anything happen to me.

He has their last known address.

You have both been so kind to me since I was taken to hospital and I am extremely grateful for everything you have done. I could not have been shown more kindness.

By now you also know I have left you a little something in my Will and I hope it gives you some pleasure in your lives. It will also provide for food and any vet's bills for Scruffy. I don't doubt for a moment my dear dog is being loved by your family, as I loved him, and I am equally confident he will soon come to join me in Heaven.

Father Shaun O'Malley of Saint Peter's knows me pretty well. He is such a kind man. Please go and speak with him.

Over the years we have had many conversations, and the odd glass of wine too, at various church social events. He has been a special friend.

God has a place in His heart for all of us. I urge you to go and find out just how much God loves you.

Throughout my life, I always found help, peace and solace in speaking with Him whenever events became almost too difficult to bear.

I know He will give the same peace to you both, if you ask him.

Over the last month or so I have come to rely on
you for so many of the little things in life. Frankly, I
don't know how I would have managed without you.
    I have been truly blessed and have become very
fond of you both, as a mother loves her own children.
    I am sure we will all meet again, one day.
    Until then, God bless you both.

All my love,
Margaret

Anna's hands were shaking as she placed the letter face up on the table in front of her. She started to shiver, turning suddenly cold as the sentiment in the words of Margaret's letter and the events of the previous days sank in. The young couple sat in silence at the table for quite a while, their minds in turmoil.

They'd never expected anything like this. The letter was upsetting and exciting at the same time, as were the terms of Margaret's Will.

They had coped with more than enough excitement for one day. A decision was made not to open the package for a while, at least not until they received the next letter from Joe Parson.

This particular evening they were supposed to be going to dinner with Jim and Sarah, giving them only a few moments to freshen up, get changed and compose themselves.

"We must make an effort to go, Anna. Sarah will be so disappointed if we cancel."

"Yes, I know, and it will cheer us up anyway, won't it? I would love to show them this letter. Would you mind?"

"Of course not. We must be the luckiest pair in Tillshott today. So that's fine with me. We should be happy, Anna, and here we are, feeling almost miserable as sin and in the depths of depression..."

"No, it's not depression. More a sense of sadness at Margaret's death and the incredible emotional rollercoaster of it all... I expect everything will look different and feel better tomorrow morning."

"I bloomin' hope so. We ought to be able to look forward to getting that money and whatever benefits it may bring."

"Hey! Hang on. We haven't got anything yet. I know what Joe said, but this might still turn out to be a big mistake."

But it was no mistake. A lot would happen over the next two weeks before the letter arrived from Joseph Parson.

On Sunday, at a quarter to seven in the morning, their phone started ringing. It woke them with a jolt. It was Gina calling. She was in a terrible state.

Anna, who answered the phone, couldn't make out what she was trying to say.

"Mum, please calm down – I can't hear you. What on earth has happened?"

"It's Scruffy, he's... We found him in his bed half an hour ago, and he's gone... he's not breathing, Anna. Little Scruffy is dead."

She was crying hysterically as she spoke.

"Mum, I'll be round in five minutes. Go and sit down and have a cup of tea. Is Dad with you?"

"Yes. Hold on..."

"Hello, Anna, it's very upsetting seeing him lying in his bed, but he just looks to be asleep. He's very peaceful. Look, I'm going to make your mum some tea now. We'll see you shortly." Then Tom hung up. It was apparent he was pretty upset as well. Anna rushed about, scrambling into her work clothes. Lee felt sick.

"I'm going to work," he said. "I don't think I could face seeing Scruffy, knowing he's dead. I don't even want to think about it at the moment."

"OK. I know it's difficult. I'll go and see Mum, and we'll need to take Scruffy to the vet's once they are open."

After the initial shock had receded a little, Anna left for work leaving Gina, who had now calmed down markedly, to take Scruffy to the vet's. She wrapped him lovingly in a blanket and placed him with great tenderness in her car.

They decided to bury his ashes right by Margaret's headstone if Father O'Malley agreed, which indeed he did.

A few days later, one evening after dinner, Anna, Lee, Tom and Gina went into the churchyard, found Margaret's recently dug grave, made a small hole near the headstone, and placed Scruffy's ashes there. They laid a square piece of stone over the top. Tom and Lee led Gina, who was crying, away from the graveside, leaving only Anna who stood there for a few moments to say a little prayer for Scruffy and Margaret, before she too turned to leave.

With slow deliberate steps, and deep in thought, she followed the others back home.

It was a sad moment and marked the end of this extraordinary chapter in their lives. Margaret and Scruffy were indeed reunited, exactly as Margaret had said they would be.

A shiver went down Anna's spine as she thought about the words in Margaret's letter. Anna could not understand how she could have been so sure she would see Scruffy again soon…

A week later, there were two identical letters waiting on the doormat when Lee arrived home from work. He knew what they were without even opening them. He placed both letters on the kitchen table and waited for Anna to get back from the hospital.

It was 9 p.m. when she got home.

"Hello, love. How was your day?"

"Oh, you know, the usual." By now Anna knew better than to tell Lee any details about her day at the hospital. They made him feel ill and preyed on his mind for hours.

"We've each received a letter. Found them on the doormat when I got home."

"From the solicitor, is it?"

"You got it in one! They're on the table in the kitchen. I haven't opened them."

"Wait a min, I'll come and read mine. I just need to go to the loo. I won't be a moment. Put the kettle on and we'll have a cup of tea while we see what Joe says."

"OK, love."

As Lee poured the tea, Anna sat down and opened the letter addressed to her.

After scanning the page for a moment or two, she started reading it aloud.

Dear Mrs Agazzi,

It was very kind of you to visit me in my office recently.

As you are aware, I have known Margaret for many years and she spoke at some length to me about how kind you and your husband have been to her throughout her last illness.

I would personally like to thank you on her behalf.

I am pleased to inform you that the total amount bequeathed to you, after taxes and other costs are taken into account, is £456,270 and a cheque for this amount is enclosed.

Please will you sign and return the enclosed document to me in the envelope provided?

Now the formalities regarding the Will have been dealt with, and following Margaret's wishes, I am also attaching a Contract Clearance sheet from the storage company relating to her personal belongings. Everything's been taken care of. Either you or your husband needs to sign the form and send it to the storage facility and then everything will be delivered as arranged during your visit to my office.

I do hope this is all in order.

If you have questions regarding any of the above, please do not hesitate to contact me.

Yours faithfully,
Joseph Parson,
Solicitor, acting for and on behalf of the estate of Mrs Margaret Sanders-North.

Lee then opened his letter and handed it to Anna. It was precisely the same in content and with a cheque for the same amount made out in his name.

They sat and looked at each other in total disbelief.

They stared in amazement at the two cheques on the table in front of them, which totalled a little under a million pounds.

Lee was first to break the silence.

"Hmmm, well... shall we go out for a meal tonight, to sort of celebrate?"

He wasn't smiling though, and neither was Anna.

"If that's what you want. We could go to the Indian restaurant in the High Street."

"Yes, we could, or we could go to a posh place like the Five Horseshoes."

"Hmmm. Yes, we could, I suppose." Anna, like Lee, was feeling rather subdued.

"Would you like me to phone them and book a table?" Anna looked up at Lee and then back to the papers lying on the table.

"OK, let's do it."

"Why are we so down in the dumps? We've just been given almost a million quid! I'm looking right at it. It's sitting here on the table."

"I know, but somehow it doesn't feel right to celebrate. Though I suppose we can afford it... now."

Anna's face was expressionless.

Ever since they'd first met, Lee and Anna had had very little spare money. They'd always carefully saved up for special things throughout their time together, and the thought of this vast amount of money at their disposal now didn't make either of them feel too comfortable.

"Do you think Mum and Dad, Sarah and Jim would like to come? Celebrating this with them would be nice. They have given us so much over the years."

Without speaking, Lee got up to fetch a bottle of wine from the kitchen. He always kept wine in the house and loved a glass of red with his evening meal, as did Anna. He opened it and poured each of them a large glass.

"We'll take a taxi tonight, I think. Then we can both have another nice glass or two with our meal."

"But we can't afford... Oh, well, I suppose we can..." Anna's voice trailed away.

"I think it's going to take quite a while for this to sink in, you know. Even having a taxi to take us there and back doesn't feel right. It's not something we would even consider normally, is it?"

"How about... How about if we get a big car organised? Then we can collect Mum, Dad, Sarah and Jim too, making it really special."

A short while later, after a few phone calls, both the Slaters and Anna's parents were booked in at the restaurant, and a big saloon car arranged to collect them all and take them back home later in the evening.

"At least no one has to drive. So we can relax." Lee smiled as he went to change into something a bit smarter than his jeans and jumper.

"And don't forget..." he called from the bedroom

"... we have the parcel to open too. It might be full of gold nuggets. Ha-ha, we should be so lucky."

"Oh, ha-ha to you too… very funny. Perhaps we can open it tomorrow evening after work."

"Good idea. I wonder what Margaret would say if she was a fly on the wall?"

"I bet she would be pleased and happy. She was always jolly and cheerful in the hospital ward, even at the end she had a smile…"

Anna had to go and fetch a tissue then so she could wipe her eyes.

This whole episode with Margaret, a patient of hers, had upset her more than she would admit. Normally, she didn't become at all involved in a personal way with any of the patients. This time everything was different. It was as though Margaret's sudden appearance in their lives was somehow planned, deliberate. Almost as if she had been sent to them. Once again a cold shiver ran down Anna's spine.

The meal at the Five Horseshoes was excellent. They found a round table in a quiet corner. Lee and Tom chose ribeye steak with all the trimmings, Anna and the other three ordered roast pork.

Tom ordered an expensive red wine and a special bottle of champagne to celebrate.

As they came to leave the restaurant, Anna insisted on paying the bill, despite there being quite a lot of resistance from her father.

All six of them were rather "merry" as they clambered back into the car to go home.

Once they got back, Lee sat laughing aloud as he lay on the sofa,

"I think I could get used to this lifestyle. It's great."
Anna went to get ready for bed, as she was tired. So

much had happened in the last twelve hours, making it a very long day.

"Don't you get too used to it. We have to go to work tomorrow."

That broke the spell, and they quickly went to bed.

"It was a lovely night, wasn't it?" Anna said.

"Yes, it was exceptional."

"Thank you, dear Margaret, wherever you are," Anna whispered into the air.

In bed, Lee cuddled up to his wife, pulled at her nightdress and started to run his hands over her body. Then, as his passion grew, he gave her a long lingering kiss. Propping himself up on his elbows, he looked lovingly into Anna's eyes and told her:

"Do you know, Mrs Agazzi? You are the sexiest and most beautiful wife I've ever had."

Chapter 20:

The Legacy

June 1982

It would not be till the weekend that Lee produced the brown paper-wrapped package. They both looked at it intently.

Neither of them wanted to be the one to cut the string. It felt like a kind of desecration.

Anna went and got a small penknife and carefully prised the seal away.

"This must have been put on here a long time ago. The paper underneath is a much lighter colour, look..."

It was a light buff below the seal whereas the main wrapping had aged to dark brown.

Eventually, the seal was painstakingly lifted clear and the string carefully undone.

Inside was an old shoebox also tied with string in a bow. It opened at a gentle pull. As the lid was removed, they saw inside a folded envelope. This contained some official-looking documents. There was also a bundle of old photos and a rusty tin, about seven inches by five, which was locked.

"Can you see a key anywhere?" Lee asked.

"No, there's not one in here."

Lee lifted the tin out and shook it a little.

"I'll get something to open it… a bent nail might do. There are some old keys in a drawer in the kitchen your dad gave us. One of them might work."

"Those are suitcase keys for the ones we borrowed from him when we went to Iceland. I don't think they'll unlock this. We ought to return them to him."

"Well, it must be worth a try." Lee went and found them.

"You're right. I don't think these will fit at all."

After trying various other keys and some assorted bits of metal, he got up and went to have a look in his van.

"Got it. This might work."

He held a packet of assorted pieces of bent metal which resembled a burglar's lock-picking kit.

"We use these on a machine in the works. It's worth a go, isn't it?"

After about ten minutes the old lock squeaked, moving enough to enable him to prise the lid open without causing any damage. Inside were some small leather-covered medal cases, quite a few tarnished silver coins, half a dozen old French banknotes, a significant cut-stone ring in a damaged setting, what looked like an old dented 9mm bullet and a small broken artist's paintbrush. Almost unnoticed and wedged into one end of the tin was a splinter of wood about five inches long. It didn't seem to belong there.

Anna prised it out of the tin, looking at the split end.

"Look at this, it's been hollowed out, and there's something inside... it's tiny." She laid the bit of wood on the table and went to get some tweezers and a needle from the bedroom.

She managed to ease out a small, rolled-up piece of paper. They both gazed at it as Anna unrolled it. There were some faint markings on it, which looked like drawn lines. There were also some tiny numbers here and there.

"It looks like a map of something." Anna went to get a magnifying glass.

"It *is* a map. There's a tiny arrow with 'N' on it in a corner and some lines and numbers. What do you make of it?"

"Don't know. Might be something from the war when Margaret was in France, I suppose. Let's look at the other things."

As they opened the old leather-covered cases they were even more amazed.

"This is like something from a James Bond film, isn't it? It's bloody exciting!" Lee enthused.

The first small case contained a medal with a ribbon and he was sure he knew what it was.

"I think this is a VC – a Victoria Cross. Wow! The other one is French. It might be a Croix de Guerre."

There were two other medals and Lee considered these to be the War Medal for 1939–1945 and an Air

Force Cross or something like it, although he wasn't quite sure.

Anna picked up the Victoria Cross, holding it with great care in her left hand and staring at it. As her fingers moved over the surface, she felt a cold shiver go right through her.

"It feels wrong to be handling this. I don't think these medals belong here. These are incredible – why didn't Margaret ever mention them?

"I think Dad might know what these are, you know. He's got a box of medals and coins he's collected over the years."

They placed the medals back in the cases and started looking at the papers and photos.

There were documents of various kinds from the British Armed Forces and different government bodies, one from Buckingham Palace and several papers in French including some that seemed to relate to an award.

Underneath one of the large official envelopes was an old passport. As they picked it up and peered inside to see whose it was, a small white wrap of thin paper, about two inches square, fell onto the floor. Written on it, in extremely tiny script, was a name: Sofia. It wasn't sealed.

Cautiously, Anna unfolded the paper. Inside was a tiny lock of very fine curly blonde hair. Anna beamed lovingly at it.

"I wonder how old Sofia was when this was put in here. I'll bet she was a young girl then. What a beautiful keepsake."

Placing the small packet back inside what turned out to be Margaret's passport, they started to look at the photographs.

A cream-coloured ribbon surrounded them, again tied with a neat bow.

The pictures were black-and-white as was typical of old photographs, many of them sepia-toned.

The majority had writing on the back, in a neat tiny script, some with dates written on them, some not. The handwriting looked similar to the letter in Margaret's Will, although the script was much smaller and neater. They were sure it was Margaret's own handwriting.

A larger picture had inscribed on the back, "Jack and Maggie – Wedding"; sadly, there was no date.

"This was probably taken during the war. They're both in military uniform," Anna said.

Another photo, clearly older and quite faded, was of a young girl in school uniform standing in front of a church porch. On the back was an old typed sticker that said, "Margaret Sanders, St Margaret's Church, Church Street, Swindon". Sadly, this was not dated either.

Other pictures were of an assortment of people, mostly with names on the back.

Taking their time, they looked at the photos in chronological order. They stopped to study one in particular. It was of a small farmhouse with a couple standing by an open door. It was labelled "Sofia and Marc Leroux at La Ferme de Leroux, Northern France, July 1945". The French couple, who'd come to the funeral had told them the farm was in north-west France, near Vouvray-sur-Loir, around 50 kilometres south of Le Mans.

"It's a bit north of Tours." Josette Leroux had written her address on a scrap of paper under the hotel letterhead and given it to Anna after Margaret's funeral, and she had stuffed this in her bag and then somehow forgotten where she'd put it. She did remember the name of the farm, however: La Ferme de Leroux.

There were several similar pictures of the farm and a close up of Margaret with Sofia. Margaret looked so young, with such a pretty smile.

Anna smiled to see this picture, handing it to Lee.

"I'd recognise that smile anywhere."

Lee, though, nearly jumped out of his chair on seeing it.

"Oh, heck. It can't be! The other woman could be my dad's sister, Anna. She looks… she looks… exactly like him. I didn't recognise anything familiar in the couple at the funeral. But Sofia…"

There was another picture of Margaret taken in 1943, but she was unrecognisable in this. On the back was scribbled "Margaret 1943 – only survivor", and there was another picture of a bomb-damaged building with a swastika flag half buried among the rubble.

This too had writing on it, but in a different hand and only stating the year: "1943".

After they finished looking at all the photos, they put everything back in the box.

Anna's emotions were in tatters again, her eyes wet and red. Lee sat gently holding her hand. He was looking down at the floor, his mind elsewhere.

It must have been at least ten minutes before he got up and started to make some tea. It was approaching midnight. They were both dead tired and couldn't believe they must have been sitting there since 7:30, over four hours.

Taking their tea to the bedroom, they turned in for the night.

"We must send off the form to the storage company," Lee said. "I meant to talk to you about it yesterday."

"OK. Not now, Lee, please. I want to go to sleep. I think we've been through enough for one day."

They snuggled up together. Lee was soon snoring, but Anna lay there sleepless. Images of Margaret, the Leroux family and their farm kept going round in her head. There was Sofia, with Margaret smiling next to her, and then the bombed building. Those images haunted her; she felt they were trying to speak to her.

Anna was almost nodding off when she glanced over her shoulder at Lee and said,

"We must go and see the farm. We have to go there – to Vouvray-sur-Loir." He was still snoring, and didn't hear her.

It must have been well past three in the morning when Anna finally went to sleep.

In a flash, it seemed, morning came, and she was first up.

She was dressed and ready to leave for work. It was a little after seven. She took Lee a cup of tea and found him sitting on the bed looking a bit the worse for wear.

"I'm off to work now. Don't go back to sleep, will you? I've made you some toast, it's on the kitchen table."

Due to Anna's shift hours, they didn't get much chance to talk again for several days.

Meanwhile, Lee got in touch with the storage company and arranged for them to deliver Margaret's property to Tom and Gina's house. The furniture and crates were to go into their garage for the time being.

Lee remembered mentioning to Joe that most of the furniture looked new. "Well, it's because it *is* new.

Margaret only ever kept things for a short time, then gave them away to a charity shop and bought new. I doubt if anything here is more than a year old, and it may well be even newer. She never kept anything for very long, not furniture, cooking utensils, cutlery or anything else, certainly since I've known her. I asked her once why she didn't keep things longer. She abruptly changed the subject. I never asked again."

The storage company vehicle arrived at the Parkes' house early on a wet and dull Friday morning, with an array of different-sized packing crates. Neither Lee nor Anna knew what was in any of them, even though they'd helped Joe Parson get everything packed before the lorry turned up at Margaret's house to clear it.

The furniture and large items were placed at the back of the garage, and the smaller crates partly piled on top and towards the front. Gina, who saw it in, considered how little there was; she'd expected there to be quite a lot more.

"Is that the lot?"

"Yes, that's it. Can you sign here, please?"

After leaving work, Lee went to visit Tom and Gina to see what the storage company had delivered. He was on his own as Anna was working lates all week.

This evening Lee was invited to eat with his in-laws. After the meal, Tom and he wandered into the garage to have a look at the crates and boxes. There wasn't much to see as the single fluorescent tube didn't give much light and their small torch didn't prove to be much use either. They only managed to look in a few of the more accessible items

Lee was fascinated to see what they might discover. There were quite a few small items of furniture at the front of a stack of crates.

"Joe Parson cleared the loft and back bedroom of Margaret's place before we got there. Most of this lot came from the loft, I think."

Tom carefully slid a picture frame out of one of the larger crates.

"This is a good painting."

"Can you hold it up a bit? The light isn't too good. Oh, yes, I recognise that place. It's the farm in France. Looks similar to one of the photos in Margaret's box. Is it signed?"

The Leroux farm in France

Tom took a good look but couldn't make out the signature.

"It looks like N and N and a number – possibly 'forty-five."

"Are you sure it's N and N?"

"Not really. It's not very clear and it's pretty dim in here."

"Can we take it indoors for a better look?"

"OK." His father-in-law passed the picture across the crates to Lee and then clambered back to the front of the garage.

Once in Tom's brightly lit kitchen, everything became much clearer. This was a light, colourful oil painting, on canvas, and it was clearly signed MSN '45.

"I think it's Margaret's signature. Margaret Sanders-North… MSN." Lee was convinced it must be her work.

"Very nice painting, Lee. This would look good hanging in your lounge. It's quite a nice size. I think it must be about… thirty-six by twenty-four inches. Nice frame as well. There's some writing on the back in pencil, but it's difficult to read…"

Lee decided to take it home to show Anna.

Tom mentioned there were several smaller paintings in the same crate as well but they were tied together with string, and he couldn't easily move them.

That was left for another day.

Gina told Anna they could store it all in the garage for a while, at least until a home could be found for everything. This would probably be in their own house, or if there were items they didn't want, they would give them to a local charity shop.

Chapter 21:

The Problem with George Welford

November 1982 – December 1983

After the constant upheaval of the previous few months, life started to settle back into its former smooth routine, with all the usual work commitments and family events.

Even though Lee and Anna had now inherited an unbelievable amount of money and the many items of furniture left to them in Margaret's Will, it didn't change Lee's tendency to panic or worry about certain situations. If anything, it made things worse. His expectations increased, but the inner feelings and worries hadn't improved. He could go, inwardly, from being happy to a wreck in a split second.

One day he was working on a Council Building Regulations form, which had to be correctly filled in or the application might be turned down. As he struggled with it, all the print on the page vanished from his sight. The rest of his office and the other papers on his desk were still perfectly visible. So he looked away, blinked several times, shook his head – but the form he was working on was still a blank. He thought he was going mad and started getting very upset. As he got to his feet to walk away from the desk, in his panic he walked straight into the doorframe, hitting it so hard he almost fell over. He was always walking into doorframes or pillars or anything near him, but not usually this hard. As a result his elbows were often bruised.

It was at least fifteen minutes before the writing "reappeared" and he could return to the job in hand. The incident frightened him, but he never spoke of it to anyone.

About five months after the inheritance was finalised, Tom asked Anna if she thought the two of them would like to become more involved with the running of the company and be prepared to help it out.

"The joinery has serious financial problems. We… well, to be honest, I… have let an outstanding debt get out of control. If we take the customer to court, we stand to lose all or most of the money owed. We are not a big company, as you know, and this has the potential to cause us a serious problem, or as a worst-case scenario, force us to close down.

"Your input would help the company out of a jam, Anna, but in the long term, the big winners would be you

and Lee. That's something that would make Jim and me
very happy. We aren't getting any younger, you know. I
hope, as you are now in a better financial position than
you used to be, this could prove to be of substantial and
long-term benefit for you both. It would also inject new
blood into the top of the company, and I think this is
what is needed. Things have changed a lot since Jim and I
started up. Maybe we haven't been quite as smart as we
should have been."

The firm's problem was with a local man, George
Welford, who was a well-known landowner in the
Tillshott area. He owed a lot of money to Slater & Parkes
for work done to several of his properties. This included
renovations carried out on a large farm he owned in a
nearby town. Over the last twelve months, this work was
completed, together with other substantial works on two
further buildings he part-owned in Tillshott High Street.
As a result, he now owed far more than he could ever
pay.

Unexpectedly, George had announced he was about
to go into a care home. He had insufficient money to
pay them, so rather than go through the disgrace of
being declared bankrupt had asked Tom if the company
would consider taking the property he currently lived
in, in full settlement of his debt. This was known locally
as Grove Farm and now consisted of the farmhouse and
its surrounding plot of land, the farm's original arable
landholding having been sold many years before.

George told them he was going to sell his other
properties nearby, and a villa in Spain, to pay his care
home expenses. The total he owed Slater & Parkes was a

staggering £28,540. How this colossal sum was never paid over the last year was a long story. He'd evaded it by lying repeatedly to them with false promises of extra work. A town councillor for years, he'd dealt with Tom and Jim for almost all of that time. The company trusted him. Unfortunately, they let things get to the state where they now found they stood to lose their money, and maybe the business, as well. The situation deteriorated every month and as time passed by it became a real worry.

Tom had several long discussions with Jim about the problem and, desperate not to lose the joinery, between them they came up with a plan to reimburse Slater & Parkes all of the money owed. At the same time, it would provide Anna and Lee with security for life, which was something they both dearly wanted.

Tom had always wanted his daughter to benefit from his stake in the company. He'd asked her to join the firm on leaving school, but Anna always wanted to be a nurse, it was her dream. The idea he and his business partner came up with would solve their immediate financial crisis and at the same time keep the business in the family for the near future.

Jim was in total agreement with the plan, saying that Lee, apart from being darn' good at his job, was as close to him and Sarah as their own son. He suggested they should have a family gathering to discuss the whole situation with them.

Jim's son Georgie had made it clear he did not want to join the business as his dreams lay elsewhere.

So the plan was that Lee and Anna were to become directors and partners in Slater & Parkes. The company would take Grove Farm as it stood to pay George Welford's debt. They, in turn, would sell it on to Lee and Anna for the same figure of £28,540. This way the company would get the debt cleared. Also, if they decided to invest further, Lee and Anna could each put an additional £10,000 into the company. This would match the figure Tom and Jim initially put in when they started the joinery, making them all equal partners.

This was to be drawn up in a legal agreement arranged by the company's solicitor.

Over coffee and a glass of wine, they put the idea to Lee and Anna.

"Well, what do you think? It would give you a nice large house in about five acres of land. The farmland has covenants on it so no one can build too near you. All the land at the rear is Forestry Commission, so it's unlikely to be built on either. No houses may be built within the current acreage of the farm, other than where the existing farmhouse and the old outbuildings are now. The original farm was much larger. The land was split up and sold off a long time ago."

Both Tom and Jim thought it would be an amazing investment for them.

The farmhouse was in a poor condition, but it was still a fantastic opportunity. The farm, house, outbuildings and land were worth far more than the figure they would be paying. The old man had lived in one room almost all the time. The rest of the property was in a dreadful state.

It was a building ripe for renovating. It could provide Lee and Anna with a superb house and an excellent plot of land at a fraction of its real value.

It would set them up for the rest of their lives, and if they chose to, it would make them part of the company too. This had been Tom's dream for Anna, ever since he'd started the business with Jim.

Sarah looked over at Gina.

"What do you think?"

She looked at Anna and Lee.

"It's a brilliant idea. But rather than repair the farmhouse, I think it would be better to knock it down and build a new one. That's what I would do. Looking at house prices today, I think you could do the whole thing for a load less than its real value and maybe less than the cost of doing it up to a standard you would want. Then you could sell your cottage, keep it or rent it out, and I'm pretty sure you couldn't lose out whatever you chose to do."

It sounded like a great opportunity. But Lee was still worried.

"Can we sleep on it, please?" he asked, looking at Anna.

"Of course you can. We don't want to encourage you to do anything you're not comfortable with. We love you far too much to do that. If push comes to shove we will refinance the company another way, if it's what we need to do."

Sarah added she thought the idea of making Lee and Anna full partners a brilliant one, regardless of the debt situation. It would be an exciting development and keep the business within the family.

The incredible inheritance they'd received was starting to open up new life opportunities for them, almost too fast though. Lee's problem was getting his head around it.

It was well after midnight when he and Anna turned out the light for the night.

"Well, what a shock. I wasn't expecting that. It could be an amazing opportunity." Lee had to admit, he found the whole concept appealing.

"Yes, it sounds almost too good to be true. Can we forget it till tomorrow? I want to get some sleep," Anna told him.

She was required to be at work early the following morning. With all the recent events taking over their usually quiet lives, everything was spinning around in her head. The latest proposal was a step too far. Anna was so tired, she wanted to shut it all out and pretend, for a few hours, that none of this had ever happened.

"I think the world's gone mad. I've had enough for one day."

Lee lay there too, his mind in a turmoil. Thoughts of every kind flooded his head. He didn't know what time he went to sleep, but it wasn't for quite a few hours.

For the next two days Lee and Anna's endless discussions about the amazing offer became more and more exciting. They opted to take the whole deal – head on – and another meeting, to confirm their decision, was hastily arranged.

They would buy the old house, Grove Farm, and join the company as full partners as soon as possible.

Anna would still remain in her nursing role. Leaving that was never going to be an option. She loved nursing far too much to give it up.

It was in their best interests to go ahead, though. Buying the farm, even if they didn't know quite what they would do with it in the long term, would be a clear benefit to them. A local surveyor offered to provide a report on the condition of the existing building and land at a reduced cost… another bargain. Lee went through all his concerns regarding the considerable task of renovation. After many hours of discussion with Anna, and as a direct response to the survey, they decided it would make more sense to demolish the old house and build a new modern home in its place. The two quotes they obtained, both to take on a possible extensive renovation and to tear down the old building and rebuild, were roughly similar. The decision was taken to build a new house with all mod-cons, which they felt would be much more practical and suitable for them. Anna was wildly excited at the thought of the new house and having a fantastic new kitchen.

So in the end, it was an easy decision to make.

Grove Farm was in fact, only a stone's throw away from Anna's parents.

Lee hadn't fully realised how near it was until they went to have a good look at the farmhouse and surrounding land. Although he'd passed along this section of road hundreds of times before, the house itself was tucked away at the end of its own curved drive and almost obscured behind woodland. He'd never noticed it.

The company solicitor agreed to sort out the purchase for them, including the removal and rebuilding of New Grove Farm. At the beginning of spring in the New Year everything was cleared and approved so that work on the first phase could commence.

At the same time, the solicitor also dealt with the legal documentation to make them full partners in

Slater & Parkes. The farm and their investment into the family business would cost them a total of £48,540 – a large sum, but good value for money. They felt this was affordable and, of course, they would not require a mortgage. Margaret's legacy was starting to change their lives in a dramatic way. Anna couldn't believe how thrilled she felt. She was nervous, too, but optimistic at the thought of their new home.

"What do you think of this design, Lee?"

"It's not bad, but I like one of the others better. Perhaps we could mix and match? You know, put parts of one design into one of the others."

"Sounds like a good idea. I've got half a ton of interior design brochures to go through as well. It's so exciting, isn't it?"

With the help of a young local architect, who seemed almost as excited by the prospect of the new build as they were, two full sets of blueprints were prepared and submitted for consideration. To speed up the process and start the ball rolling, Lee asked the young fellow to manage the entire project on their behalf. After a series of amendments and resubmissions, the town council's planning department finally approved the designs. Permission granted, Lee could at last give the instruction to proceed.

New Grove Farm was to have four bedrooms each with an en-suite bathroom, a large lounge with an open-plan kitchen-diner at one end, opening on to the back garden. The kitchen appliances, cupboards and worktops all now had to be agreed and finalised. They both went for the same solid stone worktops. Lee had to explain to Anna some of the practicalities of the actual stone they chose and the technical specifications of the ovens, hobs, refrigeration units and the dishwasher... the list seemed endless. But so was the thrill of it.

There were, of course, initial disagreements over the colours chosen and the finer points of the design. Visits to various suppliers eventually solved the problems.

Then, after weeks of indecision, everything was agreed and the orders were placed.

New Grove Farm

The modern kitchen, a separate utility room and a study, would give them ample space for anything they might want to do now and in the future. There was going to be a large double garage at the front with enough space at the rear for a small workshop. Anna was ecstatic, so was Lee, but he worried about the expense and any potential problems that might crop up along the way. His worries were well founded as it turned out. Although not in a way he could ever have foreseen.

Two weeks after signing the contracts, building work on their new home commenced as planned.

Lee, on the same day, decided to order himself a new car: an E-class silver Mercedes-Benz saloon – it was the vehicle of his dreams. He wanted Anna to buy a nice new car as well, perhaps a little sports car. She, though, decided as her car was almost new, and as Margaret had left it to her, she wanted to keep it. Apart from the fact she enjoyed driving it, its sentimental value meant far more to her than any snazzy sports vehicle ever could.

About two weeks into the demolition, a round concrete block about three feet in diameter was unearthed several yards from where the old kitchen door had been. It was about twelve inches below the surface and seemed to serve no purpose. As the workers dug around it, they found a circular brick structure below the concrete slab.

Assuming this to have been an old well, they decided to remove the capping block to see if they were correct, and soon found there was a brick-lined shaft below. Some stones were dropped into the void to see how deep it was. It was only a second before the pebbles hit something. It wasn't the splash of water they heard though. It was something much more metallic.

The well, or shaft, was deep, dark and emitted a horrible smell. Whatever the pebbles had hit, it was a fair way down, and it wasn't water. The building contractor decided to contact the council to see if there had been any mining in the area or if any official documentation would show up a well or evidence of tunnelling.

Work continued on the main site while they waited for a reply. A few days later two council officials, having not found any documentation of a well or of any mining in the area, arrived at the site to have a look. Of course, they couldn't see anything and the torch one of them had brought was of no use at all.

"Typical council officials… useless at anything remotely practical."

The builders laughed at the idea of a torch. They decided to get a small crane jigged up and lower a grab claw with a proper light on it, to try and bring up whatever was there.

The following day a steel line was lowered into the void, with a powerful light attached.

What they grabbed and managed to raise to the surface would astonish not only the site workers, but also the entire town.

It was a large metal box entangled within a mass of old steel cable. Slowly, the collection of wire surrounding the box and various other decayed artefacts came to the surface. During the journey upward, the box constantly snagged on the rough masonry wall, making a dreadful grinding sound as it did so. Finally, the jumbled collection emerged into the daylight. Foul-smelling stagnant water was pouring from the accumulated mass.

About thirty minutes later, the rusty metal case, after a thorough hosing down, was prised open. The builder estimated it to be about two foot six inches by four foot six.

What they found inside shook them to the core.

The box contained a revolting mess, but you could easily see what appeared to be human remains. One of the workers threw up on the spot and was helped out of the area. Several others had gone a greenish colour and walked away. The smell was terrible. Everyone began to back off.

A military style of uniform, severely decayed, still covered some of the bones.

Work stopped and the police were called.

The whole area was cordoned off and no one allowed near.

Lee, who was at work, received a phone call informing him of a problem. As he was now the legal owner of the farmhouse, he decided he should go and have a look for himself.

When he arrived, the whole place seemed to be heaving with people. Among them was Ted Manner from the local paper, the *Echo*. Lee went over and spoke to him.

"Hello, Ted. How are you and Ellie? And what are you doing here?"

"We're OK. You seem to have an interesting story here, Lee. What's going on?"

"Wish I knew, Ted. I had a call at work and came over to see for myself. Bloody annoying, though, it's going to hold up the work."

Everyone present was eager to see what else had appeared from the shaft.

Ted laughed, saying they could speak later in the Scuttle. Wandering off, he tried to help his photographer to obtain a better viewpoint.

The local police declared the area a potential crime scene and the remains were taken to the coroner's office for closer examination. That left just the last bits of debris to be cleared from the shaft. There were some other, rather interesting bits and pieces, including the remains of an old .303 calibre rifle plus a couple of rusty ammunition cases containing two old pistols and several pouches of 9mm live ammunition. One of the handguns was a Walther P38 in a bad condition; the other an old Webley revolver. Both pistol grips had disintegrated long ago.

After clearing the shaft, the demolition team was given permission to continue work, apart from on the area adjacent to the shaft, which remained taped off.

The following afternoon a local Police Superintendent made a brief statement, which he released to the press.

He said that initial forensic examination showed the body had probably been in the shaft since the Second World War. It was possible the remains might have been that of one of the crew of a German bomber, shot down by fighters from the RAF base near Wroughton. Being about four miles south of Swindon, it was probably the nearest airbase to Tillshott at the time. Fragments of the military uniform retrieved with the remains were identical to that issued to the Luftwaffe, the aerial warfare branch of the combined German Wehrmacht military forces, during World War II.

Further bulletins would be issued in due course as more information became available.

The police representative thanked everyone for their patience and said he hoped to be able to remove restrictions from the site in the next few days.

This was the most exciting thing to have happened in Tillshott for a long time.

The police made no mention of the fact a damaged nametag with part of a name, "Unteroffizier Otto...", had been found within the remains. Official records were checked to see if someone with this name and rank was recorded as having been on board the crashed aircraft.

What was even more disturbing was it also appeared the airman might not have died as a result of the crash. He had almost certainly done so from a gunshot wound to the head; a single bullet hole in the left temple was the cause. As a result and considering the unusual circumstances, the site was declared an official crime scene, possibly that of a murder.

Investigation then started into how the officer had ended up in the shaft.

Some time later, after searching through various archives, it was confirmed that a young German named Unteroffizier Otto Schulz was the only member of the aircrew in the downed bomber whose body was not recovered.

A local man, George Welford, was reported to be helping the police with their enquiries regarding the aviator's ultimate demise. He had lived on the farm at the time of the plane crash.

It appeared from official police interviews with him that a day or so after the bomber had crashed, the wounded enemy officer had hobbled in through the back door of Grove Farm, waving a pistol in a threatening manner.

George Welford, then serving with the local Home Guard, was enjoying a cup of tea with some members of his unit when the German appeared. He remembered how shocked they were to see an enemy soldier in Tillshott. This was the last thing they'd expected.

He didn't remember much more about the incident, it seemed, other than some of the men grabbing their weapons and scattering. He wasn't sure which, if any of them, even in fear for their lives, might have shot at the "Nazi sod". In fact, George didn't remember any shooting at all. He did not know how the German had ended up in the well shaft. He couldn't even remember there being a well, there or anywhere else on the farm…

Over the last month or two, George it seemed had become mentally feeble and his condition was not expected to improve.

Due to his personal circumstances and the fact that his statement broadly seemed to fit with the evidence, a decision was taken not to pursue the matter further. All the other members of the Home Guard in Tillshott had passed away a long time ago.

The incident would now pass to the relevant military authority. They would arrange for the remains to be returned to the Schulz family in Germany, for proper burial, if they could be traced.

Ironically, within twenty-four hours of being questioned by the police, George Welford died in the care home. Whatever he did or didn't know about the incident would go to the grave with him.

The police cordon was removed within the week and work on Grove Farm recommenced. The shaft was filled with bricks, rubble and soil from the demolition, and sealed.

The incident, though, would be a talking point in Tillshott for some time to come.

Chapter 22:

A Trip to France

September 1983

On 9 June 1983 a general election was held in the UK. The Conservatives won a decisive victory, making Margaret Thatcher the nation's first female Prime Minister. For some strange reason this victory became the catalyst that prompted Anna to go and visit the farm in France. Maybe the name Margaret had something to do with it. She was determined to go and visit the Lerouxs.

The idea became an obsession and Anna wouldn't stop talking about it, trying to push Lee to accompany her. The more Anna went on and on about it, the more annoyed he became.

One morning, in sheer frustration, he asked her to

write to Josette and see how they would react to the idea
of having visitors some time in the autumn.

Anna was wild with excitement. She found the
address buried at the bottom of her handbag and wrote
to Josette, asking if they could come and visit the farm
sometime in early September.

A reply from France was eagerly awaited, and one
arrived on their doormat within two weeks. It was a
long letter in surprisingly good English. Josette loved
the suggestion and offered to put them up, adding they
would enjoy showing them the farm. Over the last
couple of years, two luxury holiday apartments had
been created from some farm outbuildings and this was
where they would be able to stay. Some of the original
farm buildings were still almost untouched since the
war, and it was in these older parts that Margaret had
been hidden during those troubled times. Josette and
Marcel were both very young at the time, and they and
the whole family had lived in constant fear of German
military raids. At a neighbouring farm, the elderly
owner, his wife and the entire family were arrested and
not seen again. The large farmhouse was burned to
the ground and left in ruins as a warning to others. Its
remains were still visible.

In response to one of Anna's questions, Josette
asked her brother if he could remember seeing Margaret
painting while she was with them. But it seemed neither
he nor she could.

She added they would love to see the canvases and
also the photos of their parents, if Anna would be kind
enough to bring them.

A time and date in September was agreed.

Lee arranged to take a week's holiday that was long overdue. He booked a ferry crossing from Portsmouth to Caen, and calculated it would take two or three hours to get there travelling south. It was about 220 kilometres from the city centre of Caen to Vouvray.

Josette told Anna the lane to the farm was not easy to find, if you were not familiar with the area, and it would be better if they could meet in the car park of Église Saint-Martin, their local church.

This was on the main road through Vouvray-sur-Loir. It was at a road junction with Place Arsène Baussant and almost opposite 5 Rue Oscar Moneris. It would be easy for them to locate.

Église Saint-Martin was apparently only a few minutes drive from the farm. The location given was so precise Lee was sure they would have no trouble getting there.

Église Saint Martin – Vouvray-sur-Loir

On a warm September afternoon, he pulled into the car park of Saint Martin's Church in Vouvray-sur-Loir.

Josette was waiting for them, standing by the entrance. She was excited, greeting them in surprisingly good English, and could hardly wait to start showing them around.

Minutes later, they were heading down a rough muddy farm track, following her rather old and dirty green Citroën, heading for the farmhouse. Josette had been right; they would never have thought this was where they should be driving. It was almost impossible to keep the car from sliding into the ditches that ran either side of the track. The farm looked picturesque in the sunshine as they arrived, but nothing like the one in Margaret's paintings. Disappointed, Anna wondered if she had painted some other view instead.

After settling into the holiday accommodation, they went up to the main house with their arms full of Margaret's possessions.

Marcel saw them approaching and opened the door to greet them.

"*Bonjour, bienvenue dans notre ferme.* Welcome to our farm."

"You do speak some English, I see," Anna laughed.

"Yes, but just lit-tle bit… she, Josette, she speak more than me. This is good, *oui?*"

"Yes, it's excellent, Marcel. *C'est très bien.*" Neither Lee nor Anna spoke more than a few words of French.

For the next couple of hours, three of them chatted almost non-stop over a constant flow of wine and coffee. Every now and then, Josette would stop for a moment or two to explain, in French, some of the discussion Marcel didn't understand.

After a superb evening meal, Lee opened the package containing the paintings and photographs.

There were five framed canvases. One was a lot larger than the other four.

Josette loved the pictures and babbled away in French to Marcel about them. She thought that after breakfast the next day Anna and Lee might like to see the spot where she was sure Margaret might have painted two of them, including the largest study. Lee explained that they would like to give them three of the paintings, as a thank you and to remind them of Margaret and the time she'd spent with their parents, Sofia and Marc.

They were surprised, delighted and amazed Lee and Anna could bear to part with such beautiful pictures.

Over the next couple of days, the visitors were able to see the main farm buildings, including the areas where Margaret was in hiding for over two years during the war.

The next day while Marcel was working, Lee, Anna and Josette went on a walk through some woodland nearby. This was the view Margaret had reproduced in her paintings. The trees had grown up considerably since the war, but they could see the overall scene had changed little over time. Margaret portrayed the scene so well; the hedge-lined fields, the gentle rolling landscape and hazy blue distant background. She had captured it to perfection. Anna stood there in silence, breathing in the rural atmosphere, trying to see it through Margaret's eyes. She shivered as she looked.

Once back in the farmhouse, Josette produced a box of old family pictures, some going back to the 1920's. Anna started to become a little tearful as the photographs were passed between them. The ones taken of Sofia Leroux with Margaret during her recovery were the most difficult to deal with.

The day before they were due to return home, Josette once again took them out from the farm gate and across some fields to another location where Margaret had produced at least one of the paintings.

The view from here was like a glimpse of heaven. It was another beautiful vista of the French countryside, fading away into the pale blue distance.

Josette then made a point of taking hold of Anna's hand and leading her and Lee to a tiny area of brightly coloured flowers growing in the right-hand corner of the field. It seemed out of place as it was so small, only about one metre square.

"I want to show you, so much, this place. It's where Maman and Papa buried Margaret's baby, Sofia. Our family has looked after it ever since and we keep it like this, so little Sofia is never forgotten and..."

"What did you say?" Anna's jaw had dropped open. She was finding it hard to take in what Josette was saying. She felt a violent cold shudder run right through her body, as if the blood was draining out of her, making her feel slightly faint.

All the colour in her face drained away.

"B-But... Margaret said she had no children. In her letter, she said..."

Lee, standing next to Anna, gripped her hand tightly. He had an expression of shock on his face.

"You didn't know about her baby?"

"No… No. She…" Lee was holding on to Anna as he turned his head away.

"Oh… I'm so sorry, I thought you must have known."

There was a short silence before Josette continued to explain.

"After Margaret was rescued from the bombed building, her injuries were so severe the doctor couldn't believe she would survive. A couple of months later she gave birth to a baby girl, but she was *mort-née*. I think, in English, it means already dead? Until a week or two before the baby was born, we didn't even suspect she was pregnant. Her injuries were, well, you know… it made it difficult to see her normal shape. The doctor was astonished she hadn't lost the baby after she was first brought here, she was so badly injured.

"Following the birth, Margaret was again dangerously ill. The doctor told my parents he didn't think she would live for more than a day or two. She was unable to deal with, or do, anything. The baby was so tiny. Papa took the little girl away. During the night, he laid her here. He called her Sofia after Maman. Before he buried her, Papa cut off a bit of her pretty blonde hair and kept it…"

Hearing this, Anna remembered the tiny packet of hair with the name "Sofia" on it. They had assumed it was Sofia Leroux's. The shock realisation it had almost certainly belonged to Margaret's own child hit Anna hard.

She dropped to her knees, placing her hands gently between the flowers on the tiny grave, tears streaming down her face.

Josette, by this point, had started crying as well.

"I'm sorry. I didn't mean to… to upset you. I'm so sorry, I had no idea…"

Lee knelt next to Anna. He put his arm around her and turned to face Josette.

"It's OK. It isn't your fault. We are so grateful for everything you and your parents did for Margaret and her baby daughter. It was amazing kindness on your part and it must have been so difficult."

"It was dangerous and complicated during the war, you understand. Everything had to be done in secret. If the Germans had ever found out, we would all have been shot."

Later, the three of them strolled back in silence to the farmhouse.

The Lerouxs refused to take any payment for the Agazzis' stay. The only money they were to spend was left in the collection plate at the local church. Before they started for home, Anna bought a small flowering tree and planted it in little Sofia's grave.

As Lee drove back to catch the ferry home, Anna kept looking at a set of five photos Josette had given her as they were about to set off. They were of Margaret at various stages of her recovery. Anna started crying every time she looked at them. Marcel also handed them a letter from Jack, Margaret's husband. It must have arrived in the last few days of the war and would have been written a short time before he died. Lee placed this in his jacket pocket. Neither of them could face reading it.

Another interesting fact they learnt was about the mysterious damaged 9mm bullet — the one they'd found in the tin box. The doctor had removed it from

Margaret's chest at the farm and given it to Sofia as a grisly memento. After her recovery Margaret kept it as a good luck charm. It had missed her heart by five millimetres. Anna searched for a tissue to wipe her eyes again as she felt she could almost hear Margaret's voice...

"God was watching over me."

Anna desperately tried to sleep for the rest of the journey, but the upsetting memory of the little grave in the open field weighed heavily on her mind.

A few days later, back in Tillshott, it felt like an incredible dream. Once they returned to work, life was back to a kind of normality.

Lee and Anna now had two new friends in France and hoped to keep in contact with them for the rest of their lives, as Margaret had done with their parents. Josette and Marcel Leroux had been so kind to them and treated them like royalty.

But were the Lerouxs in fact a real part of their family tree, on Lee's side? They were not certain, but it looked distinctly possible that this could be the case.

Chapter 23:

New Grove Farm

Summer 1984

It was late August 1984 and Lee and Anna were getting ready to move into their new home.

Anna was so overwhelmed with excitement she thought she would pop. The house they had built was now a constant and overwhelming part of their conversation. In fact, they hardly talked of anything else.

"This is better than any dream. Who would ever have thought little old you and I would have a place like this to live in? It's like a palace!"

Anna was jumping up and down with joy.

Lee also was in a high state of excitement, tinged with his usual worry.

"I can't believe it either, Anna. It's all too good to be true. I hope everything's been built properly. You know what builders are like these days. It certainly looks great. The colour you chose for the bedrooms looks amazing."

The landscaping had only been finished two days before Lee started to organise a surprise party for Anna, their family and friends. He arranged for the caterers at the Five Horseshoes to provide the refreshments and drinks.

It was almost a year and four months after the building got started that the move into New Grove Farm began to happen. The preparations were started some weeks before, but today was the big day.

Lee drove over to their new home very early on the Saturday morning, to have a good look around and check everything was finished so they could move straight in. Apart from some carpets and underlay in the smaller bedrooms, which were still in their plastic wrapping, it seemed to be ready. He checked to see the phone line was connected. Finding it was, he called Anna to give her an update.

"It's great news. We can move in today."

"Oh, I can't wait. I'm on my way…"

Within the first couple of months of living in their new home they decided to sell the little house at Railway Cottages.

Chapter 24:

Alpha

January 1985

Lee and Anna couldn't believe it would be Christmas soon. The shops had been full of seasonal gifts for months. The year had gone by at such a pace.

Having been for a short walk and wrapped up in thick coats and scarves for protection against the cold air, they were now well on their way back home.

On passing St Aidan's Church, they noticed a long banner pinned up outside advertising an event called The Alpha Course. "Explore the meaning of life", it read.

So, with Margaret's words ringing in their ears, they made an impulsive decision. They looked at each other, grinned and decided to see what this was all about. The church office was open, so they walked in. Without looking up, the secretary said,

"Hello. Can I help you?"

Then glancing up, she recognised Lee.

"Oh, hello. What can we do for you today?"

Anna chirped up,

"We've come about the Alpha Course, saw the banner outside."

They soon found out it was a very new concept. Jim Hordram had met the curate, who had taken over Alpha and asked if he could trial it at St Aidan's. They would be the first to run it in this part of the country. This would be in conjunction with St Peter's Catholic Church from the other side of town.

The Alpha Course was to be a series of evening sessions, one per week, over ten weeks. It included an Away Day called a Holy Spirit Day. Each session would start with a sit-down meal, and this would be followed by a talk. Then the participants would split into small groups to discuss the points raised.

The aim was for it to be a journey of discovery so that participants would examine the way in which the core Christian beliefs worked in our modern world. Also, how to relate faith in Jesus Christ to the way we conduct our busy lives today.

Having got the general idea, Lee wasn't sure it would really be for him. Religion was not of any great interest to him, which was his perception of what the course was.

"I'd like to think about it, please, before saying yes. Is that OK?"

"Of course it is. Please remember it begins in a few weeks, so if you could let us know fairly quickly, before the sixteenth of this month, it would help with the planning. We start the course on the fifth of January. It's all free, including the meals. There won't be any vicars there or anyone with a white collar on. It's designed to be relaxed and non-intimidating, and will be run by the members of Tillshott's two churches. You won't be committed to anything, so no pressure. You can also leave at any point you wish."

Anna felt the same way as Lee. She too was unsure, but her conversations with Margaret had raised many unanswered queries in her mind. Anna wanted to try and understand what made Margaret so sure about her faith and had given her the overwhelming conviction that their coming together, in the manner they did, was not by accident.

Anna was intrigued enough by these questions to feel she needed to investigate further.

One thing they both agreed on was that Margaret had, without a doubt, looked after them well, so the Alpha Course seemed a right and proper thing to do in her memory. After a short private chat outside, they went back in and asked to be enrolled onto it.

Even before the start date arrived, Lee was getting cold feet.

"I'm not too sure I want to do this course."

"Well, it's too late to back out now, Lee. They've included us in the catering numbers."

"OK then. S'pose we could just not turn up, though?"

"No, it wouldn't be right. We said we would go, and we will. After all, we owe it to Margaret to try. It won't kill us, will it?"

The first day of the course arrived and twenty-two people in total turned up. Some volunteers from the parish served the meal to them. The food was delicious and they all had an excellent glass of wine too.

After the meal was cleared away, they listened to the first talk and then split into three small groups to discuss the issues raised.

Lee was very quiet, saying almost nothing. He didn't know what to say, but in complete contrast Anna was in full swing, asking all sorts of questions and saying what she thought about the night's topic.

After they left to go home, Anna was still full of what they had discussed, commenting on how interesting she'd found the discussions and how she liked most of the others in her group.

Lee, on the other hand, made little comment but for some grunts here and there, as he felt appropriate. As the weeks went by, however, he started to show a bit more animation. He would begin to say when he agreed or thought something wasn't right.

Sometimes the discussions grew quite animated, even heated, as various factions agreed or disagreed on specific points. By the third week, four of the original twenty-two attendees had stopped coming.

Everything was going pretty well until the last session: the Away Day. After lunch, the delegates were asked if they would be prepared to make a commitment to Jesus and become New Christians.

Anna felt very comfortable with the idea, but Lee was a lot more hesitant. He thought of leaving the course at this point as he felt he couldn't make such a decision at the moment.

One of the team leaders asked if Lee would mind if he prayed for him.

Lee was OK with prayer, so he didn't feel too uncomfortable about it. This, though, was the point where things started to worry him. The man began to pray over him in the weirdest language Lee had ever heard. He sat there saying nothing for a while, feeling more and more uncomfortable. The words sounded more like a ritual than anything he considered Christian.

"Please excuse me," he said, then stood up and slowly moved out of the room towards the front entrance where he sat on the steps outside in the cold sunshine, not knowing what to make of it. Anna was still in there, and he wondered what she might be going through. What was going on?

Some of the strange-sounding prayers had also upset her. She didn't understand them at all. She had already made up her mind to join the Christian community, but this latest development caused her some severe doubts. Neither of them had ever thought of the Church of England as in any way strange; quite the opposite, in fact.

The last part of the day had caused them so much upset that they didn't talk until they arrived back home.

"It's not supposed to be like this…" Anna said, becoming emotional.

"No, it's not. I didn't understand what on earth they were saying. I was shocked, to be honest. What did you make of it?"

"For me, everything was OK before that happened, Lee… Oh, this is crazy. Now, I'm not so sure."

Two hours later the doorbell rang. It was Jim Hordram.

It took many hours of talking over many weeks for him to dispel Anna's remaining doubts. But Lee was not convinced and decided this wasn't for him. He refused to discuss it further. The problem was over something Jim called Praying in Tongues, as guided by the Holy Spirit. This was mouthing spiritual thoughts and prayers in a manner that defied language. It sounded different every time. In fact, this wasn't a real language; it was speaking deeply felt prayers and thoughts in an audible spiritual way.

Lee was not convinced at all by this explanation, saying the Bible clearly stated the Apostles were given the ability to speak in other tongues. But these were spoken languages, to enable them to spread the word.

"But not in gibberish." With a shrug, he withdrew from the conversation. He went into the kitchen and put the kettle on.

Anna, though, listened and seemed to have more understanding of what Jim was trying to explain to her.

Two weeks later, she started going to St Aidan's Sunday services.

Lee stayed at home. They hadn't talked much about it over the preceding two weeks, but Anna felt it was what she wanted to do.

It would be some considerable time before Lee would set foot in St Aidan's again. It became a bone of contention between them as the months progressed.

Anna went most Sundays, and sometimes, if it was cold or wet, Lee would pick her up after the service in the car. She never pressed him to accompany her or tried to make him rethink his decision, instead reassuring him that she loved him whether he attended church or not.

"Maybe I'll come along with you one day, but I don't know when that might be… and certainly not if there's any more mumbo-jumbo," he told her.

Some months after the Alpha Course, Anna was baptised. Lee went with her to the service, but it didn't change his own attitude towards the faith. He decided, however, he did believe in God, and would support Anna in her decision to join the Church. Any commitment beyond that he felt he couldn't make. At least, not yet.

Shortly after Anna had been baptised, she woke early one morning feeling nauseous. She skipped breakfast. It was the third day in a row this had happened. She glanced at the calendar – 4 March 1986 – and recollected seeing in a newspaper a day or so ago an article about an American submarine running aground in Ireland. Why on earth did she think of this? What an odd and totally irrelevant thing to remember… Anna felt spaced out, disoriented and most certainly more than a little strange.

She turned to speak to Lee, but suddenly dashed into the bathroom where she was sick.

"You know, this feels rather like morning sickness. Hope I'm not preggy…"

Lee dismissed the idea and thought it must be something she'd eaten.

But it happened again the following day, and Anna was sure by now that she was pregnant. She decided to ask the hospital if they would run a check to put her mind at rest.

The result was a surprise. It was positive. The idea of a child appearing on the horizon was quite a shock.

This was certainly not part of their plan for the future. After ten years of marriage, the idea of having a family was not yet even on their agenda.

Nature had, once again, produced one of its little surprises.

Chapter 25:

The Funeral

March 1986

Jim was with Lee working on a contract in the planning office, for the supply and fitting of a series of new stairs and windows in an extensive renovation project of eight local houses. They were starting to discuss the timing of the deliveries when the phone on Lee's desk began to ring.

"Can I speak to Lee, please?"

"It's Lee here. Is that you, Anna?"

"Yes, love. Sorry I didn't recognise your voice. I'm calling from work and it's a bit noisy here today. Can you hear me?"

"Yes, perfectly."

"Your mum has just been brought in. I think you should try and come to see her as soon as you can. I don't want to alarm you, but I don't think she looks too well."

"OK. It's almost twelve now so I'll come in the next hour or so."

"See you then. Love you lots."

Jim knew Anna would never call from the hospital unless it was urgent.

"I think maybe you'd better get off to the hospital straight away, Lee. I'll finish this. We're almost done anyway. Hope it's not as bad as it sounds. Give Anna our love."

Lee needed fuel, so while he was in the filling station, he grabbed a pork pie to eat for his lunch. He proceeded to gobble it down while driving, giving himself chronic indigestion. As he entered the hospital car park, he was burping and his stomach was rumbling like a cement mixer.

Luckily for him, the car park wasn't full and he found an empty space almost immediately.

On approaching the ward, he was prevented from going in by Sally, a staff nurse he knew who was a good friend of Anna's. She asked him to wait as the doctors were with his mum.

Screens were around the bed, and it was apparent there were a couple of nurses and at least one doctor in attendance.

He was alarmed by the activity and went to sit by the nurses' desk to ask various questions. He received few answers, though, which didn't do his anxiety level any good whatsoever.

Lee didn't like hospitals one bit. He even found visiting them stressful. He didn't want to be here, or anywhere near.

When he was finally allowed to go in and see Maureen, he didn't think she looked too ill. He had thought she would be in a lot more distress, and was delighted he was able to hold a normal conversation with her.

Her voice was a tad slurred, and she seemed tired. Otherwise she was a reasonable colour, not looking as bad as he had imagined he'd find her.

Over the following days, Lee went to visit his mum every evening, sometimes with Anna. On one occasion, he dodged behind a corner in the corridor when he thought he saw his father walking out of the ward.

That night Lee found it difficult to get to sleep. He hadn't seen his father for so many years that the sighting unsettled him. Anna was on night duty for a week, filling in for one of the other nurses who had gone sick, and he missed not having her to confide in.

Before leaving her bedside today, a smiling and enthusiastic Lee had told his mum that Anna was pregnant.

"Mum, you're going to be a grandma."

Maureen put her hand on his arm and squeezed it tenderly as a tear ran down her face.

"I'm so pleased, Stanleigh. You are so lucky to have such a lovely wife."

"We only found out for certain yesterday. After all these years... it was a bit of a, well... a bit of a surprise."

"I'm sure it will be fine. Anna will be a wonderful mother."

"How do you feel about looking after a little one like me all over again?"

Maureen smiled at him, closing her eyes.

"I'm tired, Stanleigh. I'm going to have a sleep now. I'll see you tomorrow."

"OK, Mum. I'll see you tomorrow evening. I'll make sure I ask Anna to pop by in the morning."

Lee leant over and kissed his mum. He pulled up the bedcover to keep her warm, smoothed it neatly and left for home. He hoped she was pleased with his news.

At 3.15 the following morning, 11 March, the phone started ringing, waking Lee. It was Sally from his mother's ward. She seemed upset and he guessed from the tone of her voice what she was about to say.

Maureen, the mother he loved so dearly, had passed away in her sleep at a little before 2 a.m. She was only sixty-four.

There was a second's pause. Lee swallowed hard and fought to stay calm.

"Thank you for phoning, Sally," he said calmly.

Then he replaced the receiver and burst into tears.

For the next hour, he sat on the bed, crying his heart out.

He blamed his father for his mum's death and himself for not trying hard enough to protect her from his dad's bullying and vicious behaviour.

He blamed himself for not going back home for so long to see her.

And he blamed himself for a million other things he imagined he should, or could, have done.

But it was too late now. Maureen Agazzi would never see her grandchild.

"Oh, Anna, where are you? I need you here with me," he said aloud.

Anna was hard at work in Casualty and no one was able to tell her of Maureen's death until a few moments before her shift ended at 7.30 a.m. when her friend Sally came down to let her know the sad news.

Both girls were upset, but Anna was more worried and anxious about how Lee would have taken the news of his mother's death. He was at home on his own, and she was sure he would be in a dreadful state.

As she came in the front door, Lee almost collapsed into her arms.

He was utterly distraught, crying and asking her over and over, "Why... Why did they let her die?"

Anna couldn't answer him in a way he would have accepted at that moment, so she held him until he went to sleep in the comfort of her arms.

In spite of having a dreadful night, and against Anna's advice, Lee insisted on going in to work, although arriving late, saying he would be better off with his usual routine rather than becoming depressed and upset sitting around at home.

Jim and Tom, fully aware of the situation, kept a close eye on him throughout the day, albeit from a distance.

On the face of it, Lee appeared to have done well in life, but hidden only a little below the surface was the old Stanleigh. Sometimes he would get fixated on something, which in his mind seemed to be an insurmountable problem. It would override everything else, and it wouldn't let go of him. Small, sometimes insignificant, things would assume unreasonable proportions inside his head until he felt it would burst. He couldn't talk about it, and to help himself deal with whatever the problem was, he would blank things out of his mind, upsetting Anna at times. That did agitate him, and although he wanted to explain things to her, he couldn't find a way to do so. He was terrified that one day she would leave him, think he was an idiot or stop loving him. There were times he wanted the world to stop so he could get off. He sometimes wondered whether the trauma would go away if he were dead…

A few days later Anna opened a letter addressed to Mr and Mrs S. Agazzi.

This formally advised them Maureen had passed away and the funeral was to be held at St Peter's Church at 11:30 on 2 April 1986.

She knew Lee was not going to find this easy to deal with. He dreaded the thought of meeting his father again, but nothing was going to stop him and Anna from going to his mum's funeral.

Lee hadn't seen or spoken to his father since that terrible day thirteen years before, 5 August 1973, a date he could not eradicate from his mind. Each and every year it became a big unspoken anniversary, though one that was never mentioned. Every year, on the dot and like a never-ending tape recording, it played out in his mind, minute by minute.

Lee never said a word about this and kept it to himself.

The morning before the funeral, Father Shaun O'Malley, who was taking the service, called him at work. Lee's father had asked the priest if he could arrange a meeting with his son, in the church offices, about an hour before the funeral.

Lee didn't know what to say, so he mumbled a load of nonsense into the phone, forcing the clergyman to ask him to calm down and repeat it.

After a while, Lee said he would agree to meet his dad but only on condition Shaun O'Malley, Jim Hordram and Anna would be present as well.

"Well, that may be a bit difficult, Lee, but I'll try."

Lee couldn't admit to anyone, even to his darling Anna, after all these years, that he was still afraid of his father.

His enduring memory of their last encounter was not a happy one. He did not want to be left alone with this man, not even for a single moment.

The following morning at a few minutes before ten, Lee and Anna arrived at the church office. "Your father is already here, Lee," Father O'Malley told him. "Please be careful what you say. I understand how you must be feeling, but this is your dear mother's funeral. It mustn't be remembered for the wrong reasons. Oh, and I forgot to mention, Jim has arrived too."

Lee looked and half smiled at Anna, squeezing her hand tightly. He made no comment. They went into the office together.

Sitting to one side of Jim was a tall, thin, balding old man.

This certainly wasn't the person Lee had seen in the hospital, the one he'd thought was his father.

The elderly man glanced up as the young couple entered the room. His eyes were red and sunken in his head; his expression one of complete devastation.

His clothes were clean and smart, but somewhat old-fashioned. He bore not the slightest resemblance to the well-built, bullying, and prosperous bank manager Lee remembered having for a father.

In stark contrast to his father's appearance, Lee and Anna were in dark new modern attire and looked smart and sophisticated.

Lee was shocked by the change in his father. He hardly recognised him.

His memories were of a larger-than-life arrogant bully who'd tried to destroy Lee's life and his mother's too.

A tear started to run down John Agazzi's face as he looked up at his son.

Shaun O'Malley was the one to break the silence.

"Lee, your father wants to speak to you in private before the service. If Jim and I go into the kitchen for a while, please will you listen to him?"

"Only if Anna stays with me." Lee was adamant on this point. He was looking daggers at his father as he spoke.

John nodded his agreement, so Shaun tapped Jim on the shoulder to indicate they should go into the kitchen.

"We'll be next door, Lee, OK?"

"OK."

Lee and Anna sat down a few feet away from John and Lee stared at the father he hated and feared, now seeing a man he didn't know or recognise.

"Stanleigh... I... I want to say I'm so sorry for all the trouble I have caused to you and Mum... my little Maureen. I never wanted to hurt either of you.

"I let my temper and my pride get out of control far too many times, and I am truly sorry. Father Shaun has tried for years to help me put things right with you. I did try to come when you got married and many times since I try to go and see you, but I was too proud to back down, and I couldn't try explaining to you these things. I walked round to your house so many times, but I always went back home. Mum never knew... my little Maureen never knew. I never told her."

Tears had started rolling down John's face.

There was an awkward silence.

"So why now, Dad? After all these years. Feeling guilty, are you... sorry for yourself, eh?"

Anna squeezed her husband's hand, making him turn his head to look at her.

"Lee... not now, love, not today. Please. This day is in memory of your mum, don't spoil it."

But her husband wasn't listening to her. She could see it in his eyes, the suppressed loathing and resentment, the thirteen years of hurt, all simmering inside him.

John spoke again.

"Stanleigh, if I could change things between us... I would die before I make them any worse. If I told you I have always loved you, and that after you left my house, I cried myself to sleep at night, would you believe me? Because I did. And many times since as well."

Anna could not help pitying the old man.

She could see John Agazzi was trying to apologise to his son and at last come to terms with all the damage he'd caused... and see too how Lee was fighting to control his reactions after suffering a lifetime of rejection and bitterness at the hands of this wreck of a man.

Lee stared at the pathetic figure in front of him. He wanted, needed, to feel some love and affection for his father, but couldn't let himself believe any of the things he was hearing.

His father could have spoken to him on many occasions over the last thirteen years, but he hadn't.

So why would Lee want anything to do with him now?

Suddenly, his pent-up emotions erupted. He leant forward, pointing an accusing finger at his father, eyes streaming. He screamed:

"You killed my mum… didn't you? DIDN'T YOU? You bloody rotten bastard. You fucking killed her!"

Anna stood up and tried to pull him out of the room, frightened by his reaction. She had never seen him in such a state. But Lee wouldn't budge. His face turned dark red and he was shaking in a violent rage.

For the first time in his life, he had his father hemmed into a corner and wasn't going to let him out. He wouldn't lose this opportunity to ram home his advantage after all the years of misery and pain. Lee wanted his father to know how it felt to suffer.

John was weeping now, his head held in his hands.

"Mi dispiace … so sorry," he sobbed, almost inaudibly.

"I bet you are. Well, too bloody late now… too bloody late, isn't it? I'd like to… to…"

Lee jumped up, startling Anna. She grabbed at his arm to try and restrain him, terrified at the thought of what he might do. He shook her off, such was his anger. Lee stared at his father, and for a split second, with his fists squeezed so tight his fingernails almost cut into the palm of his hands, he wanted to kill him, to tear him apart with his bare hands. He wanted to beat him to a pulp.

Lee screwed up his eyes; banged his chair back against the wall with such force it split the seat. Turning, he stormed out of the room and into the fresh air.

Anna rushed after him.

It was now well past 11, the funeral was due to begin in the next few minutes.

Lee had felt the need to claim a moral victory.

But what a dreadful hollow feeling it turned out to be. It wasn't at all how he had imagined it. It didn't make him feel any better or give him any of the satisfaction he'd thought or hoped it would.

Instead, it made him feel ill. He'd wanted to be loved and accepted by his father. Now, after all this time, when his dad had at last tried, in a way, to put things right, Lee couldn't take it. He couldn't handle the situation at all.

He leant back against the stone wall and banged his head three or four times hard against it while struggling to settle his breathing.

Years of suppressed emotion and pure frustration filled his eyes and heart.

Anna held his hands and tried her best to comfort him.

"It's too late, Anna… it's too late for me now. I can't let it go. I want him to suffer like he made Mum suffer… I hate his bloody guts. I hate him, Anna…"

Lee's head dropped forward as tears ran down his face, leaving a wet patch on his shirt.

All Anna could do was to hold him in her arms until the storm of misery was over.

What upset Lee the most was that he hated himself even more than he hated his father. He wasn't much of a man, was he? He felt ashamed… humiliated by his own weaknesses. In his mind he was still where he had been thirteen years before: outside the front door of the family home as it slammed shut in his face. Lee knew he wanted to put the past behind him and move on. He was thirty years old now, not a boy anymore, and should start acting his age as a responsible adult. He couldn't remain a frightened child. The loss of his mother and the stress of today's events made him feel ill. He wanted to run away and hide. He felt a complete failure.

After a short while, Jim Hordram came out to find Anna and give her a gentle reminder. He whispered,

"The funeral is about to start."

"OK, Jim. Thank you. Please can you tell Shaun we won't be a moment?

"Come on, love," she said to Lee. "We must go in now. You are loved by everyone here. Remember, we have a new family member on the way too. This isn't the time to spoil the memory of your mum and the happy thoughts we have about her grandchild. You wouldn't want that, would you?"

"No. I… er… oh, no. Never mind."

Lee put his arm around Anna. He hugged her tightly to him and gave her a gentle kiss. Slowly they walked into the church and sat down. Lee leant towards her, speaking close into her ear.

"I love you so much. Don't know what I'd do without you."

The smile she gave him then warmed and strengthened him to face the ordeal of his mother's funeral.

"And I love you too," Anna whispered in reply, taking his hand and not letting go until the Funeral Mass was over.

Chapter 26:

Creaking Doors and White Lilies

May 1986

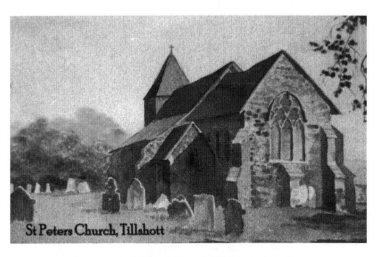

St Peter's church Tillshott

A month or so after his mother's funeral, Lee felt drawn to enter Saint Peter's Church again. As he went in through the main door, something at the corner of his eye caught his attention.

He swung around.

"Mum, is that you... Mum?"

He started to scan the church's interior, feeling panic-stricken. Was he alone?

"Mum?" he called aloud.

There was no reply. Lee had been sure he'd seen her, standing gesturing to him from the far side of the church. However, there was no one visible there, and only an eerie silence within the building.

He walked the length of the nave, wondering if he was imagining things. In the next moment he thought he saw her again, this time up near the altar. He was frantic now, staring in every direction.

"Mum..."

But there was only the same eerie silence.

He hesitated, moving up towards the altar rail, his senses on heightened alert to hear even the slightest sound. He bumped into a pew and almost tripped on a loose floor tile. After a moment he reached the rail where he stood still, holding his breath.

He looked into every corner of the building. He was sure he was alone but felt drawn to the altar rail where he stood and looked around once more. He was feeling pretty spooked, and his pulse was racing. He'd started shaking; he was sweating. Strange thoughts were running through his mind. Was he going mad? Was he dreaming... or was he himself already dead perhaps?

A sudden creaking noise broke the calm. The solid old church door seemed to be opening of its own accord, the hinges squeaking in protest as it did. Within seconds, a tiny and rather elderly lady dressed entirely in white appeared to glide through the doorway.

Lee almost fainted. Then the apparition spoke to him.

"Hello, are you OK? Is there anything I can do for you? I've come to replace the flowers. I won't be more than a few minutes."

"Er... no... well, yes, I'm alright, thanks."

Lee was breathing so fast his hands were tingling.

He decided it was time for him to leave. Saying goodbye to the elderly flower arranger as he went out into the daylight, he heaved a great sigh of relief.

As he walked up the path, he was sure he could hear a voice calling to him from somewhere behind him.

"Stanleigh, don't go... please."

He swung around, looking over the entire churchyard. There was nothing, nobody. There was no one anywhere in sight, not a single soul.

He was sure it was his mum's voice that had called to him, but it couldn't have been. She was dead.

He briefly stood still, wondering what to do. As he started walking towards his mother's grave, he noticed another recent burial only a few yards to the right. He glanced down and saw some red carnations leaning against the headstone. They looked fresh, almost as if they had been placed there within the last couple of hours. He bent down, lifting one of the flowers to his nose before replacing it.

It was quite a chilly day with a stiff breeze. Lee pulled up his jacket collar to keep himself warm. He walked on.

Within a short distance, he was standing by his mum's grave. A great sadness filled him. As he stood there, looking down, he mumbled to himself, "Mum, why are you calling me, what do you want?"

There was, of course, no answer. He stood there looking down at the ground for the moment and then closed his eyes.

Slowly, over the next few minutes, he became aware of an increasing warmth spreading through him. With it came an intense feeling of calm and a peace he could not comprehend. It seemed to overwhelm him until his arms and legs felt heavy.

After a while, the sound of approaching footsteps made him jump.

He heard a familiar voice.

"Hello, Lee, I thought it was you. How are you, my boy? And how is your lovely wife?"

It was Father Shaun O'Malley.

"Anna is fine, thank you, how are you? I thought I would come to see Mum's grave and pay my respects."

"Oh, I'm OK – on my way to see if we can come up with some good ideas for how to use dear Margaret's money. I'm going to see Joe Parson now, and I'm late, as usual. Oh, dear, please excuse me. I can't stop. God bless you two! And remind me to have a chat with you both when we can get a moment together. Don't forget now, will you?"

Shaun dashed away, muttering to himself. As he did so, Lee felt the stillness return. He lost all track of time. A sense of complete tranquillity and warmth flooded through him, almost making it feel like a lovely summer's afternoon. After a while, he turned away from the grave and began walking back to his car. As he did so, he felt the natural chill of the day returning.

He was aware of feeling completely at peace within himself, something he hadn't felt since the first call he'd received from Anna telling him his mum was very ill. This was unlike any sensation he'd experienced in his entire life, and he could not explain it.

St Peter's Gravestones

As Lee drove back to work, he decided not to mention any of today's events to Anna. What could he say? She might think he'd been in the pub and had one too many.

A week went by, and Lee still hadn't made any reference to his strange encounter.

Late on Saturday afternoon he and Anna decided to go shopping as the fridge was almost empty.

Anna's working hours made it difficult for them to find the time to go to the supermarket together, so this was quite a rare event. Over the last year, she'd got into a routine of shopping late in the evenings on her way home from the hospital.

As they were pushing a trolley piled high with food towards the checkout, they noticed Shaun O'Malley waving at them.

"Hello, you two. By Jove, that was a magnificent display of flowers you put on your mum's grave the other day, Lee. Grand altogether they were. White, of course. Very suitable. Well, won't hold you up – cheerio for now. God bless you both."

Anna looked at Lee, who had gone rather pale.

"You never mentioned you'd visited the grave. That was a nice thing to do."

"It wasn't me. I… er… I mean, I went to see it but I didn't leave any flowers there. There weren't any when I visited and I didn't have any with me or anything…" his voice trailed off.

"So when did you go there?" Anna asked him encouragingly.

"Oh, it was a few days ago. Can we… er… talk about it later?"

She was puzzled by his reaction.

"Well, yes, of course. No problem."

"I'll tell you about it when we get home. It isn't easy to explain. Something strange happened to me there. Spooky even. Let's get back, shall we?"

Anna was becoming more curious by the minute. Nothing was mentioned about his graveyard visit again until well after they returned home. Sitting with some tea and a nice big slice of Bakewell tart, Lee started to tell her what had taken place and Anna listened carefully to every word.

He finished his story and sat back with a sigh. He was relieved to have told her all about it and thankful Anna hadn't laughed or made him feel even the least little bit stupid.

"I don't think it's so strange," she said. "I hear similar stories from people in the hospital all the time. Your mind may be trying to find peace after a sad event, or it could be a spiritual awakening. I think you should go and speak to either Shaun or Jim – see what they make of it. I wouldn't worry about it in the meantime. It's left you feeling a lot calmer, hasn't it?"

"Well, yes, but it doesn't explain the flowers, does it? And since we've been together, there was only ever my mum who would call me Stanleigh."

"Well, I can't explain it. I suppose Shaun could have been mistaken about the flowers?"

"Maybe. I think I will put some there," Lee said. "I should have done it before now."

On Tuesday lunchtime as Lee went to buy a sandwich, he also bought a big bunch of white lilies in a paper wrap.

He removed the attached card with the price on it, stuffed it in his pocket, and wandered up the road to St Peter's churchyard, to place the flowers on his mother's grave.

He looked over the area for a sign of anything being moved, but there was nothing strange that he could see – although he did notice there was no sign of any flowers having been there at all.

One or two of the nearby graves had vases on them, but they were empty and looked as if they'd stayed untouched for quite some time.

Chapter 27:

Denise

April – December 1986

Over the months following Maureen's funeral, Anna became larger, and there came a point when she had to stop work as the physical effort her job required made her so tired she could no longer cope. As the big day drew nearer, she discussed with Lee the idea of having the baby at home, but her doctor advised against it and the suggestion was rejected, much to Lee's relief.

He told Anna he didn't want to be at the birth or anywhere near the hospital either. The very thought of it made him feel sick and faint.

Anna laughed understandingly and told him,

"I couldn't cope if you were there anyway."

Secretly though she was a bit upset. But she knew

Lee and had always realised this would be the way of things.

Lee had never wanted children. They'd talked this over many times during the first years of their marriage. But now was hardly the time to discuss the matter any further. It was a little late after all.

Over the last few months, they had started to think about names. If it was a boy, it might be so-and-so, and if a girl it could be... Denise. Of all the names they considered, they both opted for Denise. And so it was. Lee was sure Anna was going to have a baby girl.

As the due date was getting nearer, Anna's waters broke.

It was Lee's lucky day. It happened during an ante-natal check-up his wife was having at the hospital.

After that everything proceeded pretty quickly and at about 5 a.m. on 12 December 1986, Anna presented her husband with a seven-pound daughter: Denise Suzanne Agazzi.

Lee got a phone call soon after the baby was born, from Anna's nursing friend Sally Sturn.

"Hello, Lee, you OK? You have a lovely baby girl! She weighs seven pounds exactly. Anna is fine but very tired. You can come and see her and Denise whenever you want. If you ask for me at the main desk, I'll come and take you ."

"Thanks for phoning me, Sally, I'll get there as soon as I can," he said.

"You'll easily recognise your new daughter, Lee. She's a mirror image of her mother."

"Wow," he said. "That will be a sight to see."

Before he was due to leave, Lee phoned Tom and Gina to tell them they were now grandparents. His mother-in-law answered after one ring. "Is Anna alright? Is the baby OK? Are you OK?"

"Yes, Mum," he laughed. "Stop fretting, everything is fine. You have a seven-pound baby granddaughter. Her name is Denise."

"Oh, thank goodness everything is alright. We were so worried!" Gina said. "Denise is a lovely name. Do you need anything, Lee?" she added.

"No, thanks, Mum. I'm off to see them both for the first time. I'll call you in an hour or so." Then he dialled Jim and Sarah to tell them the good news before the short drive to the hospital.

Family life soon overtook the Agazzi family. What had always been a quiet, orderly lifestyle, changed out of all recognition as the months rolled by. The demands of their young daughter made sure of that. Lee became a doting father. He'd adored his daughter on sight and was always happy to play with her at every opportunity. Anna blossomed in her new role. She enjoyed seeing Lee so happy and joining in with day-to-day family events. He even changed Denise's nappy sometimes. Anna had never thought to see the day Lee changed a dirty nappy. It made her laugh, always trying to make sure he didn't notice.

They were the picture-perfect healthy family until one unforgettable morning. Denise had developed a very high temperature and was somewhat listless. Anna thought she might need some antibiotics to help reduce her fever, but considered this to be typical of the infections most young children seemed to contract, so was not too worried.

Denise, now a little more than eighteen months old, had never before suffered from any real health issues other than the occasional cold.

Anna telephoned her GP and made an appointment for twelve o'clock.

Lee went off to work as usual, leaving Anna at home with Denise. This wasn't their regular routine as more often than not one of them would take the baby to her grandmother Gina, who often took care of her during the daytime.

Anna had changed her working hours at the hospital and now only worked three days each week. Although she was still working shifts, Lee had no more lonely nights to contend with.

After kissing her husband and seeing him off to work, Anna started getting herself and Denise some breakfast, as she did most days. This morning the baby was refusing food and crying more than usual. Then she was sick down her nice new pink jumper. This was very unlike Denise, who was rarely under the weather.

As Anna tried to encourage her daughter to eat some breakfast, she became aware Denise was having breathing problems. She was struggling, her chest labouring, and it seemed to be getting worse by the minute.

Anna became so concerned that she wrapped Denise in a warm blanket and decided to drive her straight to the hospital instead of going to her GP.

On arrival at the Casualty department, Denise was admitted at once and placed in an isolation unit as a precaution. The doctor suspected measles and performed some tests to confirm this diagnosis. Meanwhile, Denise had become even more agitated and was given oxygen to help with her breathing. She turned a purple-red colour, and her face started to appear blotchy and wet with perspiration. She was moving in an awkward manner and it was obvious she was in considerable distress.

As her young daughter struggled, Anna watched from the other side of a window. There was nothing she could do. Two nurses and a doctor were trying to make Denise comfortable.

A doctor popped out to ask Anna if her baby had received the full quota of vaccinations. She confirmed every single one had been given, and at exactly the prescribed time.

A few years ago, Anna recalled, she had seen a young child with similar symptoms brought in by ambulance to the Emergency unit. A few days later, the child sadly died. The cause was meningitis.

Anna tried to remain calm but was terrified that something similar could happen to Denise. She felt waves of nausea within her as she fought to cope. As a nurse, when dealing with her patients she could remain detached and professional, but this was now her own child in distress, and Anna found it difficult, if not almost impossible, to deal with. This was not at all like her. Anna had always been a sensible, logical and confident person, and not one who was prone to panic. Her nursing colleagues went to her if they felt unsure about any situation. Anna was always the dependable one.

But now she felt out of control and helpless.

Lunchtime came and went. Anna's friend Sally heard on the hospital grapevine that Denise had been admitted to the Paediatric ward. So she popped over to see her, bringing a sandwich and something to drink, and to offer her some support.

Anna thanked Sally but didn't feel much like eating anything.

At 6 p.m. one of the senior paediatric doctors came to speak with her.

"Mrs Agazzi? Ah, Anna... as you are well aware, Denise has a nasty infection. We are certain it's measles. Has your daughter been in contact with anyone you know of who might have contracted a fever during the last ten days?"

"No, no one at all. She's only been with me, my husband and my parents, and we are all fine."

At first, the hospital had thought Denise might have meningitis, but the tests said otherwise, much to Anna's relief. Now on antiviral drugs plus antibiotics, Denise was responding well to treatment. The doctor felt it was unusual for measles to take this form, but the blood tests confirmed it was the correct diagnosis. He was certain Denise would be much better in a day or two.

As the doctor was leaving the office, Lee appeared at the door. He'd arrived home from work and picked up the message Anna had left on their answering machine for him an hour earlier.

"What the hell's going on?" he asked her. "What's wrong with Deni?"

Lee was in a panic. As he peered through the glass at his beautiful daughter, the colour drained from his face, forcing him to sit down and put his head between his knees.

The next thing he remembered was someone tapping him on the cheek. It was Anna. He had fainted, and she was trying to bring him around. His feet were up on a chair, and Anna was on the floor, holding his head in her lap and smiling at him.

For a brief moment, Lee couldn't remember where he was or how he'd got there.

Although his fainting created an additional problem, it was a brief but welcome distraction from Anna's concern for Denise.

As soon as Lee was sitting back on a chair and drinking some water, Anna explained to him what the doctor told her, but Lee still felt so embarrassed about fainting, he didn't react or say much.

He hoped Denise would be home in time for Easter. It was Monday, 13 March, and Easter was only two weeks away. He would be able to spend more time at home then. He laughed to himself as he struggled to rationalise his scattered thoughts.

Twenty-four hours later, Denise seemed to be feeling better. Her breathing improved, and she started causing mayhem, throwing toys on the floor and calling out for her father.

The following morning Anna sat on her daughter's bed, reading her one of her favourite stories about Pooh Bear. Denise lay there, eyes closed, sucking her thumb and listening to the story. As soon as Anna noticed she had gone to sleep, she decided to pop out for a bite to eat herself since it was past lunchtime. Twenty minutes later, upon returning to her daughter's room, her whole world was turned upside down. Denise was lying still on the bed, covered in wires and tubes.

Something had gone wrong. A young nurse was standing by the bed, adjusting one of the monitors.

As Denise was still behind a window in the isolation unit, Anna tapped on the glass and the nurse came over and spoke to her.

Within a few minutes of Anna leaving to get some food, Denise had taken a sudden and unexpected turn for the worse. The nurses were trying to keep her vital signs monitored and they were running another round of tests to ascertain what had caused the relapse. Anna felt a real sense of panic. The thought of losing their daughter was unthinkable. She was fighting back frightened tears as a ward doctor, one she didn't recognise, approached her.

"Mrs Agazzi?"

"Yes, I'm Anna Agazzi."

"May I speak with you in the office for a moment, please?"

"Yes, of course. What is the problem with Denise? She was quite happy an hour ago."

"Yes, I know, but she has become increasingly stressed and her breathing is very laboured. The next few hours could be vital. I believe you are a nurse here at St Andrews? I think it would be helpful if you could stay with your daughter for the next day, please."

"Yes, of course I will. Although I should just phone my husband."

Only a short while ago Denise was calling for her daddy. Now Anna felt that things had taken a definite turn for the worse.

She panicked, not knowing what she was going to say to Lee. Not knowing how he would react, worried her.

She phoned his office number.

A lady with a classy-sounding voice answered the call. Anna didn't think they had spoken before.

"Good afternoon, Slater and Parkes, can I help you?"

"Is Lee there, please?"

"Who is calling?"

"It's his wife. May I speak to him, please? It's urgent."

"Of course, I'll put you through."

There was a click on the line. Lee said hello, and Anna tried to ask him as calmly as possible if he would come to the hospital as Denise wasn't as well as she had been. Lee at once felt hot and sweaty. Anna sounded shaky and not at all like her usual self.

"What's the matter with Deni… and you?" he asked.

"They don't know, and I'm a bit worried."

"Er… OK, I'm on my way. I'll be as quick as I can."

The ten-minute drive to the hospital felt like the longest he could ever remember. The traffic lights were against him, roadworks slowed him down, and once he arrived, he couldn't find anywhere to park.

Lee left his car with the hazard lights on next to an ambulance bay, and dashed into the hospital.

As he arrived, Anna was sitting outside the Paediatric ward.

"What on earth's happened?" he asked.

"They don't know, but I think it might be a bit more serious than we thought. I don't know what to do… I can't do a bloody thing!" Anna never swore. Never, never, ever.

Lee knew something must have gone dramatically wrong to cause her to lose control.

However, it seemed in the twenty minutes it had taken him to get to the hospital, Denise's breathing had vastly improved and the monitors were now displaying regular readings.

Lee put his arms around his wife and she wept as he held her.

"Deni will be OK. They won't let anything happen to her. Her breathing seems to be almost back to normal now. Try not to worry." He wasn't as confident as he sounded but tried to comfort Anna.

There was nothing either of them could do. It would be a waiting game.

Ten minutes later, two doctors, together with Anna's friend, Dr Carol Nathan, walked into the ward to look at Denise.

Lee could hear a muffled conversation as the doctors discussed some additional medication. Then one of them spoke briefly to the nurse before they departed.

Carol came up to Anna, smiled and gave her shoulder a light squeeze, to comfort her.

"Hello, Anna… Lee. Please don't worry, both of you. Everything is under control. I'll come back in a short while to have a chat with you."

Then she hurried away after the other doctors.

Within a few seconds of the doctors leaving, an alarm went off and all hell let loose.

Doctors and nurses flocked from all directions and curtains were pulled around the unit.

Denise's cardiac monitor was showing a flatline. Anna saw and knew what this indicated.

She leapt up and cried out in desperation. Lee grabbed hold of her to prevent her from crashing into the glass wall.

Two nurses and another doctor rushed into the unit.

Anna was in a state of collapse. Lee grabbed her as she slowly slid to the floor. He hadn't seen the monitor. He was so concerned for Anna, he hadn't realised what seemed to be happening to their daughter.

Anna was in shock now, tears streaming down her face. She looked up at Lee, her eyes staring.

"Deni's heart's stopped. She's dead, Lee, Deni's dead."

"What… How d'you know? What do you mean? No, she can't be. Oh, dear God, help us! No, no… No, please, not Denise. Please, God, don't let her die, *please*…"

Lee's whole body started to shake, and he was stumbling over his words in panic.

He watched in horror as two more nurses and a technician came rushing in with different machines. Anna was past the point of noticing anything and sat in a crumpled heap on his lap.

A doctor appeared and said something they couldn't hear before he dashed off again.

Lee sat there, feeling numb, as if something inside him had died rather than his beautiful, innocent child.

He held on to Anna, cradling her shaking body in his arms. Their whole world seemed to have come to an abrupt end.

All this happened in the space of two minutes.

It would be a long four or five minutes more, which seemed like an eternity, before any of the medical team reappeared.

Carol came through the door and pulled up a chair between Lee and Anna. She put her arms around them in a gesture of reassurance.

"It's alright, Anna. Everything is OK again."

Anna was staring into space. When Carol received no response, she grew more persistent,

"Anna, ANNA… listen to me! Denise is OK. The monitor has a fault. Panic over. Denise's heart is pumping beautifully. Please believe me, your little one is fine. Her pulse is strong and regular, and we have put in a new machine. I'm so sorry you were sitting here when it happened."

The sheer horror of a machine failing in the way it just had was not something Anna had experienced before in her entire nursing career. It left an indelible mark on her, and her confidence in the monitors would never be quite the same again.

Thirty-six hours later, Denise's temperature had returned to normal, and she was once again asking for her daddy.

Anna, who spent the last two nights sleeping beside her, now looked utterly drained.

Finally, she was so hungry she gave in, and went down to the canteen for something to eat and drink.

As her nerves were so on edge, she asked one of the nurses if she would phone Lee at work to tell him how much better Denise was. She didn't want her wavering voice to alarm him.

Lee arrived at the hospital about an hour later. All Denise's tubes and sensors had been removed, and she was playing with her fluffy dog. As Lee appeared from the corridor, Denise saw him coming and started crying and calling to him.

"Daddy... Daddy..."

She stretched out her hands to him as she sat upright in bed and Lee took her in his arms, holding her close to him as if his very life depended on it. Denise was crying as she clung on to her father, refusing to let go.

Lee held and cuddled her for a while until she calmed down enough to fall asleep in his arms, sucking her thumb. He sat with her, sitting on the end of the bed, holding and comforting his darling daughter until Anna returned about ten minutes later. That night, having made sure Denise was settled, Anna went back home to sleep. She sat on the edge of the bed as still as a statue. She didn't speak, didn't move. Anna was mentally exhausted. Her beautiful blonde hair hung limp and bedraggled on her shoulders, and her eyes looked red and strained.

Lee kissed his wife on the forehead. He undressed her with great care, laying her down on her side and covering her with the duvet. Finally, he got into bed himself, put his arms around Anna, cuddling her like a child, and proceeded to rock her to sleep. Only when he was sure she was resting did he allow himself to relax and shut his own eyes.

The shock of the last couple of days had taken a heavy toll on them, so it came as a huge relief when the following morning, the hospital considered Denise was well enough to go home.

At about eleven o'clock, Lee and Anna arrived to collect their precious daughter.

Denise was almost back to her usual mischievous self within hours of returning home, the only noticeable difference being the way she kept asking for her daddy. It became a lot more persistent than usual.

Lee held Deni, thumb in mouth, as she fell asleep in his arms. He looked down at her.

How near they'd been to losing their young daughter, he didn't know. Lee didn't even want to think about that.

He looked up at Anna and smiled as she handed him a mug of coffee.

"I thank God every day for Deni's life, Lee. I hope we don't ever have to go through anything like that again."

Then, glancing at Denise, asleep in his arms, Anna added,

"She's a little angel, isn't she?"

Chapter 28:

Memorials and a Reconciliation

In the years following Lee's mother's death, Father Shaun O'Malley asked him repeatedly to come and sit down with his father and the priest, to try and achieve some kind of reconciliation. So far, though, this had failed to happen.

He also wanted to talk to Lee and Anna about Margaret's life, as he knew a fair amount about her – maybe more than most – especially in connection with her wartime service. This part of her life story was what he thought Anna and Lee might like to hear.

Shaun was working with Joe Parson to create a permanent memorial to her, celebrating Margaret's involvement with the ATA and SOE during the war. There were some gaps in his knowledge, which needed filling before they could complete the project.

One afternoon while shopping in town, Father O'Malley bumped into Anna in the street and took the opportunity to ask her if she would mind showing him some of the things Margaret had left to them. She was delighted and agreed on the spot. One evening a week later she took Lee with her to meet the priest in St Peter's Church office. Joe Parson came along too as he wanted to see the medals, photos and other items in the parcel Margaret had left to them in her Will.

Father Shaun O'Malley had known Margaret for many years, and during that time had spent many hours in jovial conversation with her. Even so, he didn't recollect her ever mentioning the medals she'd received, from both Britain and France. Nor did he know of the paintings she'd produced while in France, or indeed at any other time.

Shaun said he would love to see these precious items. Finding out about Margaret's secret life seemed to fascinate him.

"It's amazing, really it is. The things people never speak about. Well, I'll be…"

Anna felt uneasy about holding on to Margaret's war medals with their accompanying certificates, and the tiny map in its splinter of hollowed out wood. She felt these items should be in a museum or somewhere safer than stored in a cash box back at their house.

Over a few weeks, Anna, Lee, Shaun O'Malley and Joe Parson drew up a plan to create a small secure museum display in the local library, dedicated to Margaret and showing the majority of the medals and other historical artefacts. They wanted to produce a printed presentation outlining her wartime exploits, her capture and subsequent ill treatment by the Gestapo. It would also cover her recovery in the French farmhouse owned by the Leroux family and her eventual return to England at the end of the war. Anna told them she and Lee had visited the farmhouse in France as they wanted to see for themselves where she had been.

The local town council thought it was a fantastic idea and gave it their full backing. The councillors approved the outline plans and said they would help where they could to produce an enjoyable and informative display. As the exhibition was to be in the local library, the council offered to pay for the cost of setting it up, so everyone could see it and feel proud of the dear lady who had lived in their town.

Tillshott Library was ideal for the display. It was an extraordinary building. Built in 1928 in the then ultra-new Art Deco style, it looked eye-catching, if slightly out of place situated where it was, near the railway station.

It was designed initially to serve as the Town Hall but instead was used for various local events, ending up as the Public Library a short time before the Second World War.

Ted Manner was going to run a big article about Margaret and her amazing life in the *Tilshott Echo*. It would appear in print on the opening day of the display.

Anna and Lee were thrilled to loan all the items of hers they possessed for display on a permanent basis, but felt they should retain legal ownership of them as this was clearly what Margaret had wished.

Father O'Malley again broached the subject of a meeting between Lee and his father. It was now some time since his mother's funeral and Lee's father was apparently looking older and frailer. The priest thought this was a good time to try for a reconciliation, however slight, to give both John and Lee some peace in their lives.

Father O'Malley spoke firmly to the younger Mr Agazzi.

"You know, Jesus always forgives our transgressions, Lee, and teaches us to forgive those who hurt us. I know it will be hard for you to forgive your father for his past actions, but I'm asking if you feel able to give it a try? Would you do that for me, please? I have spent many hours with John and the talks I've had with him started a long time ago, before your dear mother passed away. I feel he is ready to show you some of the love I know he feels for you. Can we not try and heal the pain you have both lived with since everything went wrong between you? Are you finally prepared to listen to your father and try to forgive him?"

Anna looked at Lee. She was convinced he would want nothing to do with his father, even though she prayed every day for something to happen that would end his inner anger and bitterness.

There was a long silence before Lee said anything. He took a deep breath before answering.

"OK… But only if you are there the whole time, Father. And Anna, of course. Would you agree to this?"

"Of course I would, yes, of course."

"I don't want to be alone with him, I don't think I could handle that, and I don't want any pressure to carry on if I decide to quit, OK? Oh… and one last thing. Please can you move any tables away from the area we will be using? I do not want to sit at or be near a table of any description if we are going to do this. Too many bad memories."

"Yes, Lee, I understand only too well. I give you my word, and will not press you to stay if you choose not to. I will be praying that won't happen though. The table here can easily be moved, don't worry. I think you will find your father has changed a lot over the years and now deeply regrets his past actions. I shall say no more than that. Perhaps we could meet here next Friday evening at, say, about seven... Would that be OK with you both?"

Lee looked at Anna, and for once his facial expression gave no hint of his feelings.

In fact, he felt surprisingly calm and comfortably warm inside. This was not how he'd expected to feel at all. He had been dreading the thought of any attempt at a reconciliation, but somehow, now the day of reckoning was near, he seemed relaxed about it, even positive. He nodded his approval to Anna as she smiled at him, squeezing his hand tight.

Over the last few years Father O'Malley as parish priest of St Peter's had met John Agazzi many, many times and had influenced John greatly.

Father O'Malley had urged him to contact his son on many occasions. Now at last it seemed that a meeting might take place.

Believing their business was at an end, Lee moved towards the door but Father O'Malley caught his arm, saying he wanted to explain one thing to them both, quickly, before they left.

Several of the discussions he'd had with John seemed to point to one of the root causes of his anger. Ever since he'd arrived in England in 1945, John had been uncertain of his new identity. Changing his name to its anglicised form had seemed to be a good idea at the time, but he'd found that he hated it. It made him feel isolated, a non-person. His real name was Giovanni, and he thought it was time to reclaim that. It would reunite him with his Italian heritage, giving him a feeling of belonging and self-worth.

After thinking about this for a moment, Lee said he wasn't surprised. Knowing his father as he did, he was amazed he'd ever agreed to change his name in the first place.

It seemed a strange coincidence that Lee felt the same about his own change of name, from Stanleigh to Lee, but in his case, in reverse.

As they drove home, he started to lose his initial confidence. He wasn't at all sure he would be able to cope with a face-to-face ordeal next Friday evening.

After collecting Denise from Tom and Gina's, they went home. As they opened the front door, the phone started ringing.

Anna quickly grabbed the handset.

"Hello…"

"Anna? It's Jim… Jim Hordram. Rather glad I got you. I've been talking to Shaun O'Malley on the phone. Given your impending meeting with Lee's father, I think if you could persuade Lee to come to the nine o'clock service this Sunday, the sermon I have planned might help him. Or at least make him think a bit before he meets his dad.

"It's based on two Bible verses, *Romans* twelve, verses nineteen to twenty-one, and *Deuteronomy* thirty-two, verses thirty-five to forty-three. The sermon's theme is forgiveness. I know Lee has found believing in the Lord difficult at times, but I would love him to hear this. I will try to make it particularly applicable to him, Anna, though he can sit anonymously with you at the back. It will come over as a regular Sunday sermon to everyone else. There won't be anything to embarrass him in any way."

"OK, Jim. I'll see what I can do, but I'm not sure…"

"Quite understand. I'll leave it with you."

"Thanks for phoning, I'll do what I can." Anna replaced the handset.

"Who was on the phone?" Lee asked.

"It was Jim Hordram… letting me know about a change of arrangements for Sunday."

"Oh. Is everything OK?"

"Yep. No problem."

Anna was unsure how to approach the subject with her husband. She decided to ask if he would come with her on Sunday to look after Denise as there would be no playgroup for her to go to this week. To Anna's utter amazement, he agreed without a word of protest.

Sunday came and he sat in the church with Denise on his lap. She was sleepily sucking her thumb. Anna kept glancing at him, but he seemed quite calm, and she felt sure he was listening to everything.

As the sermon started, she began to feel a little agitated. Would Lee grasp its meaning? Might he feel a little embarrassed?

"… our natural human instinct in responding to hostility is to react with even more hostility, and to kindness with more kindness. In the Bible, *Romans* twelve, verses nineteen to twenty, it says: 'Do not take revenge, my dear friends, but leave room for God's wrath, for it is written: It is mine to avenge; I will repay, says the Lord. On the contrary: If your enemy is hungry, feed him; if he is thirsty, give him something to drink. In doing this, you will heap burning coals on his head.'"

Jim went on to try and explain how this could affect our thinking in a positive way within our everyday lives.

After the service, Lee was walking around by the church door, talking to Denise, who was still in his arms, when Jim came up to him.

"Great to see you here today, Lee. Hope you liked the service."

"Yeah, it was… er, well, I suppose it could have been written for me, couldn't it?"

Jim smiled at him.

"Glad you liked it. You should come more often. Are you and Anna going to stay and have coffee? I think there's some cake too and it's a chocolate one this morning."

"OK… Thanks. Try keeping me away from coffee and cake."

Nothing more was said. A bit later as Jim was saying goodbye to some members of the congregation, he caught Anna's eye and gave her the thumbs up.

She was happy and smiling as they went home for lunch.

Friday evening seemed to come around like lightning, and Lee was very nervous when he, Anna and Denise entered the empty meeting room at St Peter's.

They'd decided to leave Denise with Anna's mum and dad for the evening, but Tom and Gina, having been out all day, said they wouldn't be home until about 7:15 in the evening. They'd offered to collect Denise from the church rooms on their way home. Gina laughed at the idea of a noisy young child being at the meeting and didn't think it would help the delicate discussions about to take place.

Shortly before Anna's parents called to collect their granddaughter, Giovanni arrived.

Shaun O'Malley introduced him to Anna and his granddaughter Denise, who started to cry. A few seconds later, Gina popped her head around the door, came in and scooped the child into her arms.

"We could hear you from the car, young lady. I think you need to come and have some fun with Grandma for an hour or two. See you later, Anna." With that Gina vanished through the door and all was quiet again.

Shaun ushered them to some comfortable seats.

"Would anyone like a cup of coffee or tea before we start?"

The three of them politely refused.

"Right then, before we get going, I think Giovanni has something to say… if that's OK with you?" Shaun said, looking directly at Lee.

Lee felt calm and reasonably relaxed.

He'd expected to feel anything but.

Anna was more nervous than usual as she sat looking at her husband, trying to stop her hands from shaking. Giovanni coughed and started to fidget with the buttons on the front of his jacket.

In the end, it was Lee who spoke first. He wanted to feel in control.

"Dad… I don't think you have ever properly spoken to my wife, Anna. I want you to say hello and shake her hand before we say anything else. Whatever happened in the past has nothing to do with her. We are now a united, solid family unit, and we will love and support each other to the very end, regardless of what is said, or not said, here today."

Giovanni hesitated, then holding Anna's hands and looking straight into her eyes, he spoke to her.

"I am very pleased to be able to speak at last to you, Anna. I have seen you in the town with your sweet child, my little granddaughter, many times over the last year. I wanted to say hello to you but I… I…" He spluttered as he tried to speak. After a moment or two, he continued,

"I keep your wedding photo by my bed, so I recognise you easily. You are so pretty."

Lee and Anna glanced at each other in surprise.

Giovanni then pulled some folded pieces of paper from his coat pocket and sat looking at the creased sheets for a few moments, his hands trembling.

"Stanleigh, I… I want to… to…" He stopped abruptly as his eyes once again filled with tears. He was stressed and knew his English would suffer as a result. He tried hard not to be upset.

"I apologise to you for what I said and what I did to you when you were a boy. After you were born, I was so proud of you. But over the years as things didn't go as I expect it would, I get angry. As you got older, it got worse. My dear Maureen always tried to help you, so I resented it and got in bad moods."

He shuffled his papers.

"When I got angry, I lost my temper, many, many times. I was more worried about what people think of me than anything else. I'm very sorry. I was wrong, very wrong. After I made you go from my house, I cry all night, and in the morning I go looking for you to bring you home again. But I do not know where to go. I went to see Father O'Malley, but he hadn't seen you, so I was angry with him too. After, everything got worse. I blame everyone else but me. I was wrong, and all I can do today is tell you how sorry I am. I don't know what else I can say. I do not blame you if you never want to speak to me anymore. I deserve my sorrows. But when I hear you have a little girl, my grandchild, I see what terrible things I have done more clear, as I will never see her, or know her, or even hear her voice. It breaks my heart, but I know it's my own fault. I drove you away with what I said and did… I'm sorry, so sorry. I can't undo it, and now my little Maureen has gone, I have nothing left to live for. I beg you to…"

Giovanni was by now sobbing so hard he could barely get out his last words.

"Please forgive me, Stanleigh. I always loved you and my Maureen, even though I couldn't show this to you both."

There was complete silence in the room, apart from the sound of quiet weeping. All four of them were tearful.

"I don't know what to say to you, Dad." Lee, although upset, was still remarkably calm; far more relaxed than he'd expected to be. He was nervous, as was Anna, who kept blowing her nose. She sat very close to him, gripping his hand.

Shaun got up and went to get some glasses and a jug of water.

They all had a drink, and there was a short spell of silence.

After a while, still crying, Giovanni said:

"Please, can you try to forgive me, Stanleigh? I don't want you to hate me. I don't know how or what to do, to make things better. What can I do?"

Lee looked into his father's eyes and saw nothing but sadness there. He was a broken old man, destroyed by his own stupid, selfish actions.

Lee tried hard not to feel angry with him but couldn't accept the way his father had mistreated his mum. His own tone grew louder and more assertive for a while, before it calmed down again.

"I can't understand why you behaved like that, Dad? Why? If you were angry with me, well, OK. I can live with it. But what had Mum ever done to you, to deserve what you did to her? It's not for me to forgive you, Dad, only God can do that. I can forgive you for what you did to me, and I can sit here and say… *I FORGIVE YOU.* I know I can't go on for the rest of my life being screwed up over this. It's killing me. I don't want or need this bitterness in my life anymore…"

Lee, holding Anna's hand tightly, looked intently at his father.

A while later he added, in a quieter tone,

"Dad, I forgive you for what you think you did to me. That's all I can do for now."

Even the battle-scarred old priest had a tear in his eye by now.

"I will offer a prayer for us all," he said, "and then I think it would be better for us to go home and meet up again another day, to see if we can build some more bridges. Lee, can you shake your father's hand? Then we should say goodnight. I'll take Giovanni home. Thank you, Lee and Anna, for coming tonight. I will be in touch with you to arrange another meeting. I think we have made a good start this evening, and I thank the Lord for His intervention. I trust you will all draw hope and encouragement from the time we have spent together today."

Lee stood and went over to the crumpled figure that was his father. He took Giovanni's hand, holding it gently, then reached for his other hand as well. Holding them lightly in his, Lee looked directly at his father, holding his gaze for a moment before speaking.

"I'm sorry too, Dad. So very, very sorry."

Lee nodded to Shaun then. He took Anna's arm and together they left to collect their dear little Denise and go home together for an early night.

After their initial meeting, Shaun O'Malley did as he'd promised and organised several more evenings for Lee and Giovanni so they could try and mend their broken relationship.

Although he managed to at least partially forgive his father, the bond between them remained somewhat frayed.

Lee felt Giovanni was trying to overcome his inner demons and reach out to him, but over the years he had lost so much respect for his father that the love and trust between them he'd hoped to regain were slow to return.

It seemed unlikely this would happen any time soon, if ever.

Over the next few years, Lee tried hard to remain in contact with his father by having periodic chats with him, normally in the church meeting room. Sometimes Anna and Denise would be with him, and at others it would be only Denise, as Anna's work schedule got in the way.

Sometimes Giovanni would try to play with the child but she appeared wary of him, tending to go off and play on her own in another part of the room, even though Lee tried hard to encourage her to stay with her grandfather. He wanted Denise to know Giovanni and for them to have a real and loving relationship. She didn't have a shared past to contend with as Lee did.

On other occasions, they would meet in town. This would always be for coffee at the weekend as Lee was too busy during the week. A few times Anna took Denise to see her grandfather on her days off, and this continued until the little girl started school when things again became more difficult.

Lee tried to see his father at least every month or two, even if it was just for a short visit.

Sadly, it was more from a sense of duty than out of love or affection, which was what he needed and wanted it to be.

Over time the visits became fewer and of shorter duration. The demands of family life and Lee's difficulty in feeling real affection towards his dad seemed to get in the way more and more. As he assumed more responsibility at work, his free time became scarcer.

Since the first meeting with Giovanni, however, Lee

had started to feel considerably more relaxed inside; he was visibly less stressed, and in far better control of his personal feelings. His decision-making too was vastly improved... or so he thought.

Chapter 29:

Investigations

1994 – 1995

Ever since she had started to walk, Denise had been a happy and confident child, very much like her mother.

Slowly though, over the last year or two, almost imperceptibly at first, she became more difficult to handle at home and this was a lot more noticeable when she started at her senior school. Anna and Lee observed the differences in her but, as always in life, small changes taking place over a long period are often underestimated.

The number of Denise's school chums, who used to come and play weekly at their home, was slowly declining. Then one day, the week before her eighth birthday, there was a reaction from Denise that was totally out of character.

She was a pretty young girl with the same colouring and large eyes as her mother, and similar mannerisms. Denise was growing into a happy, confident little girl and seemed very grown up for her age.

Lee imagined Anna would have been much like this at the same age. The sudden change in his daughter's behaviour therefore was all the more noticeable and took both parents by surprise.

Anna asked Denise if she would like to have a party on her birthday and invite some of her friends. The child became quiet and seemed unwilling to say anything.

On similar occasions, she had always been enthusiastic at the prospect of a party and had enjoyed socialising with her friends. This time, though, the idea appeared to unsettle her in a dramatic fashion.

Anna put this down to her daughter growing up and told her not to be so silly. But Denise, rather than going along with Anna's ideas, as she usually did, grew upset and said she didn't want a party and wouldn't invite any of her friends as she hated all of them.

Anna gave her a big hug to reassure her.

"OK, Deni. You don't have to have a birthday party. We thought you would enjoy it, but never mind."

Deni sobbed.

"Well, I don't want a party ever again! I hate parties."

Anna sat her down and tried to coax the reason for this out of her.

Denise just cried and shook her head, saying nothing. Anna concluded this was an eight year old having a tantrum or perhaps trying to assert her own independence.

Either way, Anna thought it would be a good idea to take her to the doctor for a check up as this behaviour was very unlike their daughter.

She decided to speak to the teachers at school as well, to see if anything there had upset her child. Perhaps Denise was being bullied?

Anna was convinced something specific must have happened to cause such a sudden change in her behaviour.

The doctor at the local surgery ran all the usual tests and reported everything to be completely normal and healthy.

The same result came back from the school.

Anna spoke to both her daughter's class teachers and then the head teacher. Everything, it seemed, was perfectly normal. The class teachers' remarks were similar, saying Denise was a popular girl, pretty, bright, and doing well in most subjects.

They made a point of saying they would observe her closely for a while, to make sure all was well. The teachers commented this was the beginning of a new class year for Denise. The more advanced curriculum sometimes caused anxiety in children. They would keep a more careful eye on her, to see if anything showed up. They promised to let Anna know if it did.

Denise's birthday became a quiet affair with only Anna and Lee in attendance. They bought in some cute-looking chocolate cookies, trifle, and other things they thought Denise liked.

Anna had made her an adorable birthday cake. Denise would only eat a tiny bit.

Lee tried to cheer her up but it didn't work out as he hoped.

She looked down at the floor, mumbled,

"I don't like cake or jelly," and sat there growing agitated and tearful. Lee tried again.

"But you love jelly usually, Deni. Mummy's made this specially for your birthday, so you'd better eat some of it or she will be upset."

"I don't want any and I don't care!" Denise cried. She sat there with her head still down, looking miserable.

Lee told her not to be so ungrateful.

"Let it go, Lee. It's OK, leave her." Anna looked straight at him, nodding her head warningly to try and prevent any further conflict.

Sadly, Lee didn't notice or take the hint, adding that this wasn't a good way for Denise to behave and she was to stop it at once.

"I don't want any, and I don't care! I don't... I don't want *anything*."

Denise started crying in earnest then, got up and ran out of the room and up to her bedroom.

Lee and Anna looked at each other in real astonishment. Nothing like this had ever happened before. Lee could feel himself getting stressed. He worried that he should know how to deal with this situation... but when it came to it, he didn't. He didn't know what to do.

This was new territory.

Anna said she would leave Denise for a little while then go and sit with her, to try and find out what the problem was.

This birthday would not be remembered as anything but unhappy.

Lee sat at the table, shaking his head and with a puzzled expression on his face. Kids always enjoy birthdays, don't they?

Over the following weeks, Denise's behaviour continued to fluctuate between her usual self and an unhappy, depressed child. Lee found her behaviour increasingly difficult to deal with and at times became less tolerant with her.

Up until now, Denise was always happy to turn to either Anna or Lee if she was hurt or upset about something.

Now she would only go to Anna, and it was becoming ever more obvious and hurtful to Lee, who felt she was rejecting him. He could not believe his little Deni, his darling daughter, would hardly speak to him.

Why? He couldn't understand it, and found it most upsetting.

Lee found himself starting to become a bit firmer with her. Denise wanted to get her own way all the time, about everything.

Lee talked to Anna about the various things they could try to resolve the situation.

"Lee, you could try talking to her instead of shouting," Anna rebuked him. "It's not like you to shout so much. You're normally more tolerant. She is only doing what all young children do. She's growing up, and we have to give her space and understanding."

"I know we do. We also have to provide rules and discipline."

"Yes, I know that, but shouting at her isn't helping to achieve anything, is it?"

Over the next few days, they had some difficult conversations on this subject.

During one rather heated exchange, Anna and Lee disagreed over Denise's future schooling.

Lee wanted her to remain in familiar surroundings at the local school, but Anna considered the nearby grammar school would provide a better education.

Lee put his foot down.

"That's not going to happen. I went to a grammar school and hated every moment of it."

He did not want Denise to suffer as he had done. The pressure to achieve at the grammar school he'd attended became far more intense as pupils grew older. The constant competition and need to perform well had screwed him in knots and made him feel awkward and looked down on, when he failed to reach the required levels.

Anna's view was quite the opposite. She too had been sent to a grammar school. She'd enjoyed most of her schooling, which she had found both enjoyable and rewarding. She couldn't understand his objection to it and in secret started making enquiries at the local grammar school without telling Lee.

A few weeks later, on a Monday morning, Anna received a phone call from one of Denise's teachers to say there were concerns that she wasn't coping as well with her classwork as expected. She was also skipping some lessons.

This was a new development. They needed to find out why it was.

During one harsh confrontation with her parents, Denise shut her eyes, pouted and put her fingers in her ears, refusing to listen to them. Lee slapped her lightly on her arm to get her attention.

Denise, though unhurt physically, looked shocked, instantly started to cry, got up and ran out of the house, down the drive and across the road.

Anna and Lee were left distraught. Anna tried to calm her husband down, and they ended up blaming each other.

Anna, now in a panic, went rushing off to find Denise, returning a couple of hours later. In floods of tears, the child had run straight round to her grandparents', and that was where Anna found her. After they returned home, Denise wouldn't speak to Lee and went straight to her bedroom.

It didn't make him angry, but saddened and upset. After all, he'd acted as he had for her own good, or so he thought.

During the following days, Denise was even more subdued than before and was not very forthcoming in any conversation whatsoever.

One morning she refused to go to school, saying she wasn't feeling well and had a tummy ache.

Anna checked her temperature. It was normal, but she decided to keep her daughter in bed for the day.

When Lee got home from work, Denise was still in bed.

"Lee, I've had enough of this now," Anna told him. "We have to find out what is upsetting Deni. It must be something at school, I'm sure of it. This is so unlike her.

She's always been happy there before now. I can't imagine what's gone wrong. Please can you get some time off work and come up to the school with me? We need to get to the bottom of this, and quickly."

"Yes, I agree. I'm sure I can arrange it. I'll speak with your dad or Jim tomorrow morning."

They arranged a visit to the school and spent over an hour with two of the teachers, but there wasn't a positive outcome. It appeared that although Denise had certainly become more reserved of late, there wasn't any major educational problem.

Her marks in certain subjects were quite a bit lower than a year ago, but her teachers could not detect any apparent reason for this.

Over the next few weeks, Denise seemed to perk up, and for a while life returned to a more even keel. She, though, was still not too happy about going to her father with problems or about anything else. She was being polite with him, but not much more.

Anna suggested it would be a good idea to go and have a chat with Jim and Sue about the situation as they both knew Denise well. Perhaps Sue might have noticed something, or maybe Denise had said something to one of them. Anna was sure this was an avenue worth exploring.

Lee phoned to see if Jim would be available for a chat later on that same evening. After dinner, he walked down to the vicarage.

Sitting in their lounge, Jim and Sue sat holding Lee's hands and offering prayers for him, Anna and Denise.

Then he tried to explain the problem.

"We are at a loss to know how to deal with Deni's recent odd behaviour. We only want the best for her, and deciding what to do is becoming more difficult by the day. I know I may have been a bit hard on her of late but she is only eight and extremely self-willed. If we let her do whatever she wants, she will have no real discipline whatsoever. I know it's a modern trend to let a child learn by experience, but neither Anna nor I agrees with that. There has to be a better way – like creating boundaries that can't be crossed. We were wondering if Denise has said anything to either of you that might throw some light on recent events?"

"I can't recall her saying anything about this. I know it's difficult, Lee, but you can't just impose things on her without explanation. She's an intelligent child. Far better to sit down and discuss things with her, try to get her to understand your reasoning," Sue said.

"But she's only eight years old."

"Of course she is, but you still need to sit and talk to her in a calm fashion and try explaining to her any problems you have. Kids grow up fast today – a lot quicker than we did," was Jim's advice.

In fact, Jim and Sue had got to know Denise very well. Ever since Deni was quite young, Anna had always taken her daughter to church with her.

Every week at the Sunday school sessions, Sue taught about ten children of various ages, including Denise, and had noticed the recent change in her behaviour. She had her own theory about this but decided to bide her time.

Meanwhile Jim asked Lee what his relationship with his father had been like at a similar age.

"I'm not prepared to discuss that. Anyway, it's not relevant."

Lee fell very quiet after making this retort. He could feel his heart pounding; it seemed to be getting louder and faster.

There were many events from his childhood buried deep in his subconscious mind, and he would prefer they remained there.

Jim coaxed him to come clean about his own behaviour as a child. Lee did not handle this query well.

"Why do you want to know about my past, Jim? It's over… history. It has nothing to do with Deni."

"Lee…" Jim began, trying to be tactful,

"yes, it has, because you are trying to impose your own life experiences on Denise."

Lee started to get angry then.

"No, I'm bloody not! She's a young girl in a loving home. This… this is nothing like my childhood, this *is now.* My dad didn't show any love to me, or even want me there at all. I love Deni, very much. There is NO comparison."

Jim thought about things for a moment or two before he continued advising Lee.

"Even a gentle slap on her arm to correct her, or shouting at her to attract her attention, won't help because she doesn't understand why your behaviour towards her has changed. This gulf in understanding between you sounds a little bit too much like your own childhood experience to me."

Lee sat there considering the implications of Jim's words. When he spoke again, he made himself use a calmer tone.

"Anna and I don't know what else to do. Deni has become so challenging and, well, as you know… difficult. She won't listen to either of us. Anna and I try to help her, but she ignores us. What the hell else can we do?"

"Have you tried listening to her? I mean, really listening and trying to see what is upsetting her?"

"Of course we have. It's a waste of time. Deni won't talk to us, Jim… and she definitely won't listen. It makes me so bloody angry! I've tried everything I can and it's made not one scrap of difference."

"Do you remember the day your father asked you to leave home?"

"Yes, of course I do. That's one I won't forget in a hurry."

"Do you remember your mum's reaction?"

"Yes… Please, let's leave my mother out of this." Lee felt his insides starting to twist with apprehension.

"I remember it far too well. Please, please, don't go there, Jim. I don't want this discussion. If you push me too far, I'm telling you now… I'll walk out."

There were a few moments of silence.

"Well," said Jim. "You… are driving Deni away from you. In a way, it's the same thing as your father did to you."

"NO… it's not like that at all!"

Lee could feel panic rising within him, threatening to stifle him.

"My bloody father didn't love me… or my mum. He was full of hate. We love Deni more than anyone else in the world could ever do."

"I think your father probably did love you, Lee. In fact, I'm sure he still does. But like you now, he couldn't handle a difficult situation. Please be very careful how you deal with Deni. We don't want history to repeat itself. If you feel you can't cope..."

"What do you mean – can't cope? Of course we can cope, don't talk rubbish! But Deni won't listen to either of us."

Lee was beginning to see white lights flashing in his eyes.

He could feel his pulse racing. He thought his heart would explode.

He sat staring at the wall... closed his eyes, and there was a long silence.

Within the silence, Lee imagined he saw a frightened little girl sitting opposite him at the dining table. Then he saw his father shouting at her – or was it Lee? He felt very confused.

All of a sudden he turned away from the wall, feeling as if he'd been looking into a giant mirror.

It was not his father but Lee himself who was sitting there, pointing his finger and shouting in a rage, and he was doing this to his own dear Denise. It seemed horribly similar to the way his father had spoken to him, if not as violent.

"This can't be real. It just can't be... I can't be doing this to Deni! I would never harm her. She is so very precious... she means the world to me."

Lee slumped forward in the chair, his head in his hands. He could hear his mum crying, pleading...

The pain he'd buried inside for so many years, suddenly returned full force.

The reality of what he had unwittingly been doing hit him so hard he started shaking uncontrollably.

Sue came and sat next to him, putting an arm around his shoulders to comfort him, but his distress was so great he felt he couldn't breathe.

Quite a while later Lee had calmed down enough to continue. He agreed their way of dealing with Denise would have to change before things got out of hand.

He could never allow anything to come between him and his daughter. Even imagining her going through the same trauma he'd suffered was unthinkable to him. It was so shocking, Lee visibly shuddered. He loved his daughter far too much to let such damage be done to her.

Even though he was sitting with friends, in their comfortable, warm home, he started feeling cold, shivering. Right now he felt alone and afraid.

Jim and Sue offered to help in any way they could.

"Thank you. I think we need as much help as we can get."

After this dramatic revelation, life at home started showing signs of improvement.

Lee started to sit down and talk to Denise, listening to her responses and asking about her schoolwork and her friends in a different, more conciliatory way.

He tried so hard to have a calm and constructive dialogue with her, to understand the workings of her young mind, that Denise started to respond to this approach.

After their evening meal one day, she came and put her arms around her father, hugging him.

"I'm sorry I've been so horrid, Daddy. I do love you."

Lee couldn't say a word. He put his arms around her and hugged her tight to him, kissing the top of her head, breathing in her fragrance and running his fingers through her velvet-soft hair.

Lee started to think. Maybe his mind had been in a sort of time warp. Society had changed a lot since the 1960s but he hadn't paid much attention to that.

Could he still be living in the same bubble as when he'd turned up on the Slaters' doorstep all those years ago?

By reasoning more with Denise, he felt he might start to understand his own emotions better. Over many evenings, after their child had gone to bed, Lee talked this through with Anna while they sat in front of the TV with the sound turned off.

A semblance of peace returned to the home of the Agazzi family.

Denise's problems at school, though, and some of the difficulties with her former friends, remained unresolved.

A while later the annual school health check took place. Denise's medical file recorded the discussions about her that had taken place over the recent months, so the doctor spent a longer time with her than in previous years. She decided to ask Denise a variety of different questions regarding her schoolwork. These were not usually part of a school medical. As she was about to let Denise go, the doctor changed her mind and decided to ask the girl if she would read a page from one of the schoolbooks lying on the desk. The result of this small exercise gave the doctor a slight insight into a possible problem. The doctor thought it sensible to send the girl for some initial eye tests in the

Ophthalmic Department in the local hospital. This would necessitate speaking to her parents.

She dictated a short letter to initiate this course of action before calling in the next pupil.

By the time Denise got home from school she was thoroughly frightened and in tears. The doctor had asked her lots of different questions, she said, and she didn't know why. Anna put her arms around her daughter and gave her a big hug to comfort her. She tried to tell her everything would be OK and it wasn't anything to worry about.

Anna was well aware Denise had been seriously alarmed by the questions. Since the school medical service was not a part of the health profession she was familiar with, she decided she would mention her daughter's recent experience to a colleague of hers, a paediatric doctor Anna knew and trusted.

Lee got home from work quite late in the evening after Denise had gone to bed. Anna told him about the questions the school doctor had asked their daughter, about her schoolwork and the reading test. Lee thought the doctor was probably being a little over-cautious.

"I think it's a bit more than that, Lee. She suspects something isn't right, I'm sure of it."

Lee's imagination instantly went into overdrive.

The thought that Denise might have some dreadful affliction filled him with horror. He could feel panic rising inside him and felt hot and dizzy. He sat down, asking Anna for a glass of water and sipping at it until the feeling passed.

The following day, a letter regarding Denise's medical

arrived, asking if one of them would please call at the school to speak to the school doctor.

Lee thought it would be better if Anna went on her own, knowing he didn't handle medical matters too well.

Anna laughed, having experienced this on several previous occasions, gave Lee a hug and agreed to go.

She phoned her ward, explained the situation and said she would be a bit late for work in the morning.

Anna learnt that the school doctor, during her examination of Denise, had asked her to read a page of type and as a result thought she needed an eye test. In her opinion, though, the problem was far more likely to be dyslexia. The doctor recommended Denise should see a specialist in the subject. Anna explained that she was a nurse working at the local hospital and thought it would be better if she discussed it with her colleagues and tried to arrange something there.

"It might take a week or two to arrange but there really is nothing to worry about. We have lots of children around Denise's age who are experiencing similar problems. Quite often this is just part of growing up. Hormones can cause real havoc sometimes."

After a lengthy discussion, Lee and Anna decided, before receiving any diagnosis, they would try to find out a bit more about dyslexia.

They would go together to see their friend Carol Nathan, who was still specialising in Paediatrics.

When they arrived in her consulting room, Carol greeted them warmly, inviting them to sit in the more comfortable chairs on the other side of the room.

After a short chat, they were handed some leaflets while she explained more about the complexities of dyslexia. To aid her explanations there were a few trial demonstrations. Lee asked if he could have a go at one of the tests, to try and understand it better.

As he was working through the questions, it became apparent in an instant that he was dyslexic himself.

This came as a massive shock to Lee. In fact, he was devastated. He was an adult and nobody had ever mentioned this to him before. How could there be anything wrong with him?

He recalled hearing dyslexia mentioned on a TV programme sometime in the past, but that was all. He had no idea what it was.

His visible reaction alarmed Carol so much she spent the next half an hour or so trying to explain what was in fact a very complex subject.

She decided it might be best to refer both Lee and Denise to a private consultant as the NHS didn't do all the diagnostic tests she thought would be useful to them.

Lee and Anna readily agreed and Carol said she would try to arrange for father and daughter to be seen together.

On the way home in the car, having heard all the symptoms described to them in such detail, Anna said she wasn't surprised to learn Lee might be dyslexic.

"I think it could explain quite a lot of things, Lee, and I expect it will make Deni feel a bit less nervous if Daddy has dyslexia too." Anna hoped and prayed this might help to bring Lee and Denise closer together again. Both parents loved their daughter so much. The last months, almost a year in fact, had been beyond distressing for them all.

Lee looked quizzically at her, but as he was driving he decided to leave further discussion until later when they could chat without interruption.

They collected Denise from Gina and drove home. They were all tired, and after a light snack Denise went straight off to bed, followed not long after by Lee and Anna. He felt an early night would be a welcome relief after the stress of the hospital visit.

Anna was astonished by Denise's reaction to being told she and her father could have dyslexia and that they would be going to have some tests at a specialist unit. In fact, Denise didn't react at all. She just smiled and carried on talking about some schoolwork. It was almost as if nothing had happened, nothing had been said.

When the day arrived, although puzzled by some of the written tests the centre asked them to complete, Denise remained unexpectedly calm.

"Is Daddy doing the same exam sheets as me?" she asked.

"Yes, Deni, exactly the same. But they aren't exams, love, just a series of questions to test your reactions. Does that bother you? 'Cos it needn't, you know. No one is going to do anything to you. This isn't a hospital."

The visit lasted almost two hours and after all the sheets were completed and assessed, the specialist spent a fair bit of time going through the results with all three of them.

"Well, Mr Agazzi, looking at the results from the

initial tests, they appear to confirm that you and your daughter Denise have dyslexia to varying degrees. I would say you, Denise, appear to have a rather milder condition than your father. Does that please or surprise you, my dear?"

"I don't know... maybe surprises me a bit, but I don't think so really. I don't know what to say..."

Anna was sitting next to Lee, who appeared to be more taken aback than his daughter was. Denise seemed intrigued and interested in the proceedings and remained largely unbothered by the consultant's diagnosis, telling her mother to stop looking so worried.

"I don't think we are going to die, are we, Daddy?" she asked him outright, and he had to smile and agree with her about that.

In the following months, Denise and Lee went several more times to the centre. During these appointments each of them went through additional tests, to ascertain which of the methods of treatment currently available would best help them, primarily Denise, to overcome at least some of the problems they faced in connection with the written word.

The first thing to be performed was an extensive eye check. The tests gave a very satisfactory and clear result. Neither of them required glasses. Then they were asked to look at a different set of tests. The first involved placing an assortment of coloured films over printed pages, to see if this made any difference to their perception of the text. They also tried placing pieces of white or coloured card with slots in them over the print, to help concentrate the eyes on single lines or sections of type.

Lee felt this was rather a waste of time, saying he couldn't see what difference it would make.

The only thing Denise found to make any difference to her was a light brown film placed in front of the page she was given to read. This combined with a slightly larger typeface seemed to improve things quite considerably. Eventually it was suggested that, for her schoolwork and general reading, Denise should try and wear a pair of glasses containing a brown tint to the clear glass lenses, the right-hand one being slightly darker than the other.

"Oh, no, I don't want to wear glasses, Mummy. Do I have to? They will all laugh at me." Denise became fidgety and was quite upset by the suggestion.

"No one will laugh at you, Deni. In fact, I expect they will all be jealous. You can tell them it's the best way to get good results at school. Then they'll want to have a pair of glasses like yours, won't they? Tell them it's a magic formula."

The glasses certainly helped Denise to read more fluently, and it was decided to try them out for a few months and then review the situation.

Lee was not so fortunate. None of the tests seemed to improve his reading difficulties or make any other noticeable difference to him. The dyslexia centre, he felt, did not appear to be overly interested in trying to resolve his condition, real or not, maybe because he was an adult. He was disappointed, but not surprised. He felt that when none of their suggestions produced any tangible results, they rather gave up trying, and considered they became somewhat dismissive of his apparent issues. But he was delighted that his daughter seemed to benefit from the consultations.

As the year progressed, Denise's school marks improved considerably and she seemed to be much happier. Some good at least had come from the exhaustive testing as Denise no longer struggled with her homework as she had before. The occasional problem occurred, but overall life was a lot calmer for them all.

One afternoon about an hour before Anna was due to leave for home, Carol Nathan appeared on the ward. She was carrying a large folder, which she handed to her friend.

"I've been trying to find something to help give Lee a better understanding of his dyslexia. There's a wealth of information in here that I think would be useful. I don't need it back. I just hope it helps because I feel the clinic let him down, and I'm sorry about that."

"Thanks, Carol, that's so kind of you. It must have taken ages to find all this."

"Not really. Anyway, hope it's of some use. Have to dash now. I'll ring you soon. 'Bye."

"Thanks..."

Carol disappeared, leaving Anna with the heavy file.

Over the next week, with mounting interest, Anna pored over the pages, sorting them into the categories she felt would be most helpful to Lee, and maybe Denise too. As she started to read the various articles, she felt that at last she was gaining a better understanding of Lee's apparent insecurity and why some of his reactions to stress appeared so extreme.

After dinner one evening, while sitting in the lounge

with a glass of wine, Anna started to discuss with him what she had discovered.

"Do you remember me telling you Carol gave me some info on dyslexia?"

"I remember you saying something about it. Do you know what's on TV this evening?"

"TV? No, I don't. Look, I want to talk to you about what I've discovered. It's important and interesting."

"OK. Go on then. I don't expect I'll get any peace till you have, will I?"

"Do you remember your dad calling you names, like lazy, careless, and saying that you weren't trying hard enough?"

"Oh, yes. He did that all the time."

"Well, apparently those are all typical traits of dyslexia. So are other things you have mentioned to me many times. Things such as eye ache, headaches or feeling nauseous while reading, and finding the words move about or even disappear from view for a while. Were you clumsy while playing games at school? That can be caused by a problem with spatial awareness, Lee."

"I was never any good at games. Maybe that's why I'm always bumping into things now."

"It could also explain why you get so stressed when you have a problem to deal with. It might all be connected, and caused by dyslexia."

Anna felt a weight lifted off her shoulders. So many things about her husband's behaviour now had explanations. She was relieved and excited by all she had read. Lee turned towards her, smiling.

"I know this sounds silly, but do you think that's why I can't ride a bike?"

"Quite likely. Bad balance and motion sickness are also mentioned as symptoms. "

"OK, I get that, but you can't blame everything on dyslexia, can you? I thought it had more to do with reading and writing than all this stuff? That's what the clinic said anyway. They told me I didn't track lines of type properly and gave me that card with a slot in it to fix my eyes on. Bloody waste of time that was! It made things even worse."

"Do you realise how easily distracted by sounds you are? Maybe more than you think. Remember telling me you smashed up a Beatles record once because a clicking sound on it drove you mad? It got so dominant in your head it ruined the whole LP for you, even though I hardly noticed it at all."

"Oh, yes, I remember that well. I chucked out several other LPs at the same time too. They were covered in scratches and sounded dreadful."

"And do you remember you told me how you used to draw diagrams for Maths problems at school, which the teacher tore up in front of the whole class? On the other hand, your Art teacher told you how good you were at painting and drawing, didn't he? All these things relate to dyslexia. And there is another common problem: filling in forms."

"Oh, yes, of course. I hate forms."

Lee was starting to sweat, fidgeting with his wine glass and looking distinctly uncomfortable.

"Please can we turn on the tele or talk about

something else?" he asked. "I'm going to open a window. It's getting very hot in here."

"OK. I thought talking it through would help you a bit, that's all."

"I'm sure you're right, but please… can we discuss the situation a little at a time?"

Unbeknown to either of them, Denise had been sitting on the stairs listening the whole time. She felt sorry for her dad. She was fascinated by this conversation, and in her optimistic young mind she decided she would help her dad and appreciate his struggles more in the future.

The explanations Anna had given Lee went around and around in his head. They certainly gave a fresh perspective on some of the annoying problems that had dogged him all his life.

Chapter 30:

Intensive Care

June 1998

After work, late one Thursday in June, Lee arrived home feeling unwell.

He had a sharp pain in his right side and back. It had started after he and two of the machinists at work were shifting a heavy load of carpentry and packs of fixings in the loading bay.

After arriving home, Lee complained of feeling ill and said he thought he would go to bed. He must have pulled a muscle with all the lifting he had been doing.

At about 10:45 in the evening he was in severe pain and doubled over, groaning. Anna phoned for an ambulance as she thought he might have acute appendicitis. It arrived within five minutes, and Lee was taken straight to the hospital where Anna worked, St Andrew's Military Hospital.

Denise, woken up by the commotion, started to get upset. She had never seen her father unwell. He hardly ever caught a cold.

"Is Daddy going to die?" she sobbed. A young girl at her school had lost her father to a heart attack less than two weeks before, so Denise, assuming the worst, was frightened.

"No, darling. Please go and get dressed and I will take you round to Grandma's. I'm going to the hospital to see how Daddy is."

Gina answered the door to them in her dressing gown. She was surprised to see Anna and Denise at that time of the evening. After a few quick words of explanation, Anna left.

It didn't take long to reach the hospital, and by the time she got there, Lee was being prepared for emergency surgery.

The doctor informed her they believed his appendix had burst, causing acute peritonitis, and surgery should take place as soon as possible.

Anna panicked for only the second time in her adult life. She couldn't keep still, felt tearful and frightened.

As a nurse, she knew more than most people about hospital procedures.

She was very used to dealing with the patients' problems on a daily basis, some of which she knew could be quite upsetting, and always dealt with them in a professional manner. She considered herself to be in control of most situations and did not normally show her emotions. The other nurses always joked about the calm manner in which she went about her work. This was her chosen path in life – part of her daily routine.

Dealing with health problems of a severe nature within her family was a different matter. Since she had taken up nursing as a career, this had only ever happened once before, when Denise was a young child.

The situation in which she now found herself was once again beyond her control. Other than for an occasional headache, Lee was never ill…

Lee was gowned up and very drowsy when Anna reached him. She could see he was in considerable discomfort.

"I don't want to die, Anna. I'm frightened. What are they going to do to me?… I love you so much." His voice trailed off then and became inaudible.

"You'll be OK, Lee. I love you too. You won't die…"

Then the theatre staff took him away, leaving Anna a trembling wreck standing in the corridor.

One of her own team appeared and took her away to calm her down and give her something to drink.

The hospital grapevine meant everyone knew Anna's husband was in theatre right now.

As the nurses hurried about their usual duties, they came and gave her brief hugs.

"Everything will be OK soon, Anna. Don't worry, he's in good hands."

"I know, but… but…"

An hour went by, then another – still no word. At last one of the surgical doctors guided her into the nearest nursing station, grabbing a passing nurse to accompany him. He spoke hurriedly but in a calming way.

"Anna, Lee is going to take a while to recover, I'm afraid. Very simply, after we dealt with his appendix, he did not respond as well as we had expected. His blood pressure dropped so low his heart briefly stopped and had to be restarted. He will remain in Recovery until his condition stabilises and will then be transferred to Intensive Care. There is a faint possibility he may require another operation, but it's the worst-case scenario. We don't think it will be needed, but I wanted to let you know now so it won't come as a shock if it does happen."

By now Anna was crying. The doctor went back to theatre and the nurse he'd brought with him tried to calm her fears.

"Lee could die, couldn't he?" Anna mumbled between bouts of tears.

"I'm sure that won't happen. You know the doctors here very well. They will do everything they possibly can."

Two more doctors and a nurse ran past in the direction of the operating theatres.

"Oh my God, please don't..."

Assuming the worst, Anna fainted and slid to the floor, banging her head hard against one of the desks in the process.

She was taken into an empty private room and, after being checked over, given something to help her sleep.

At 6:15 in the morning, she awoke with a thumping headache. Everything seemed quiet. After a while, the nurse who'd been with her earlier returned to check on her and see how she was doing.

"Is he… is he OK?"

"Lee is still in Recovery at the moment and doing well. I expect a doctor will pop in to see you soon."

"I must get up, I want to go to him."

"No. Not yet, Anna. I've been told you must stay here at present as you might have concussion. You suffered a nasty bang to your head and it's looking quite bruised."

"I can't, I've got to go and see Lee."

"Sorry, Anna, but you need to stay here for a while longer."

A moment later a doctor she knew well appeared with a different staff nurse.

"Hello, Anna, I hope you are feeling a bit better now. I am pleased to tell you Lee is OK. He is due to go to ICU very shortly. At present, he is in a mild induced coma, to allow his body to stabilise. He has come through the worst and is doing well. In my opinion, he will make a full recovery pretty quickly. You'll be able to come and see him as soon as we have him settled in the ward.

"We know this has been a traumatic time. You are an extremely competent nurse, Anna, and know the procedures we go through. So please try not to worry about your husband, he's doing fine. I think now we should get your head wound looked at. I want you to rest for the next hour or two and take these, which will help with your headache." He handed her two small tablets.

"Everything will be alright. Trust me – I'm a doctor," he said with a cheeky grin on his face.

Anna forced a smile in return. She hesitated for a while before taking the medication he'd left for her, not knowing what it was.

She asked Sally, her staff nurse friend, to phone her parents.

"Please don't say too much."

"OK, Anna, don't worry, I'll call them myself. I'll be careful."

Within a few moments of sitting on the bed Anna started feeling strange, as if she was floating above Tillshott Stream. She could hear Lee whispering to her, "Anna, please will you marry me?" repeatedly in her head until, feeling sleepy, she closed her eyes and slid backwards onto the pillow.

When she woke up some hours later the headache was still there, but at least it wasn't as bad as it was earlier, and as a bonus sunshine was streaming in through the window. It was a beautiful day.

The hospital was as busy as usual, with nurses bustling about doing the drugs round. Anna was alone in the room, wearing a hospital gown. Her memory of the previous few hours was rather vague, and she couldn't recall getting changed. Her clothes were folded in a neat pile on a chair near the door.

She still felt rather sleepy and a little dizzy, but dressed and headed to the nursing station to ask about her husband.

"Hello, Anna, there is a message for you. Lee is now in ICU. You can go and see him anytime you like. I expect this must have been rather a shock to the system. I hope you're feeling a little better than you were earlier? You've got your normal colour back again, and that's a mighty big red bump on your head." The nurse was smiling warmly at her as she added,

"Lee's OK. They are taking exceptionally good care of him."

Anna's nursing experience had taught her what to expect when she walked up to the Intensive Care Unit.

She spoke quietly to the nurse sitting beside Lee.

"How is he, Rhona?"

"He is doing well. All his vital signs are stable. The doctor wants him to remain at this level for the next twenty-four hours. So, as you know, he won't respond to anything we say to him for a while."

Lee looked a reasonably good colour but was very still and covered in tubes and wires, all attached to a variety of different machines.

Anna particularly noticed Rhona's lovely soft Welsh accent and thought she had a gentle, kindly manner. She had briefly worked with this nurse before and had seen her sometimes in Casualty, but had never before noticed that accent. How odd, Anna thought. How could I have missed it?

She stayed for a while, talking in a soft voice to Lee and holding his hand.

The spell was broken by a phone call for her at the nurses' desk a short way down the corridor. It was her mum. Anna went to speak to her.

"Hello, Mum. Yes, Lee is… he is… Well, he's OK. I'm coming over shortly and will explain everything then. How is Deni?"

"She's alright but very quiet and not eating much. I think you will need to explain things carefully to her. She's in shock. Keeps asking when she can go and see Daddy."

"Alright, Mum, I'm on my way. Please give Deni a kiss from Daddy and me."

Anna quickly slipped back into nursing mode. Although still upset, she felt more in control of her emotions. It seemed very strange to be on the patient's side of things. She found it unnerving.

Dealing with her young daughter was going to be the difficult bit. She didn't want to convey her concerns to Denise.

How much medical knowledge her daughter might have picked up from listening to various conversations over the years, Anna didn't know, so she would have to make sure only to give minimal information and try not to frighten her unnecessarily.

It was a little after 3 p.m. when Anna pressed the doorbell at her parents' house. She was tired and hungry as she hadn't eaten since waking in her hospital bed earlier that morning. Her mum prepared some beans on toast as Anna explained what was going on with Lee's treatment. Gina thought it might be a good idea if Denise stayed with them for the next day or two. It would enable Anna to return to her nursing duties and remove the worry of getting Denise to and from school. As for meals, Gina and Tom would take care of that too.

"It would only be for a day or two after all. It will give you a little breathing space. Have you told Lee's father? I think you should do."

"Mum, I haven't had time to do anything, but, yes, I will tell him. I'll call in this evening."

After reassuring Denise her father was doing well and was in the best place, Anna drove to the house in Cogg's Path where Lee's father lived and rang the bell. There was no answer. Back in the car she found a sheet of paper in one of Denise's drawing books, quickly tore it out and scribbled a short message for Giovanni, popping it through the letterbox.

The following afternoon the doctors stopped one of the drugs Lee was having and hoped he would start to wake up within a few hours.

Anna went to see him on and off during the day, to check how he was progressing. Nothing had changed. Lee remained asleep, but at least he still looked a good colour.

Another twenty-four hours passed and there was no noticeable change. On one occasion as Anna popped in to see him, one of the doctors was present. He didn't appear too concerned, saying Lee's failure to surface from his coma was nothing for her to be worried about.

"The human body is a wonderful thing, Anna. Lee will wake up in his own good time, you'll see."

Later the same evening the consultant suggested she might like to bring Denise to see her father and talk to him as this often triggered a reaction.

The following morning Anna phoned the school and explained she was taking her daughter to the hospital.

"Daddy is fine, Deni," she explained. "He's sleeping. If we go and talk to him, he might wake up. That would be great, wouldn't it? I know he would love to hear your voice and he's used to hearing you singing at home all the time. Why don't you try that?"

"I know the words to the one he used to sing to me, when I was little... But it's a children's song, isn't it?"

"It doesn't matter, I'm sure he will love it. He knows it well enough."

As they arrived at the hospital ward, Jim Hordram walked in at the same moment, having decided he would pop in and see Lee.

ICU policy was to restrict visitors to a maximum of two and family members only, but as Jim was the local vicar an exception was made.

Lee looked very peaceful. While holding his hands, Jim said a short prayer for his recovery and then left.

Anna suggested to Denise that she could hold her father's hand and sing the song to him.

Denise looked nervous. "It's OK, Deni, Daddy will love it."

Denise still looked worried and a bit tearful as she gently took hold of her father's hand. After a few seconds, she quietly began to sing:

I'll be here, just for you,
And even if it takes my whole life through,
I'll care for you, so you won't cry,
And I'll love you till the day I die...

By the time she got to the end, both Anna and the nurse had tears in their eyes. Denise had the voice of an angel and although a bit shaky at the start, it grew stronger as the song progressed. As she finished the song, Denise turned to face her mum. Her face was glowing.

Anna pulled her into a huge hug and just held her there.

"Look, Anna... look!" the nurse said with excitement.

Lee had turned his head towards them and although he had not fully woken, his eyes flickered open for a second or two.

"He heard you, Deni! Hold his hand and speak to him again. Tell him what you are doing at school. Just keep talking for a while."

A few moments later he spoke to them in a whisper.

"I love you, Deni. Is Mummy there? I can't see…" Then Lee went quiet and still again.

The nurse adjusted one of the monitors as a doctor arrived.

He spoke quietly to Anna.

"There are signs of progress here. I need to run a couple of tests now and think it would be better if you could take your daughter out for a while. I'm sure you know what I mean."

"Yes, of course. Come on, Deni, let's get a cup of tea and pop back later."

Anna whispered to the nurse that she would call her before returning to check all was OK.

Over the next couple of days, Lee slowly improved and was able to speak with his wife for a few minutes every so often before slipping back into sleep.

Then on the fourth day after his surgery, Lee woke up at breakfast-time and asked for a glass of water and something to eat. He was actually hungry.

Even though Lee had never been overweight, he now looked considerably thinner.

He was very weak and experiencing some discomfort from the surgery, but did not seem to be suffering from anything worse.

The nurse said the morphine was controlling his pain well, and they would start to reduce this over the next day or two.

The following morning, Lee was sitting up in bed and had a nice little chat with Anna and Denise before he wanted to have a snooze. So after Denise was taken back to school, Anna went to see her mum with the latest news.

Anna felt relieved and emotional as she described Lee's progress. Tom also popped in as an excited Anna had phoned him earlier, at work, to tell him she would be coming home for lunch.

Within a few seconds, it seemed, Sarah too appeared at the door. She and Jim had been regular visitors to the hospital and to Tom and Gina's ever since Lee became ill.

Later the same day Anna went with Denise to see Jim and Sue at the Vicarage, to thank them for their kind support.

Jim said he would hold some special prayers in their next Sunday service in thanks for Lee's recovery and hoped he would be home again quickly. Denise ran up to Sue and hugged her.

"Daddy's coming home soon!" she cried in excitement.

In reality, it would still be a while before Lee was fit enough to return.

"It will be a great day for a celebration," Jim said as he held Anna's hand and murmured a few words of prayer for Lee's successful recovery.

Anna was surprised what a calming effect this particular prayer had on her. She'd often wondered if praying made any real difference. She still wasn't sure, but never said anything about it to either Jim or Sue.

After some more chatter, Denise was beginning to look tired so Anna took her home for an early night. After a long and stressful week, this would be her own first proper chance of a good night's sleep since Lee had been taken ill, which now seemed a long time ago.

She was both physically and mentally exhausted.

A day or two later, on her return from visiting Lee one evening, and after Denise had gone to bed, Anna decide to tidy up their spare bedroom. She came across one of Lee's jackets, slung over the back of a chair. As she lifted it to hang in the wardrobe, an envelope fell from somewhere inside. It was addressed to her and must have been there for quite a while, well before Lee went into hospital. It wasn't sealed so she opened it. Inside was a card with a picture of red roses on the front. She was not at all prepared for what she found written inside.

In Lee's scrawling handwriting were the words of a song written to her... Anna.

Your love's like oxygen
Always around me, it keeps me alive
Your love's like a mountain spring
I drink in your presence, it helps me survive

There's nothing I've done to deserve such affection
I seem to receive so much from you

You are the one but it's beyond my comprehension
Why you chose to love me like you do

Your love's like solid rock
Helps keep me standing, strong in a storm,
Your love's like the morning sun
Brightens my spirit, makes me feel warm
You are the love I need, you are the only one
You are the air I breathe, you are my oxygen

Already tired and in a highly emotional state following her visit to Lee, this was almost too much for her to read.

By the time she reached the dedication written by Lee she was shaking from head to foot and tears ran down her face.

My dearest Anna,
This is for you, my love. I am the luckiest man alive...

This is a song written by our friend Stuart, who we met on holiday a few years ago. These words say more about how I feel for you than anything I could ever write. I will want and need you until the day I die and beyond. And I will always love you.

Lee XXXX

It wasn't until the eighth day after Lee's operation that he was allowed home. He was still quite weak, but he was back with them, and that was what mattered. Denise was thrilled and didn't want to let him out of her sight. Her outpouring of affection touched Lee. The previous months, after all, had been rather different.

He let Denise do everything for him, even changing one of his dressings while Anna watched over her as supervisor. The sight of dried blood and stitches didn't seem to worry her daughter at all.

"Quite a little nurse, just like Mummy, aren't you, Deni?" Lee said, with a big grin on his face.

"Of course I am, Daddy. And you have to be careful or you won't get better." She wagged a finger at him to make sure he did as he was told. Lee smiled, looking at Anna, and knowing only too well where she'd learnt that little gesture. He wondered if Deni might also become a nurse one day, like her mum.

Anna was pleased and greatly relieved to see, after all the troubles of the previous months, Lee and Denise happy together again.

"You will never know how many people have been praying for you, Lee. I have prayed constantly with Deni for you to come home fully recovered. And now you have! You are a lot better already and I thank God for that every day. I don't know how I would have coped without having Jesus beside me. I'm sure it made a huge difference."

Lee said nothing. He smiled and looked deep into Anna's eyes. There was a serenity and peace in her he hadn't noticed before. Or was he imagining it? Then he remembered the warming sensation he'd experienced while standing by his mother's grave on a chilly day a while ago.

"There must be a connection here with what happened at Mum's grave," he said. "Do you remember me telling you about it?"

"Oh, yes. I have never forgotten it. I prayed the experience might bring you nearer to Our Lord as well as to your father. Do you think it helped, even a little bit?"

"If I'm to be honest, love, I don't know, but I've never experienced anything like it, before or since. I'm certain of that. So I think the answer is probably, yes."

Later in the evening, Lee decided these experiences were not random and made a decision to see what else God intended for him.

"I want to come to church on Sunday with you and Deni. I admit, I feel a bit awkward about it and find it rather embarrassing. Will you make sure you stay right next to me? Physically, I still feel rather wobbly, if you know what I mean? You will have to drive, sorry."

"Of course I will, don't be silly. I wouldn't leave you on your own, would I? And apart from your health problems, I think everyone feels a little awkward when they start going to church. I know I did. It will be fine though, you'll see."

A couple of weeks after being sent home, Lee was finally fit enough to return to work even though he wasn't able to drive himself for a while. In the office, Tom and Jim, to ensure he didn't overdo things, watched him closely. The hospital had signed Lee off and said they didn't want to see him for three months unless he developed any new symptoms.

Although he was rather tired at the end of a day's work, Lee felt pretty good and was putting some weight back on. His normal healthy colour returned, and he soon managed to get back into his old routines.

A few weeks later in the office, Jim suggested he should take a couple of weeks' holiday. Neither Lee nor Anna had discussed holidays, not real going-away holidays, for a long time. The last proper holiday they'd taken as a family was at least three years ago.

One morning Lee arrived at work and on his desk found a pile of holiday brochures. Jim and Tom started to encourage him to book up and go away somewhere special.

One of the brochures was from a cruise company and Anna, in particular, was very excited at the thought of it. The cost was prohibitive but she dismissed any objection on those grounds.

Over a week later, she, Lee and Denise were at Tom and Gina's house for Sunday lunch. The subject of holidays was up for discussion again. Denise and Lee didn't mind where they went, but Anna still thought it would be nice to go on a cruise.

"Perhaps we could find a cheaper company than the ones I've been looking at?" she suggested.

"There must be several doing short cruises to Norway and the Baltic area?"

Tom stopped this conversation in its tracks by announcing that if they found a cruise they liked – he and Mum would sort it all out for them. And by that he meant the whole thing, including tickets, transport to and from the port, plus the entire cost.

Anna looked at him with her mouth open.

"What… But, Dad, it's several thousand pounds, even for a short cruise. You can't do it. And after all, we aren't short of money, as you know."

"Of course we can do it. The company has done really well over the last few years, and a lot of our success is thanks to you, Lee.

"So it's not a problem. Mum and I can't take it with us,

can we? It's only money, you know. Nothing is too much for my girl's family."

Anna felt excited at first and then she started becoming tearful. The strain of the last few months, culminating in Lee's illness, was catching up with her. She looked at her dad, then in turn at her mum, Lee and Denise, opened her mouth to say something, but couldn't find the words so didn't say any more than,

"Thank you so much. We would love to do this. It will be like a dream."

Anna got up and went and hugged first her mum then her dad.

Later, back home, Lee, Anna and Denise were looking at the brochures again, pointing out various holiday destinations.

They were all delighted, but none more so than Denise, who was beaming from ear to ear and jumping up and down with excitement.

Anna said she would pop into the local travel agent's on the way home from work the next day to pick up more brochures.

It was well past 1:30 in the morning when she finally turned out the light. Lee was already asleep and snoring gently beside her.

She was overtired and excited too, sleep didn't come quickly. After the stress of the previous months, this break would be wonderful. Images were going around and around in her head until finally Anna nodded off with a big smile on her face.

In reality, of course, they could easily afford any holiday they wanted, but spending large amounts of money on things like cruises or other expensive luxuries still went against the grain. So they stuck with the habit of not spending money if it wasn't necessary.

A week or two passed and they eventually found a holiday to suit them perfectly. It would be a fifteen-night cruise to Madeira and the Canary Isles, or as Denise so beautifully put it, "We're going to Tenner-weef."

The weather in the Canary Isles was normally good with consistently warm temperatures throughout the year. Lee would also be able to see another volcano. This time it would be Mount Teide.

Chapter 31:

Mummy, What's an I-tie?

1998

One day, Denise was feeling upset by what some of the girls in her class at school had been teasing her about.

"Mummy, what's an 'I-tie'? Is it someone from Italy? Two of the new girls in my class keep saying I'm an 'I-tie' and I don't really know why. I'm not from Italy. They're not being nasty but they won't tell me what they mean, and run off giggling."

With the surname of Agazzi, some of her classmates pulled her leg about being an Italian by calling her an "I-tie". Denise, though, had not considered it referred to her possible Italian heritage.

She thought her grandparents were Gina and Tom, her mother's parents, and Jim and Sarah whom she had always viewed as her father's. All of them were, of course, English. Each of them had played an essential role in her life. She knew her surname was different and she knew of a Mr Giovanni Agazzi, but didn't think much more about him; couldn't remember when or if she'd ever spoken to him. Denise did ask her mother about him one day, but it had been years ago it seemed. It was only now that she started to question who her real grandparents were, on the Agazzi side of the family.

Lee and Anna had continued to have intermittent meetings with Giovanni on and off over the years. Denise, though, after her third birthday, hadn't seen Lee's father to speak to on more than a few occasions.

Anna sat her down and tried explaining it to her. Lee knew the day would come when he or Anna would need to clarify a few things about their family history to Denise. He was surprised it hadn't cropped up before now. They'd decided, a while ago, that as and when it became necessary, they would only explain whatever seemed needed to satisfy her questions. They didn't want to upset her. They would treat this in the same way as they had sex education.

Anna rummaged about in a drawer in her bedroom and found an old photo they had of Giovanni, Deni's grandfather. Denise looked at it with a puzzled expression on her face.

"Mum, it's really funny, but I'm sure I saw him in the library last term. I was doing some homework with Gwen. He said 'hello' and smiled at me. He seemed nice, but I didn't know who he was, and he didn't say his name. Gwen said he was probably a dirty old man and I should ignore him. So I did."

Two weeks after this conversation with her mother, Denise asked if she could have some Italian lessons.

Lee was surprised but said if she was serious, of course she could. He thought it was always a good idea to speak another language. For Denise Italian would obviously be a good choice.

Anna agreed wholeheartedly.

One of the congregation at St Aidan's Church, to whom they spoke occasionally, had been a lecturer at Cambridge University. Although he had retired a few years ago, his subject had been Modern European languages. Now retired, he sometimes offered private lessons from his home. His wife Molly was born in Sainte-Agnès in south-east France. The small town was only one or two kilometres from the Italian border, so she grew up speaking both Italian and French fluently.

Anna thought, if Molly was around too and speaking Italian, it would make Denise feel more comfortable and relaxed while she had her lessons.

After a brief meeting the following Sunday everything was arranged, and Denise started her first lessons in spoken Italian.

Like her mum, Denise was a fast learner and got on well with her language studies, surprising everyone. She seemed to enjoy them, had little or no difficulty with the pronunciation – even some of the more difficult-sounding words.

Lee amazed himself too by speaking some phrases in Italian with his daughter. He was astonished to find that he remembered any at all.

December arrived all too quickly and Anna started

packing for their cruise. This was to be the first Christmas of their married life spent away from home. Lee hoped Gina and Sarah would not miss them too much.

The holiday went entirely as planned. Right on time, a smartly dressed chauffeur arrived at the house to take them to Southampton docks to meet their ship.

The cruise was everything Anna hoped it would be and more. The food was fantastic, the land excursions were most enjoyable and the sea was calm most of the time. The weather was warm and dry, even hot some days, apart from while they were crossing the Bay of Biscay, when it became choppy. But the three of them were having such a great time they hardly noticed the movement of the sea at all.

A little before the Christmas season arrived, and unbeknown to Anna or Lee, Tom Parkes made several visits to his GP. During the previous months he'd been told his blood pressure was rather too elevated and that he would need to go on to medication. The doctor advised him if possible to try and reduce his workload and stress levels. Tom spoke to Gina and his partner Jim, and decided now would probably be a good time, as he put it, to "semi-retire". He discussed with Jim the various options for the company. They decided that, in the New Year, they would offer Lee the position of sales director in Tom's place.

"Neither of us is getting any younger, you know, and it would be a good grounding for him."

Tom would initially continue to guide him while at the same time taking a step back, reducing his working week to three days. He and Jim agreed that Lee should become Managing Director once they'd both fully retired.

Early in the new year, Lee was promoted to sales director of Slater & Parkes. As business started to increase the company decided they would need more space. When the engineering company next door closed down in the summer of that year, the joinery quickly acquired the premises.

Lee was happy with his new position and laughingly said to Anna one evening,

"It's only a title change. I'm doing the same work I've been doing for the last six months. You and I are both company directors anyway."

Chapter 32:

Grandpa

September 1999

A short while before her thirteenth birthday Denise, on her way home from school, noticed several people had collected around an elderly man who was lying in the road. Apparently, he had slipped on a wet patch of pavement, hit his head on the kerbstone and now seemed to be in a confused state. The onlookers couldn't understand a word he was saying.

One of the ladies decided to call for an ambulance and dashed into a shop to make the 999 call.

In his semi-conscious state, the elderly gentleman was speaking in a language someone thought might be Italian. Hearing this, Denise went to see what was going on and immediately realised who the man was. It was her grandfather, Giovanni Agazzi.

She pushed her way to him and in slightly halting Italian asked him if he was hurt…

"Hello, Granddad, it's Denise, your granddaughter. Someone has called for an ambulance. It won't be long now. Try to keep still."

"*Ho freddo*, Denise. *Ho freddo…*"

"He's cold. Can someone get a blanket or something, please?"

Denise put her school bag gently under his head as a kind lady shopworker ran out with a blanket. Denise tucked it around him.

"*Grazie, sei così dolce*, Denise."

She would generally have been embarrassed by this public display of gratitude. But she was so busy trying to keep him still and wrapped in the blanket that she didn't react at all.

After a while, the ambulance arrived, and she was helping the crew by giving Giovanni's details and translating some of what he was mumbling. A member of the ambulance crew asked if she would be willing to come with them and help Giovanni communicate.

Lee was working from home all day, certainly not something he would normally be doing, and made a mental note of the time. Denise was late home from school, and he was becoming slightly uneasy.

About an hour later the phone by his elbow started to ring. He grabbed the handset quickly. It was Denise, phoning from the hospital to explain what had happened. She was speaking so fast he couldn't get a word in edgeways.

"Hello, Daddy. It's Deni… don't panic but I'm at the hospital. Grandpa Giovanni had a fall, and I was asked to go with him in the ambulance. He was speaking Italian and they didn't understand him. He's OK but has slight concussion. They're keeping him in tonight. Can you please collect me? I'll be at the main entrance."

"OK… er, I won't be too long. Are you all right?"

"Oh, yes, I'm fine. Can you bring my coat, Dad? It's started raining… Thanks."

"Yes… well, of course, yes, see you in a bit then. Deni, how did you…? Hello… hello?" Denise had already hung up.

Lee quickly bounded up the stairs to let Anna know where he was going.

He was astounded by Denise's composure – she sounded so like Anna at work, calm and entirely professional. If his wife had not been at home upstairs asleep at the time, he would have thought it was her at the other end of the line. Denise was incredibly like her mother.

Lee bubbled with joy. His little Deni.

He couldn't believe it… she wasn't yet thirteen, he was so proud of her.

A few weeks before Christmas, Denise asked her father if Grandpa Giovanni could come for Christmas Day. Otherwise, he would be on his own, and she thought it wouldn't be good for him. Plus it would be helpful for her to get to know her grandfather better. She also thought it would be quite exciting as she would be able to speak Italian with him.

Lee wasn't sure this was such a good idea. He still didn't feel particularly comfortable being near his dad for more than an hour or two at a time. But on the other hand he loved his daughter so much, he would do almost anything for her, so he said he would consider it.

"Please, Dad. I'll look after him. It would be so nice. Otherwise he will be all alone at Christmas, and that's horrid."

Lee thought his dad had been alone all these years, so what difference would another one make? Plus it was entirely his own fault. He discussed it with Anna, though, and in the end agreed to Denise's request.

The thought of his dad being in his house over the festive season did not please Lee too much. But the more he considered it, the more he realised it could be a good thing. There were several ideas currently running through his mind.

It would be interesting to see how his father would react to seeing what he, Giovanni's useless son Stanleigh, had done with his life. And for him to discover at first hand that Lee had actually done rather well. Lee thought to himself, I have a highly paid job, a lovely wife and family and we live in a posh new house, with an expensive car... two cars in fact.. on the front drive. He couldn't think of a better way to show his dad how wrong he'd been. Lee didn't want to rub his nose in it – well, not too much – but he couldn't resist the temptation. He'd decided a while ago that he had to forgive his father – completely. He wanted to end the bitterness that had screwed him up for most of his life or it would never go away, but he still felt the need to prove a point.

He was going to try hard to accept Giovanni as a welcome guest for Christmas, and maybe on other occasions too. It would be difficult for him to do, but he was going to try his hardest, with Anna's help and support.

After all, this was their family home, and if the shit hit the fan, he could always ask his father to leave. It gave Lee a feeling of strength, the upper hand. But he hoped he would have more compassion and never treat his father in the same way as he had treated a teenage boy. He sat quietly and said a silent prayer to help him manage the situation gracefully.

He picked up a spare Christmas card and wrote out the invitation. He handed it to Denise, saying she could pop it through his father's letterbox.

"Thanks, Dad. It'll be great fun, you'll see." Denise had decided in her young mind that they should all be one happy family again. She was going to try to make sure they would be.

So against all the odds, Giovanni Agazzi, Lee's father, came to stay for Christmas.

He would arrive on Christmas Day and remain overnight for Boxing Day, precisely as Denise wanted.

It would be the first time Giovanni had been in or even seen his son's new house. Anna was picking him up in Lee's car, on her way home from collecting her mum and dad, who were also to spend Christmas Day with them. As Giovanni came in through the front door, he almost bumped into the large, lavishly decorated and sparkling Christmas tree. He and Anna's parents were warmly welcomed with some Christmas cheer... a tray full of chilled glasses of Champagne.

Tom and Gina wandered into the kitchen with Anna, Denise and Lee, leaving Giovanni, for only a few moments, on his own to look around in wonderment. He was amazed by how big and expensive the house looked and by all the pretty and festive decorations. Giovanni stood looking at everything, remembering vividly some of the things he'd said to his son before throwing him out of his house, all those years before. He now felt more than a little embarrassed. His son, it seemed, had made a fantastic success of his life. What's more, he'd made a far better job of being a family man than his father had done. Giovanni stood there and in fact, felt pretty stupid.

If life can ever be said to be a power game, it was at this point he finally realised he was the real loser... not his son. After a few moments, Lee came to find his father with a glass of champagne for him. Despite all his misgivings, everything remained calm and the day was a great success.

Giovanni was enjoying himself. He was quiet, polite, and seemed to be very grateful to Lee and Anna for having him, even saying he realised it must be difficult for them to accept him into their home after such a long time.

The conversation was relaxed and jovial throughout the whole day. The turkey lunch with all the trimmings was served at three o'clock promptly after the presents were opened. It went down a treat.

They all raved about the Christmas pudding and brandy custard.

Denise got on well with her grandfather, sitting next to him on the sofa and sometimes speaking to him in little snatches of Italian. Giovanni showed a lot of affection towards her and was obviously becoming increasingly fond of her. Later in the evening, he gave her the extra Christmas present he'd kept hidden in his pocket. It was a twenty-four-carat gold and platinum necklace with a pendant of large brilliant-cut diamonds surrounding a sizeable single natural pearl. Giovanni particularly wanted Denise to have it, he said, as it had belonged to his mother.

He asked Denise to close her eyes as he placed it around her neck and fastened the clip. He so wanted to see her wearing it. Lee was astonished. It must be worth thousands, he thought. He looked at Anna with his mouth open. He was sure he had never seen this item before. It was a fantastic piece of jewellery, and Denise looked so grown up wearing it. She loved it, throwing her arms around her grandpa and thanking him repeatedly before she dashed off to look at it in the hall mirror.

Giovanni was delighted, adding he was enjoying spending so much time with them. He complimented Anna on her superb Christmas fare, adding what a beautiful wife and mother she was. He became a little tearful when Denise hugged him, saying,

"It's alright now, isn't it? We can start again, can't we? Daddy doesn't want you to be sad anymore, not ever. And I love the necklace. Thank you so much. I can't believe you have given it to me, Grandpa. I promise I will look after it and always treasure it. I will never forget today."

"I am pleased you like the trinket, Denise, my mother would be proud…"

Throughout Boxing Day, Giovanni spent several hours, on the sofa, talking with Denise. He told her of his life in Italy, and how he'd ended up in England – the edited version, of course.

After the evening meal, Lee drove his father home. He helped him into the old family home, and his father turned and hugged him, getting very emotional while doing so, saying how much he'd enjoyed Christmas, though after all he had done, he didn't deserve to be treated with such kindness. Lee stood with his arms hanging slack at his sides. He so wanted to hug his father, but somehow couldn't quite bring himself to do it. He began to put one arm out but slowly lowered it. He realised he still had some way to go, even now, though he desperately wanted to let it all go and love his dad.

This was the first time Lee had been entirely alone with his father in all the years since 1973. Although finding it awkward, he wanted very much to try and put the past behind him and move forward.

Lee told his father Denise would like to come and see him sometimes so they could get to know each other better. Perhaps they could even speak some Italian together.

"It would be nice for her to know you better, Dad, and it will be good for you too."

"I thank you, Stanleigh, for this. I don't know how I can make better what I did, but I will try to give little Denise the things I could never manage to give you."

Giovanni sobbed as he spoke. He held out his hands and Lee took them in his, holding them in a firm grip.

Then he lifted his father's hands to his lips.

"It's OK, papa."

He slowly turned away. Giving his father a last wave, he got back into his car for the short drive home.

After all the upset and bitterness of the previous years, perhaps this was the turning point, and maybe, just maybe, it could be the start of them overcoming the past and becoming a real family again.

As 1999 ended and rolled into the year 2000, Denise wanted to go and ask if her grandfather would like to spend New Year's Eve with them. It would be the start of a new millennium, and an excellent idea for the family to join forces, either watch the international celebrations as they took place on TV or go to the event the town council planned, which was to take place on the school playing fields. There would be fireworks and a huge screen to display the excitement being transmitted from around the world.

Anna thought it was a good idea. Nevertheless, they were talking about Lee's father. She felt Lee would have to be the one to decide what they would do.

Denise could nearly always get round her dad. This time, though, Lee was one step ahead of her. He had already phoned and invited his father for the evening, suggesting he could stay the night as it might be a "boozy" night and he would not be able to drive Giovanni home. Denise was overjoyed and hugged him.

"Thanks, Daddy, it'll be great fun, won't it?"

Lee laughed, agreeing with her that it would.

Chapter 33:

A Visit from France

May 2000

Anna wrote to Josette in early April to ask if she and Marcel would like to come and stay for a few days. They would arrange for Giovanni to come as well so they could meet him. He had never met the Lerouxs and this would be a good opportunity for them to try and find out if he ever knew their mother Sofia in his youth.

Lee thought there was a strong possibility Sofia Leroux would prove to be a relation of Giovanni's. He and Anna were desperate to see if there was any truth in Margaret's assertion that Lee's father and Sofia were almost certainly either brother and sister or, maybe, cousins. It would be interesting to find out.

Anna was never able to get out of her mind the idea

that their meeting with Margaret was achieved by divine intervention, as their friend had believed.

Margaret seemed totally convinced that God had placed her into the care of the Agazzi family on the two occasions when she was desperately in need.

It certainly was a strange coincidence, this possible link between the two families; almost unbelievable, in fact.

Anna asked Josette if they had any documents, like birth or marriage certificates or a family tree, to bring with them, which might confirm their speculations on the matter.

Josette and Marcel arrived on 16 May and would be with them for two days only, as they couldn't leave the farm for long. A neighbour was looking after the property while they were in England.

Giovanni came for dinner on the second day and after the meal was over and cleared away, the birth certificates and several other documents including a handwritten family tree were spread over the dining table together with some photos.

There was no doubt about it at all. The papers confirmed everything pretty conclusively. Sofia Leroux was certainly Giovanni's aunt, his mother's younger sister.

Giovanni thought he remembered her, but added it was a long time ago and his memory wasn't as good as it had been.

Josette, though, was completely certain her mother Sofia must have been a direct relative of his, regardless of any paperwork.

"Giovanni, your eyes... they are so the same as the eyes of Maman. It is hard to believe, I know, but it must be so... life is strange sometimes."

So… they were related. It was exactly as Margaret had predicted. Anna once again felt a strange tingling sensation all down her spine as she remembered hearing her say one day, from her bed in the hospital: "I am quite certain God has a plan for you both."

A week or so into the New Year of 2001, Giovanni started to get uncomfortable aching in his lower abdomen. The pain was there most of the time and it was beginning to annoy him. He was rarely ill. It didn't bother him too much at first and he assumed it was indigestion or something similar.

So he tried to ignore it and did so, pretty well, for quite a few months. One morning the ache seemed more noticeable, and he got an early appointment for the next day with his doctor.

The GP examined him and decided he would like him to have some tests carried out to eliminate the possibility of any cancerous growths, and as Giovanni seemed so depressed about it, gave him a course of antidepressants, saying they would lift his spirits.

"These will take a week or so to become fully effective. They are quite safe to be taken together with this other prescription."

The additional tablets he'd prescribed would help Giovanni's digestion.

The doctor didn't think it was anything too serious, but he wanted to be sure.

"We need to check, to be on the safe side," he said, smiling at his elderly patient.

An appointment card arrived a few days later, but it was for a date in several weeks' time.

Giovanni reflected that it couldn't be too bad or they would have made the appointment much sooner.

The tablets had helped considerably, and during the following week, he began to feel more comfortable.

Over the following weeks, his life went on as usual.

He continued meeting Denise most weeks on Saturday for an hour or so, and was invited to join the family for dinner several times, at Lee's invitation. Lee always insisted on driving his father home, chatting with him during the short journey. Giovanni never once mentioned the constant ache in his stomach, either to Lee or to any of them, and carried on as if everything was perfectly normal. If anything, he was more cheerful than usual.

Anna was pleased to see Lee finally forming more of an attachment to his father. He was inviting him to dinner himself, rather than at her or Denise's suggestion, which was previously the case.

In Giovanni's mind, anxiety over his looming hospital visit was mounting. He was convinced he was suffering from an incurable cancer. He started to get all the paperwork with his bank details in order and also updated his Will. He wanted to make sure his dear little granddaughter Denise would not be forgotten should anything happen to him.

Several visits were made to his solicitor to ensure everything was in order and his wishes would be carried out correctly.

He was formulating a plan in his head, which was wildly out of proportion to the medical problem. Always assuming there was one in the first place.

His appointment was at 9:30 in the morning at a hospital in Swindon, and he arranged for a taxi to run him there in plenty of time then bring him back home later in the day.

By three in the afternoon, a series of tests and procedures were completed, and he was asked in to see the consultant before going home.

"I wish you had come along a little sooner, Mr Agazzi... even so, from what I can see, the preliminary results do not appear too serious. However, there are a couple of small areas of abnormality in your lower bowel. Until we get the results back from the lab, we won't know exactly what this is. I wouldn't worry unduly at this stage. I have taken several biopsies for checking. Whatever the tests reveal, I am hopeful we will be able to sort something out to improve the situation for you. We will be in touch in the next couple of weeks when we have the results. Personally, I'm hoping you won't have too much to worry about."

Giovanni though, far from feeling reassured, returned home from the hospital in a dismal mood. And this became more sombre as the hours passed. In his mind the diagnosis was bowel cancer and he was as good as dead. He imagined all sorts of dreadful horrors. Operations, radiotherapy, pain and misery. He was not going to wait until it was too late, or until he had no strength left.

During the following few nights, he had constant nightmares. He would wake up covered in sweat. By the third morning, he'd managed to work himself up to fever pitch.

Chapter 34:

Full Circle

July 2001

It was a beautiful sunny Saturday morning in mid-July when Denise, singing to herself, walked round to Cogg's Path, to see her grandfather, as she now did most Saturdays. She was excited today, as during the week Anna had bought her a new pair of light blue jeans with attractive embroidered motifs on the lower legs. She felt a million dollars in them and was so thrilled. She wanted to show them to her grandfather. Denise was sure he would like them too.

She was feeling happy when she rang Giovanni's doorbell. But there was no response. So she rang again, several times in fact, but no one came to the door.

She looked through the letterbox but couldn't see anything that seemed out of place.

As it was a beautiful warm day, Denise thought he might be in the garden, so she went through the side gate and wandered across the paving covering this end of the garden. She peered in through the patio doors, the kitchen windows and even into the garden shed. It all looked clean and tidy as she expected it would. Her grandfather had a place for everything.

She retraced her steps and, after trying the doorbell one last time, gave up and decided to go home, feeling more than a little deflated.

Anna was in the kitchen emptying the dishwasher when Denise arrived home, coming in through the back door.

"Is that you, Lee, have you got a moment?"

"No, Mummy, it's me. Grandpa isn't home. I rang and rang, but there's no answer."

"I expect he's gone shopping, Deni."

"But he knows I'm coming. It's Saturday."

"Perhaps he forgot what day it is. I wouldn't worry. You can call him later."

Denise tried phoning her grandfather several times, on and off, all during the day, but there was still no answer.

By eight in the evening, she was becoming frightened something had happened to him.

"Mummy, there's still no answer. Do you think he might be ill or had a fall?"

"I suppose that's possible, but I would have thought, even if he was ill, he would still have answered his phone. If he hasn't answered by tomorrow morning, I'll see if Daddy can pop round to check on him."

Unusually for a Saturday, Lee had been at work all day and was late getting home, arriving back at just after eight-thirty in the evening. He was knackered. Two of the company's best workers had gone down with 'flu, and they had another on holiday in Europe. There were not enough machinists to fulfil an urgent order, so Lee had filled in.

Denise rushed up to him.

"Daddy, can we go and see if Grandpa is OK? Please?"

Lee kissed Anna.

"I'm hungry! Sorry I'm late. It's not been an easy day. My arms ache like hell. What were you saying, Deni?"

Somewhat annoyed, she repeated her question.

"I said… Grandpa isn't answering the door or his phone… so can we go round and see if he is alright?"

Lee wasn't too keen to go out again, but Denise was persistent.

"Oh, all right. We won't be long, Anna. Can you remember if Dad gave you a spare key when he came at Christmas? I seem to remember him saying something about one. If he did, can I have it, please… just in case?"

"Yes, he did. I think I put it in my handbag, the black one. It's in the wardrobe. Please can you get it for me, Deni?"

A few moments later, Denise came back with the bag.

"I'm sure it's in here somewhere… Yep, it is… Here you are."

Lee took the key with its Italian flag key-fob and stuffed it in his trouser pocket.

Denise was urging him to hurry.

"Thanks, love. I'll call you if there's a problem…

Calm down, Deni. We'll get there… all in good time."

Lee tried the doorbell, but there was still no reply. A few moments later, he unlocked the front door of his dad's house and he and Denise went in.

"Hello, are you there, Dad… Dad?" Lee called several times in a loud voice. There was no reply. Everything looked to be in place, but there did seem to be a strange kind of silence.

"You look around down here, Deni, and I'll look upstairs." So, calling out to her grandfather, Denise looked in the kitchen, then the dining room, the lounge, and noticed the table with a pile of neatly placed envelopes on it. Finally, she checked the loo by the front door. Giovanni certainly wasn't downstairs.

Lee had gone upstairs where first he checked the bathroom. There was no one in there. He guessed which room was his father's. He opened the door, and before it was even halfway open, froze. The sight before him was horrific. It was so utterly unbelievable it shocked him to his very core. The room looked like a war zone. Blood splatter was all over the walls and the bed where his father was lying, slumped on his side.

Lee suddenly felt faint and thought he was going to throw up. He had never seen anything like this in his life. Then, out of the corner of his eye, he noticed an automatic pistol lying a few feet away on the floor. It was almost out of sight near the edge of the bed.

Clearly, Giovanni had been shot. Some of the blood looked quite dry. Lee guessed his body must have been lying there for at least a day or two, maybe longer.

In his shock, he must have called out or made a noise, loud enough to have alarmed Denise. Hearing her footsteps pounding up the stairs, he slammed the bedroom door shut, spreading his arms out to hold her back so she wouldn't see the horror inside.

As Lee turned towards her, he was shaking like a leaf and as white as a sheet. Denise looked up at him. She could see the shock on his face and was frightened.

"Stop, Deni… Don't go in there…You can't go in… don't…" Lee grabbed her by the arm when she tried to push past him.

"Dad, you're hurting me! What is it?"

"It's my dad… Grandpa… He… he's dead, Deni."

"What?… He can't be." Denise started crying and becoming frantic. She tried several times to push past.

"He's dead, Deni. I'm so sorry. Please, come downstairs with me. We need to phone the police… now."

In her panic, Denise tried to evade him again, but Lee held on and pulled her away, turning her towards the stairs.

He sat on the bottom step. Denise sat on his lap. Her head was resting on her father's shoulder, her arms around his neck. She was crying, tears running down her face.

Lee was hugging her, holding her as close to him as he could. Denise was so, so precious. He rocked her in his arms, exactly as he had when she was a young child, and as he had when he held both her and Anna in the hospital only twelve years earlier. He reached for the phone and with a shaky hand dialled 999.

Fighting back his tears, he asked for the police and an ambulance.

Epilogue

Some weeks after the police investigation into the death of Giovanni Agazzi was completed, the coroner's office handed Lee a large bundle of envelopes, full of documents.

On the top was the envelope marked "Private and Confidential". It contained the letter written with such care that Lee's father had placed among the other documents on the morning of his death.

Dear Stanleigh,

There are so many things I would like to say to you I cannot put into words. So many things I regret in my life, but the worst was the way I treated you, my precious son, and Maureen, my dear wife. I cannot ever forgive myself for what I did so many years ago to drive you away, and for all the torment I must have caused both you and my little Maureen. At the time, I felt sure all your problems at school reflected on me. I thought the bank would blame me, and that I would lose my job because my character was bad.

I was so wrong, Stanleigh, wrong about everything. Mum knew.

I caused so many bad problems, and she tried so hard to help, but I would not listen to her. I had horrible temper, and I blamed her for that too.

Even though I also blamed Father O'Malley, he never gave up trying to help me and years later he managed to arrange the first meeting we had. It was the first night for many years I had no bad dreams. I so wanted to be your father again, a good father. I wanted to make up for what I had done. It took many more years and in the end it was your dear little Denise who brings us together again.

Now, as you will see from the doctor's letters, I am not so well, and I not want to cause any more hurt or be a problem to you as an old man. I am very sorry for all I have done. I do not want to pile any more pain on you.

When you look in my Will and the solicitor's letters you will see I have provided for you and Anna. And you will also find I have set up a trust for little Denise, so when she is 21 years old she will be able to have secure future, and maybe buy a house or something else she like.

As I said to you once, I would try to give to my little Denise the things I could never find a way to give to you. Well, some shares I bought for a small sum in the 1980s, when I worked in the bank, have grown into a big amount.

I had not looked at these since the day I bought them, not until this year. I had forgotten about them. The solicitor had everything made up to date as you will see. It is incredible, but it made me so happy that finally I had something to give you and your beautiful wife Anna that was better than my words.

Please remember that in my heart I always did love you and my Maureen, far more than I could ever explain to either of you. I don't want you to think badly of me, I want you to be happy and now accept the love I could never show to you when you were a young boy.

> *Goodbye, Stanleigh, my dear son.*
> *So sorry for everything, figlio mio.*
> *All my love,*
> *Giovanni (Dad)*

Postscript

Father Shaun, after a long discussion with Lee and Anna, took it upon himself to organise Giovanni Agazzi's funeral. Lee was traumatised by his father's death and the shock of witnessing its aftermath and Anna was only too grateful for some help.

"I think you can safely leave it all to me," the priest told her. "Don't worry, I'll keep in touch to make sure it's as you would wish."

"I'm very grateful, Father. Thank you so much."

Ten days later the service took place at Saint Peter's Church. The priest had done a marvellous job and after a Funeral Mass, the small group of mourners followed the coffin out to where a grave had been dug for Giovanni next to Maureen's.

After the coffin had been lowered into the ground, some prayers were offered and then the group of mourners dispersed to the priest's house where he had laid on some refreshments.

Only Lee, Anna and Denise remained at the graveside for a few moments on their own. Anna whispered to Lee how warm and peaceful she was starting to feel. He said he felt the same.

"This is how it was when I came before – remember me telling you?"

As they started to turn away, Father O'Malley called from somewhere behind them. Lee and Anna were surprised to see the old priest waving to them from the far side of the open grave.

"Hello. By Jove, that is a magnificent display of flowers you put on your dad's grave, Lee. Grand altogether they are. White, of course. Very suitable. Well, won't hold you up – cheerio for now. God bless you both."

Lee and Anna glanced back to the open grave but there were no flowers anywhere to be seen as they had been taken to one side by the undertaker's men, to await the filling in of the grave. They glanced briefly at each other, then quickly back to where the old priest had been standing, but there was no one there. Lee suddenly turned white as a sheet and Anna said urgently to her daughter,

"Deni, did you see Father O'Malley walk by just now?"

"No. Of course not… He's over there, talking to someone." She pointed in the general direction of the church buildings.

Shaun O'Malley was about fifty yards away, holding a cup of tea, deep in conversation with one of the mourners.

Author's Note

The song 'Oxygen' is taken from an album by Stuart Anderson called *Discovery*.

It is a beautiful song, as are the others on this CD. For more information on Stuart or the album go to: https://www.pianoman.biz/newcd